Other Novels by Brian Cleeve

Violent Death of a Bitter Englishman

Violent
Death
of a Bitter
Englishman

by ━━━━━━━━━━━━━━━

BRIAN CLEEVE

Random House
New York

In remembrance of *Vera Anderton*

Violent Death of a Bitter Englishman

1

IT WAS very quiet, very dark. The trees leaned their shadows over the grass track, toward the car. What moon there was, was hidden behind clouds. The two men listened, feeling the dark, the silence creep into the car like a tide, enclose them, until they belonged to the wood and not the road, until their eyes and ears belonged to it. They began to hear the small sounds of the wood, see the outlines of the trees.

They listened for a long time. Until the driver touched the other man's arm with his gloved hand and they both opened the doors of the car and stood on the grass, still listening. After another minute the driver went to the back of the car, unlocked the trunk and opened it. The second man joined him and they bent down and lifted out the man who had been inside it. They laid him down very gently on the grass and the driver relocked the trunk and pocketed the key. Then they picked the man up again and carried him into the wood.

There was a path, and they followed it. They went a long way into the wood until they came to a clearing. The moon came out from the clouds and there was the glisten of water.

It ran very softly over stones and moss. They stood the man on his feet, supporting him between them, and then let him fall. He fell with his head toward the stream and his face turned up to the sky. The driver took a revolver out of his coat pocket. The other man stopped him with a small gesture, knelt down by the fallen man and lifted his wrist, feeling for the pulse. After a moment he nodded, satisfied. He took the fallen man's jaw between finger and thumb and adjusted the angle of the head a little. Even in unconsciousness the face seemed both intelligent and bitter. The face of a man who had had much less from life than he had once hoped for.

The man with the revolver knelt down in his turn, folded the unconscious man's right hand around the butt, eased his index finger onto the trigger, through the trigger guard. He pushed the limp thumb against the safety catch until it gave, clicked free. Put the muzzle of the revolver against the man's temple, and holding the limp hand and the butt of the gun enclosed in both his own gloved hands, squeezed the trigger.

The noise was not outrageous. Like the breaking of a rotten branch from a tree. A smell of burning, very slight, lingering for a few seconds. Not much longer than the flat echo of the shot. The silence came back, settled. The driver took off the dead man's shoes and then his own, and changed one pair for the other. It was oddly difficult to lace the warm shoes onto the dead man's feet, although they belonged there, and the driver grunted a little with effort and concentration. When he had finished he put his own shoes into the outside pockets of his coat. The other man had worn no shoes from the beginning, only thick fisherman's socks, pulled over his trouser ends.

They shone a torch on the ground where their knees might have made marks beside the body, brushed the grass gently with their hands. When they were satisfied the driver put the keys of the car in the dead man's pocket, and they

—

4

stepped carefully across the stream and walked away in the opposite direction from the abandoned car. After half a mile the wood came to an end and they crossed an empty field. There was a gate in the far corner and beyond it a parked car with the interior light burning. When they came close they could see a man and a woman sitting in the front seat. They whistled softly and the woman looked toward them and nodded. They opened the gate and got into the back of the car.

"Is—is it all right?" the man in the front said. He had limp fair hair, long thin strands of it brushed up and over his bald head, like yellow seaweed over a white rock. His cheeks were fat and sagging, and they shook with fear as he spoke, his small, plump hands gripping the wheel, holding him rigid. He smelled of sweat and terror.

The man who had driven the first car leaned forward and the woman gave him a cigarette. "Why shouldn't it be?" he said. His face dark in the sudden flare of the match, like bronze, the flesh smooth as burnished metal over powerful cheekbones, the mustache black, sleek and animal. He touched the woman's cheek with the back of his fingers as she lit the cigarette for him, and she shivered. But she didn't move her head.

2

"*Yea, though I walk through the valley of the shadow of death, I will fear no evil: for thou art with me; thy rod and thy staff comfort me.*"

The voice rich and musical, like an actor's voice. White

—
5

lawn surplice, lace, embroidered stole. Flowers and shadows and the warm fire-glisten of brass. Sean knelt three rows behind the widow and the chief mourners, watching them, his hands joined in front of his face as if he were praying. No one had asked him who he was, why he was there.

"I will keep my mouth as it were with a bridle; while the ungodly is in my sight."

The coffin lay on the high draped table in front of them, on hidden rollers. In a little while the brass doors at the end of the table would open, the rollers would revolve and send the coffin through the brass doors to the fire.

The man lay in the coffin, the shattered side of his head resting against a white silk cushion. Flowers on the polished mahogany lid. "From his loving wife Mary Elizabeth." "From his friends in Midland Television." "From Edward Bryce, Esq." "From Miss Eva Lund."

Sean had tried to identify who was who, but it was impossible. The small man with the large domed head, thin fair hair brushed up and sideways over the ridge of the skull, hiding baldness, kneeling beside the widow—brother, brother-in-law? On the other side of the widow an elderly woman in a veil. The mother? Next to her a girl with a black mantilla over a black and shining mass of hair. Her traveling companion beside her, a fat young-old man with a pasty and yet boyish face. Sean had seen them arrive in a red sports car. Were they "his friends in Midland Television"?

The friends of Olaf Redwin, television producer, who at about 3:00 A.M. on June 17, while the balance of his mind was disturbed, did, in the place known as Goff's Wood, near the town of Learham, kill himself by discharging a revolver against his right temple.

"For I am a stranger with thee and a sojourner, as all my fathers were." The clergyman lifting his white sleeves, lace and lawn and a hint of lavender; voice filled with compas-

—

6

sion, with the eternal sorrow of death. Did he feel it? Sean wondered. Or was it just a job?

Like mine? he thought, with a sudden stab of bitterness. He put his hands over his face, crushed the heels of his palms against his mouth, the mouth of a man living on his nerves, harsh, down-curving, making his face look savage, dangerous, the black eyebrows hooked over the deep-set shadowed eyes, one of the eyebrows scarred across, the nose straight and powerful. He dug his fingers into the flesh of his forehead. Why did he go on with it?

Loyalty? To what? He felt his mouth twist under his hands. "Oor maircenary" as old Mr. Drybergh used to say. "Oor gallant Heeberrnian soldier o' fortune." The old sheep's mouth twisting with silent laughter, the long yellow teeth bared to the shrunken gums. They had hated each other from the first, from the day he had been let out of prison to join the department, almost five years ago. But on his side at least it had been a hatred of respect. On both sides by the end, before the old man took his pension and his gratuity to run a fishing hotel in the north of Scotland. "Ye must come up and stay wi' us one o' these days, and I'll show ye what a real fish looks like, wi'oot the chips. Did ye ken ye could ha' one wi'oot the ither?"

He thought sometimes he'd have given a month's pay to have the old fool back, to hear his insults, see his dusty, waxen old face bent over the desk in the antique shop, making up accounts. And the major— He dug his fingers into flesh and bone until the nails threatened to cut the skin. Seeing the major as he had seen him last, his face gray with illness, his eyes deadened, his body shrunk inside his clothes with sickness. And the harshness of disillusion and frustration.

While Randall sat at what until six months earlier had been the major's desk. Commander Oliver Randall, R.N. (Retired), Head of Department, trim and clean and supple

—

and contemptuous. "I want this to be a happy ship. But a tight ship. I understand things were a little—amateur— under the old leadership. We're going to change all that. Pretty rapidly." The actor's mouth smiling, thin, curved, carved in charm and malice and condescension.

Setan took his hands down from his face, clenched them together on the wooden back of the pew in front of him. Why did he go on? For the major? "Don't leave it, Sean. The job's still there, it's still worth doing."

And Margaret? Was she another reason? Still?

"I've written my resignation half a dozen times," Margaret had said after the first month of Randall. "The only reason I haven't given it in is because he's waiting for it." And because of the major. And because of—

"What's the point of going on?" he had said often, often, and then the last time, in the small firelit bedroom, lying in the winter dark, touching her body, thinking that it would be weeks, months before he touched it again, ran his fingers over the smooth flesh, the long, narrow flanks, the sudden astonishing richness of her breast. "We could get married— there's other things I could do besides—" and she hadn't answered, only shaken her head, caught his wrist and held it against her breast. As if it was something they couldn't discuss, that wasn't worth discussing. That they could sleep together, share their bodies but not her mind. As if there were an inner privacy that he wasn't fit to enter, was too ignorant, too alien to enter. The same barrier that had always been between them from the beginning was still there.

"Because I'm Irish?" he had asked her, more than once. "Because I was in prison?" And she had smiled, but never answered. Like now. Holding his wrist against the warmth of her breast, but not answering him at all. Did she think he wouldn't understand an answer? That she was not working for Randall, or for pay, but for an idea, an ideal that she, and the major, and Mr. Drybergh could understand, but that

—

8

couldn't be explained to a "mercenary," a mere "Heeberrnian soldier o' fortune," even if he was fit for bed.

"Why not?" he had said, stupidly, savagely angry, as if by being angry he could make up for the past month of humiliation, the parting in five hours' time, the loneliness coming. "You know I can't," she had whispered, her tone ending it, making it not worth even discussing. He had switched on the bedside light, lifted himself on an elbow to stare down at her, the shadows making her mouth look contemptuous.

"I'm cold," she had said, and had pulled the covers over her, turned her head away. And he had left her; got dressed and gone back to his own flat and caught the plane without ringing her, hadn't written to her. The girl in Venice had been like a revenge, a futile revenge that he'd regretted even while it was happening. And when he got back Margaret had known. Because Massingham had known about it and told Randall. And Randall had told her. They hadn't spoken since. Except for work. Her eyes not even cold. Simply indifferent, as if there had never been anything between them. Only her mouth showed sometimes what she felt, tightening a fraction when they had to meet, talk.

Why don't I get away from it? he thought. Why, why?

"Come in with me," Niccolò had said. "We are quite mad, you and I, working for peanut money, for stupid, worthless governments that will tip us out like old ashes when we are finished." Like the major. Like the major. "A few men like us, Giovanni mio, trained, experienced, no illusions. We could make some remarkable moneys, I promise you. No need for any treasons, unpleasant things. Just straight business deals."

In other words, industrial espionage. Niccolò had kept him up till four o'clock in the morning the last day they were together, trying to persuade him. Why hadn't he let him? Lieutenant Niccolò Tucci of Italian Security's Section "S," who drove a Millecento with a ferocity of hatred and

—

9

dreamed of Mercedes cars and large obedient women. He'd be a good partner, a good companion. Why hadn't he let him?

Because of the major? I'm like a child he thought, clenching his teeth, forcing his knuckles against them. Must I always lean on someone? Dressing up lack of guts as loyalty, as ideals? And the emptiness inside him was like the dark, like agony, and he had to cram his knuckles inside his mouth to stop himself from making a sound, from making an exhibition in the hushed chapel, the shadowed gentility of suburban death.

Was that how the man had felt? Olaf Redwin, television producer? When he took the gun in his right hand in the small clearing in the wood, and blew half his face off? "One should never think too much," Niccolò had said, "or one would inevitably kill oneself. That is why God made women." His oil-dark eyes yearned after the buttocks of a German starlet passing in front of their table outside Florian's.

The same emptiness? The same ache in the bone? Why had he come back? "We do now commit the body of our dear brother to be cremated. This we do in sure and certain hope—"

Of what? He shut his eyes against the coffin, moving now, gliding slowly on the hidden rollers toward the square brass doors. The widow sobbed, the noise loud and sudden and shocking in the silence, dreadful in its reality after the clergyman's professional compassion. The coffin vanished, the brass doors closed, hiding the reflections of the fire.

The clergyman's voice rose, spread balm. "—the glorious resurrection of the life everlasting." The man with the limp fair hair put his arm around the widow's shoulders, held her for a moment.

"Let us pray."

Five minutes later they were outside in the weak sunlight

—

of the afternoon. Two men were monopolizing the widow
and the old woman: the man who had sat beside her in the
chapel, and a much bigger man, with a deeply bronzed face
and a heavy black mustache. The bald man looked white,
rigid with nerves. The fat, youngish man interrupted them,
grasping the widow's gloved hand in both of his. "—desperately sorry—one simply can't take it in—but if there's anything one can do—" His voice high-pitched and carrying.
The girl stood to one side, as if her share in the funeral was
marginal. She turned away from the others, looked toward
the chapel.

Sean moved closer, as if waiting his turn to offer con-
dolences to the widow. "I don't know what to tell you to look
for," the major had said. "I'm not even sure it's there."

The girl had a broad, high-cheekboned face, very pale
under the mantilla, the heavy mass of hair. The hair was no
longer completely black now that the sun was on it. Like
blackened copper. She looked straight at Sean and away
again, without really seeing him. Her eyes green, slanting,
almost Chinese. And crying.

She was wearing a loose black linen coat over a dark close-
fitting dress; the suggestion as she moved of a hidden richness of figure, of a dark magnificence. More than a "friend
from television"? She put up one hand, drew the edge of the
black lace mantilla forward, shadowing her eyes, the side of
her face. Her mouth was full and soft and beautiful. Mistress? No man with that kind of mistress could kill himself,
unless he was losing her. "That is why God made women."

The fat young man caught her arm, not as gently as he
might have done, pulled her away, his eyes briefly meeting
Sean's, small and bright with suspicion, like currants in
suet.

They went over to the red sports car, Italian, expensive,
the man whispering fiercely to the girl. There was something
more than funeral ill-temper about the set of his head, the

—

angle of his forearm as he half handed, half pushed her into the car. Her eyes met Sean's again as she leaned back in the black leather seat. Looking at him as if the whispering had been about him. Was the fat young man a jealous, unloved husband? The car snarled into movement, swung viciously past Sean, the flared, arrogant wing uncomfortably close to his legs, the driver doggedly not seeing him. But the girl saw him, the green, slanting eyes wide with speculation, with something more than curiosity.

The car accelerated toward the gateway, braked hard to avoid an incoming hearse, accelerated again and vanished in a roar of triumph and contempt up the London road. Sean got into his own fifth-hand, broken-down Jaguar, feeling a half-wakening of interest as if for that moment there had been conflict. He stared for a long moment in the direction they had gone, remembering the girl's face, heavy, almost sleeping—the eyes.

Other mourners were going, making way for the incoming funeral. The big man with the heavy black mustache and the bronzed face, like a Kipling soldier, was handing the widow into a vast hired car. The older woman was already in. Sean started his own car, let it roll forward, followed the hire-car out of the crematorium. It turned right, away from London, headed for the center of Learham.

Just short of the center they swung right again and made their way out through increasingly prosperous suburbs that had once been villages, to Aylesham Road, and number 37. A pleasant two-story house in mock-Jacobean style, with diamond-paned windows and a carefully shaven lawn running down from a glassed-in porch to the front gate. An expensive-looking house. Too expensive for a television producer?

Sean stubbed out his cigarette in the crammed ash tray and crossed the road to the wrought-iron gate. "I don't know what to tell you to look for. I don't even know it's there."

—

12

And if Randall found out he had been looking, there was going to be trouble. Which might be a very good thing. He found the bell—a wrought-iron bell hidden behind a hanging basket of flowers—and heard it chime inside the house. Nothing else happened for what seemed a very long time. What could he say to her? What could he ask that hadn't been asked at the inquest?

The inquest had been very quick, very simple. Everyone seemed to have thought it was perfectly straightforward. Police. Coroner. And Randall. Only the major hadn't. And the thought came to him again, forcing its way into his mind as if Randall had poisoned it, that the major was very old, much older than his age in years—very ill, very out of touch. And trying desperately to get back into some kind of touch, however imaginary?

A shadow moved behind the amber bottle-glass panels of the front door. The old woman opened it. A beaked nose. Fierce, sunken, washed-out blue eyes, wisps of gray hair, an old, thin gray cardigan over stooped, bony shoulders.

"I'm Inspector Ryan," Sean said. "If I might see Mrs. Redwin for a few minutes?"

The old woman looked at him. "We've just been to my son's funeral. We're not receiving visitors." The faintest trace of a foreign accent. The mother was Norwegian, he remembered.

"I know," Sean said. "I would much rather not have come today but—"

"You were at the funeral." Peering at him. "Why?"

"I—"

The widow came into the hall. "Who is it?"

"I'm from the Special Branch," Sean said. "If you'd be kind enough—"

A tall woman who had once been handsome. Brown hair that suggested dye. The lines of the face sagging. Eyes red from crying. "I've told him to go away," the old woman said.

—

13

She was trying to close the door. Unobtrusively Sean put the side of his foot against it.

"You'd better come in," the widow said. "Weren't you satisfied with the inquest?" Her voice bitter with hatred. "What more do you want?"

"Just a few minutes. I'll make it as brief as I can."

She led the way into a sitting room: chintz, flowers, a baby-grand piano, photographs in silver frames. Mostly of men in uniform. A wedding photograph. Her own? Sean moved slightly so that he could see it better. A tall, thin young officer, dark, almost swarthy, smiling self-consciously, his new bride looking at him proudly, an indistinct background of men in uniform holding swords above the couple's heads in a protective arch.

Sean looked away, hoping that she hadn't noticed, suddenly ashamed, as if he had looked at something that shouldn't be seen by strangers. What had they hoped for that day? Whatever it had been it wasn't this.

"Well?"

He hesitated, wondering whether to ask her what she meant about the inquest. Had the Special Branch really been onto her?

"Just before he—died, your husband tried to get in touch with—one of our departments. He put an advertisement in the *Times*, saying that he had what he called 'frightening news' for us. Before we could get in touch with him he—shot himself. Did he tell you what the news was?"

She looked at him strangely, as if she couldn't understand what he was saying. The old woman, who had come into the room behind them and taken a chair close to the door, like a chaperone, leaned forward. "Shot himself? Shot himself? My son was murdered! Don't let us tell lies about it here, in his house, whatever we must say outside."

"Mother, please." The widow closed her eyes. "I don't understand, Mr.—"

—

14

"Ryan."

"Mr. Ryan. Surely we've been through all this before?"

"If we could just go through it again," Sean said, feeling his way. "Just tell me from the beginning."

"What is there to tell? When he was making this film about colored people in England he learned too much about them. And they put him out of the way." She leaned her head back against the cushions of her chair, her face rigid with barely maintained self-control.

"What did he learn?" Sean said gently. The truth seemed to take shape in the room like a ghost, clanking the sad chains of madness.

"That there is a world conspiracy of colored people to destroy us," she said tiredly, as if what she was saying was too commonplace to need emphasis. "And that it has a highly developed organization in this country." The tension had gone out of her face and only tiredness was left. And bitterness. "How many sacrifices do you ask of one man?" she said. "To be branded as a coward during the war. As a suicide now. Don't you think you've asked enough?"

"I am sorry," Sean said, wondering how to go with the least awkwardness. "Was there—anything else worrying him?" He had said it almost unthinkingly, just words to say, preparatory to getting himself out of the house.

The widow opened her eyes wide, looked at him as if he had struck her. "Anything else?" she whispered. "Do you mean—you don't believe—?"

"I told you," the old woman said. "They have been making a fool of you. Keeping you quiet." She stood up, stooped fiercely in front of Sean. "You are laughing, aren't you?" She swept his denial aside like cobwebs from her face. "You are such a clever young man, so soothing and kind. To keep us quiet, keep everything hushed up, nothing bad said that might upset those nice colored people who love us so much." Her voice was rising, spittle struck his face in cold drops like

—

15

rain. "But will you laugh so much when the day of payment comes, when we are starving and dying, when Chinese soldiers are trampling on the broken bodies of children and women, when men like you are being driven into concentration camps, shipped away to slavery in Asia? If you are lucky. If you are lucky enough to live that long."

Sean stood up. "Please," he said. "I'm sorry to have upset you."

"Upset?" The widow was standing now, her face flushed, like rouge on paper, flesh without substance. "He's dead. And you tell me not to say anything, not to do anything, leave it to you—"

"Who told you that?"

"Major Cannon of course."

"They're going to do nothing," the old woman hissed. "Nothing. Haven't I told you, it's a trick, just a trick to keep you quiet? They are bought, bribed; they think they will be commissars, rewarded and trusted. Wait till you see, Mr. Ryan. Wait till you see what will happen to you when your masters arrive." She had gripped his sleeve and was shaking it, spraying spittle into his face, her false teeth slipping up and down.

Sean backed away, tried to say something. The old woman followed him through the hall to the front door. "One day you'll know," she whispered. "When it's too late."

He got out onto the path. "Traitor!" she screamed after him. "Traitor to your race!" The door slammed behind him. He was alone among the Gloires de Dijon, genteel lawns and privet hedges stretching endlessly on either side of him, the afternoon sunlight flashing from the leaded windows of the house opposite. He got into the car and lit a cigarette. To his surprise he found his hands were shaking. That was sadly that. Except for one thing. Who was Major Cannon?

He sat thinking about it while he smoked the cigarette. The road stretched peacefully empty, overwhelmingly sane and stable in front of him. Two children in nice red blazers and clean flannels came home on bicycles from an obviously healthy school. Madness. Suicide. Nightmares of persecution shuddering behind the privet hedges, the diamond window panes. How many of these houses hid the same kind of insanity? Retired colonels certain that the Communists were infiltrating the golf club or poisoning their chrysanthemums just before the flower show?

And for a moment he had a shocked and dreadful vision of the life in front of the two women in the house across the road. How would the major take it?

He switched on the engine, trying not to think of Major Courtenay, something else nagging slightly at the back of his mind. The other major. Major Cannon. A lunatic neighbor? "It's all a plot. Your husband was killed by a mysterious Chinaman. Don't breathe a word. Department X is coping with it. Trust me." It must be something like that. And yet—

It was still worrying him halfway to London. He saw an inn sign ahead and remembered that he had missed his lunch. The Coach Inn. The sign showing a fat red-faced coachman in a great bottle-green overcoat with half a dozen capes, quaffing a gallon tankard of ale. He turned into the parking entrance, suddenly hungry, forgetting about Major Cannon in the vision of sirloin steak and beer. A car turned into the courtyard behind him and two men got out, but there was no other sign of life. He went inside. Timber paneling and brass ornaments. Fake horse brasses and sporting prints. A brass and copper coach horn hanging above the bar in the lounge, prints of famous stagecoaches on the walls, a Dickens calendar showing Mr. Pickwick and his friends eating themselves into a jolly stupor. But no waiter, no barman.

He went through the only visible doorway and it led first to an empty passage and then to a men's lavatory. The two

—

men who had parked behind him came in, and he looked around. "I think everyone's dead," he said, for the sake of saying something. The men nodded, mumbled, moved one on either side of him to the vacant places. Sean started to turn away. The man on his right whipped around very fast, caught his lapels in his left hand, lifted and pulled.

"You dirty bastard!" he shouted. "Peter, you see what he did?" and as he was shouting his right hand was moving. Sean saw it coming, saw the man's face, young, hard, packed with muscle, eyes cold, unexcited, icily efficient; saw the arm swinging, the hand flat, fingers extended like the broad blade of a knife. He started to lift his own hands, but he was off balance, and then his arms were caught from behind, pulled back, twisted. The extended fingers hit him high up in the stomach, just under the ribs. Like being disemboweled. He folded forward and the elbow followed through, smashed him across the side of the jaw. He couldn't see, couldn't think, felt something hit him again. Elbow? Knee? He didn't even know where it hit him. Hands pulling at his coat. Cold stone under his face. Wet. Nothing.

He came around, tasting blood, vomit—a searing pain inside his body as if he had been cut in half. When he tried to think his head started opening and closing, faster and faster. He rested his head against something white and cold. There was a rushing noise, and water came flooding down on top of him, soaking his head, neck, shirt, running down inside his clothes, shocking him alive. He tried to sit up, and it was difficult to move. Nothing co-ordinated, he hadn't any strength.

Someone came into the lavatory, cried out. Voices. Hands pulling at him. Not gently, roughly, dragging and shaking, propping him upright. "Good God, he's bleeding. What the devil—" A big gingery mustache, a colored silk scarf. The other man had a white coat. Doctor? How had a doctor— lucky, lucky it was a— His head started to go around and he felt vomit flooding up his throat. He retched and twisted his head. The vomit went on the stone floor, over a pair of suede shoes, yellow ankle socks. Trouser ends.

"God damn it—"

He felt better after being sick. He was cold and sweating but he could see, he could focus. He was in a lavatory. A man in a blazer and flannels and a striped silk scarf stepping away from him, gingery handlebar mustache quivering in disgust and outrage, while the waiter—barman—made clucking noises, tried to look helpful. Sean gripped the copper water pipe, dragged himself upright. His legs were shaking but he could stand.

"Two men—" he said. "Beat me up—" He felt his pockets. His wallet was gone. He caught sight of his face in the mirror over the one washbasin. Blood still running sluggishly out of his nose. His clothes stained, sodden, his hair on end.

"We'd better get him out of here," the mustache said. They took him by the elbows, helped him walk. The mustache kept him at arm's length while they were doing it, as if he smelled. He probably did, he thought. Down a corridor, into a storeroom. Bottles in cases, on racks, on shelves; tins of potato crisps piled three quarters of the way up to the ceiling. Jars of olives, maraschino cherries. There was a wooden chair and they sat him on it. The barman fetched a wet cloth and gave it to him.

"Thanks," he said. "Did you see them? Two men, young, raincoats."

The mustache was looking at him from hostile, gin-washed eyes. Like Randall's eyes, he thought. "Look here," the man was saying. "Are you sure about this? You didn't just fall? I run a pretty decent pub here and chaps don't just beat up other chaps in the lavo—not without a jolly good reason, that is."

Sean pressed the wet cloth against his face. Cold and hideously painful and then wonderful. He didn't want to talk

—

19

or think. He must have got a knee in the face. When he put the cloth against his left temple it felt as though the bone was broken.

"If I were you," the man was saying, "I'd think pretty carefully before you start throwing accusations about." And to the barman. "Did you see two chaps in raincoats?"

"No, sir. Not been a soul in the bar since half past three, sir."

"I've been in the bar since half past three," Sean said. But the effort of thinking it out, saying it, made him feel sick again. They had known how to do it. Not amateurs. A long, long way from amateurs. He tried to think about telling the police. If they were simply thieves, it would be a waste of time; and if they weren't, it wasn't a police thing. Why had they done it?

The landlord was putting a glass of something into his hand. "You'll feel all right if you down that. Raises the dead. And I'd toddle off home if I were you and put a bit of steak on that eye."

Steak. "That's what I was looking for," Sean said. "I came in for a meal." It seemed somehow important to explain. His head was still opening and shutting.

"Don't serve food, old man. Can't get the staff. You just toddle off home and forget about it. And next time I'd go a bit easier on the throat oil if I were you. You can get a damn nasty fall in a lavo if the old legs give way."

Sean drank what he'd been given. It smelled vaguely like brandy and tasted like surgical spirit, but it cleared his head. Were these two part of it, covering up for the others? Or just protecting their filthy pub? It was too complicated to work out. He gave back the glass and finished cleaning his face.

"You'll be as right as rain in the morning, old man. Just sleep it off."

They waited while he combed his hair and cleaned the worst mess off his coat and then took him out a back way.

—

"Don't want to frighten the other guests, do we, old man?" The landlord's manner was almost jolly now that he saw there was going to be no trouble. But his eyes were still coldly watchful, like glass eyes in the bottom of a tumbler of gin. Sean felt for his keys. They hadn't taken those, thank God. He fell into the car seat, let them close the door on him.

"Cheerio, old man. Drive carefully." He wanted not to move, not to do anything, but they were standing beside the car, waiting. He drove very slowly out of the courtyard. The drink was making him muzzy. He drove a hundred yards up the road and stopped. Whenever he moved his arms the muscles of his stomach seemed to tear. He wanted to get sick again, but when he got out of the car nothing happened. He walked up and down very slowly, and then sat on the grass by the roadside. After a few minutes he lay down. Major Cannon. Major Cannon had done it. He had a huge ginger mustache and little glassy blue eyes. He had done it.

When he woke up it was twilight.

3

HE WAS stiff and cold and hungry, and when he sat up his head spun around and he felt sick. He sat with his head between his knees and tried to force himself to feel better. A car went by with its headlamps already on and the light struck him like a blow, swept over him, was followed by more lights. Somewhere at the back of his mind was the fear that they might have followed him, waited for him. He couldn't work anything out. Why, how? And the drink he'd been given. Raw alchohol? In case he went to the police? Did that mean—?

He got back into the car, glad to sink into the cold, sagging embrace of the bucket seat, feel the car around him. Like an old, worn-out friend. But still a friend. He switched on the engine and the heater, lit a cigarette and sat in the dark, while the lights flowed past, hit the car, filled it with sudden brightness, left it coffin-black. The cigarette made him feel worse and he stubbed it out. No one could have known he was going to stop at the Coach Inn. Couldn't have guessed it.

Were they just two toughies waiting for a quick roll, anyone, so long as he was alone and the place was quiet enough? He tried to remember their faces, their actions. They hadn't been that type. They had known too much, done it too well. Ex-commandos—cold, quick and brutally efficient. The kind of men who'd normally be working for big money for a big boss. Not for risky fivers in pub lavatories. They'd been after him, not just anyone. If they hadn't done it back there it would have been somewhere else.

Which meant that the landlord couldn't have been in it, couldn't have known he was going—anyone was going to be beaten up; was just protecting the reputation of his rotten pub. The police wouldn't take much notice of a man stinking of alcohol and vomit, and spewing his appendix up on the station floor.

He got out of the car and was sick again from merely thinking about being sick. He leaned against the door of the Jaguar, feeling wrung-out, drenched with cold, oily sweat and weak as a drowned cat, but clearer-headed. Why had they done it? Something to do with Redwin? And what ought he to do about it?

Tell Randall of course. Only that was going to be worse

than difficult. For the major rather than for him. He got back
into the car and started driving slowly toward London.

"I shouldn't ask you this," the major had said. This morning. Nine, ten hours ago. It seemed a lot longer. Drinking a
glass of sherry in the small, unbearably neat sitting room of
the major's house. Itself too small, like a doll's house. Queen
Anne, paneled and polished and furnished with the right
things: a pocket garden outside the bow windows, green velvet and red brick and three ancient plum trees. All of it like
a page in a magazine article about "The Real England." But
totally wrong for the major, who needed fug and clutter and
spilled ash, and big, ugly, comfortable Victorian furniture. It
was as though he had become the prisoner of his housekeeper, an old Scotch woman who spent her life polishing
and disapproving and worrying about the major's health.
Which was bad enough to need worrying about.

Retirement had seemed to make him an old man over-
night. Sean could remember almost the exact moment when
it had happened, when from being "the old man," the major
had simply become old—an old, unwanted man in a shabby
suit, his eyes faded, exhausted, with nothing to look for any
longer. It had been at the party. Not really a party but a
small, gruesome "celebration," with a bottle of champagne
and borrowed glasses and everyone standing around the
office too embarrassed to look anyone else straight in the
eyes. Old Mr. Drybergh, talking about the fishing hotel he
was going to buy; and Anthony, who had come back the
night before from some loan-assignment with the CIA in
Thailand, his face fat and pasty as ever and a jagged scar
halfway around his throat; John Trent, who was taking over
from the major, trying not to appear too pleased, too impa-
tient to get on with it; and John Trent's German wife being
silkily unpleasant to Margaret over the top of her champagne glass, obviously seeing her as an office wife who'd

need her feathers trimmed. And Sean. And the major. And two or three of the others who happened to be in town.

There was another bottle of champagne and a third, and the atmosphere had warmed and everyone was talking guarded shop and laughing at shop jokes and gossip. Except for the major. No one did it on purpose. No one but Sean seemed to notice it. He was simply by-passed, as if by unconscious consent the others had agreed that he was no longer really alive. Mr. Drybergh was still alive, telling pawky Scots jokes and spreading malicious rumors and boasting in a canny way about the tourist prospects of Sutherland, where his hotel was. But the major was dead.

When it was over, Sean followed him down the stairs and out into the street. John Trent offered them both a lift, but the major refused it and Sean and he walked together for a long way through the dark January evening, neither of them talking. And oddly enough, after years of working together it was only during that silent walk that they became something close to friends. At Hyde Park Corner, when the major finally decided to take a taxi, he touched Sean on the arm. "Keep in touch," he had said, and had given Sean his private address, the doll's house in Richmond.

They had met only four times since then, but the friendship had grown. Once it had been by accident in Piccadilly and they had had tea together in a hotel. The second time had been just after Trent's sudden, unexpected transfer to Washington. The major had sent Sean a note, asking him to dinner, and they had had an awkward, uncomfortable meal, with the major obviously wanting to ask what the new chief, Oliver Randall, was like, and not knowing how to begin.

"Ex-Navy," Sean had said cautiously when the housekeeper had at last left them alone with brandy and cigars. "Only the one now, major," she had said. "Ye know fine what the doctor would say if he knew ye were havin' even that."

"He's told us he wants to run a tight ship but a happy

—

24

ship," Sean went on. And the major had nodded as if he didn't need to be told any more. He knew all he wanted to soon enough at first-hand. Various loose ends from previous assignments called for meetings, and although Sean had been in Italy and Yugoslavia for a lot of the time, he had heard the gossip. Mr. Drybergh walking out of one conference saying that he'd not come down to London again while that "matinee pig" was performing there. Oliver Randall treating both Mr. Drybergh and the major as though they were senile. Picking out minor discrepancies in old expense accounts; finding odds and ends that hadn't been documented in quintuplicate.

Sean had met the major on the stairs one morning and the old man had brushed past him as if he didn't recognize him, his head shaking as if he had palsy, his papery, withered cheeks flushed with anger and humiliation. It was as though Randall had some mental compulsion not merely to succeed the major—John Trent had scarcely had time to read the files before he was transferred—but to destroy any image he had left behind.

Even so, he was the major's lawful successor and Sean's chief, and it had taken the major a long time and a second glass of sherry to come to the point that morning: that he wanted Sean to do something without telling Randall. To go to the funeral of a man who was supposed to have shot himself. "It's a place called Learham. Three o'clock this afternoon. And I want you to—that's the devil of it—I don't really know what to tell you to do." He had sat staring out the window at the plum trees, his head shaking a little, his cheeks an unhealthy, leaden color. Although the morning was very warm he had the windows shut and the gas fire blazing, and even so he shivered every now and then.

"I'd better start at the beginning. This chap Redwin joined us during the war for a special operation. In Norway. His mother was Norwegian and he'd worked there for a couple

—

of years just before the war. He was bilingual and he had lots of local friends, good cover. His father was something in the fish business in Yorkshire and he'd sent his son to Norway to learn the trade." The major coughed dryly, without much humor. "The poor devil hated every minute of it. He told me once he'd wanted to be a poet—"

And Sean had sat cradling his sherry in one hand, his mind recording what the major was saying but not really listening. Later he'd be able to play it back, word for word, even the inflections. But now his real mind was thinking of the past rather than the present: all the other times he had sat like this, listening to the major—being briefed, rebuked, advised, reminisced at. Until out of it had come—friendship? Respect? His mind stumbled on the word "love" and rejected it instantly. Yet he had never felt for his own father as he felt for this man, with his ragged white mustache and faded blue eyes half hidden by the heavy, drooping eyelids; cigarette ash scattered down the too-broad lapels of his old-fashioned, shabby suit. And his hatred of Randall, of what that matinee pig with his actor's profile and gutter venom had done to this man, seemed to catch him under the heart, made him clench his hands so hard that the stem of his sherry glass snapped, and glass and wine fell on the carpet, left a smear of blood on his left forefinger.

"It doesn't matter," the major said. Although it obviously did. The glass had been beautiful, threads of blue and red caught inside the twisted stem—Venetian, old. Sean picked up the ruins and put them on a small silver tray on a side table.

"Pour yourself another one," the major said. "And you might as well fill mine. Where was I?—oh, yes—his father had packed him off to Norway in 1938 and he was there when the war broke out, buying and selling fish and hating it. I think he thought the war was specially invented to get him out of it. And eventually he came to us.

"Someone had made him an officer but he was no good at it. Too many brains, I suppose. The wrong kind. All his COs hated him. But I rather liked him." The major had glanced sideways at Sean, for that moment almost his old self, the eyelids drooping with a hint of malicious humor, the straight mouth under the fringe of white mustache twitching into a half-smile. "He wasn't altogether unlike you. Always asking the wrong questions. But much cleverer." He had smiled again, very sadly. "Too clever in the end, for us at least.

"What we wanted him for was a bit obscure—I'm telling you all this because it may have a bearing—" As he went on talking he seemed to gather strength. As though he were back in authority, back in the office, had a reason for living again. He even felt for the cigarettes that his housekeeper prevented him from smoking.

Sean gave him one. "They're not Russian I'm afraid," Sean said, lighting it, and then his own.

The major drew the smoke into his lungs like air. Even his voice sounded stronger and the shaking of his head stopped. "We wanted to set up a decoy organization in central Norway—something to draw the Gestapo off what we were really doing about the heavy-water plant. And Redwin was perfect for it. Obvious enough to draw the SD's attention pretty soon after he started, because of course a lot of the locals knew him quite well before the war as an Englishman —it was a racing certainty that one or two of them would give him away, even if it was only by mistake—but clever enough to keep them chasing him for a fairish time. We were hoping for two or three months. If he was still free by then we'd have fetched him out of course. And if he wasn't—"

He looked away from Sean, his voice becoming fractionally defensive. "—it would have still served our turn. You see, we didn't let him know he was just a decoy. He thought he was setting up a real circuit. Jotun was the name for it.

—

And if it had any successes, well, why not? We gave Redwin some sabotage targets and told him they were desperately important for the heavy-water exercise. Of course they weren't, but we'd have been quite glad to see them knocked out. And if Redwin was caught and cracked—it'd do a double thing for us. Persuade the SD that they'd caught our real man, and also that we were aiming at the wrong targets."

His eyes were looking far away from Sean, and from the present—into a past where he himself was almost as young as Sean. A past in which he still mattered, still gave orders that would be carried out, had a share in the world. Sean guessed that he was talking as much for that re-creation of his own past as to tell Sean about Redwin's. Could all this matter, all this long-dead intrigue? Had it mattered even then? He thought of all the dead agents, the ones who had died anonymously and the ones who had died screaming, and the ones who had slowly starved and rotted in Dachau and Ravensbrück. For the politicians to say after the war that none of it had really mattered, none of it had made much difference.

The major crushed out his cigarette. "You might as well give me another one. She'll smell I've been smoking, anyway." Illness came back on him like a heavy shadow. His hand shook a little as he took the cigarette, tried to hold Sean's hand, to guide the flame to the cigarette trembling in his mouth.

"What happened?" Sean said, thinking the major had lost the thread of his thoughts.

"He found out," the major said, his eyes far away again. "I told you he was too clever. He found out that the targets didn't really matter and the whole thing was a fake. Only he didn't realize why—that it was just as important as if the targets had been the real ones. Or perhaps he did realize that and didn't care. I don't know. He had a streak of vanity that—"

He sat smoking the cigarette. "I liked him very much," he said at last. "Someone said once in a report about me that the only agents I ever really liked were the failures." He smiled at Sean to take the hurt out of the remark. "A good agent isn't always a very attractive character, you know. Of course you know. Randall is supposed to have been one of the best. Or so they tell me." He stared out of the window.

"Redwin should have been in SAS or the Commandos. Poets did very well in that sort of thing at times. The quick and sudden things. He wasn't really made for our kind of work. Only we thought that didn't matter."

"But what happened?"

The major looked at Sean in surprise, as if he were sure he had already told him everything. "The girl tipped him off— didn't I mention her? He had a girl friend from when he was working there before. Her father was in the local police. A sort of unwilling collaborator. They told him the Gestapo were on to him, and also that the factory he was aiming at hadn't anything to do with the heavy-water scheme. The girl got that from a fairly high-level German who was smitten with her. And Redwin put three and three together and made seven, and ran for it. He got across the border into Sweden and wound up in hospital in Stockholm with rheumatic fever."

"I don't think I blame him," Sean said.

"I didn't either, really. But the people who mattered did. Nothing was done about it, naturally. But it left a smell."

Sean thought of the widow in the mock-Elizabethan house. "How many sacrifices do you ask of one man? To be branded as a coward during the war—" What was his version of the story?

"He tried to get a court-martial to clear himself, when he

—

got back from Sweden. But there wasn't anything to get cleared of. You couldn't court-martial a man for escaping from the Gestapo. And then the war ended and the thing just died away. I heard once or twice that he tried to get back with us. But I suppose I hadn't thought of him for twenty years until I read this."

He took a folded sheet of foolscap from an inside pocket and gave it to Sean. Five newspaper clippings were stapled onto it. Three were identical. "Cora, frightening news. Reply with phone number soonest, Olga." Only the dates penciled in beside each clipping were different. The fourth was larger and dated two days after the last of the three Personal announcements. "Death of TV producer." Two short paragraphs.

Mr. Olaf Redwin, a television producer, was found shot dead yesterday morning in a small wood about three miles from his home at Learham, Surrey, A .38-caliber Webley revolver was found close to the body and one shot had been fired from it. The Learham police said that foul play was not suspected.

A spokesman for Midlands Television said that Mr. Redwin had been working under considerable pressure for some time past on a new public affairs series. "It was a major project involving great responsibilities," the spokesman added, "and it is now tragically evident that these weighed on his mind to an undue extent."

The fifth clipping was a brief report of the inquest, which had taken place two days before. Only formal evidence was offered, and the verdict was suicide while the balance of his mind was disturbed. Sean refolded the foolscap and gave it back to the major.

The major rested his head against the high back of the chair. He looked very tired. "It could be a mare's nest," he said. "It could even be some real Cora trying to find a real

Olga. But it would be a rather a coincidence—I remember when we chose then during Redwin's training someone objected that they must be the most unlikely pair of code names on record." He laid the palm of his hand against the paper on his knee and smiled. Or tried to smile. He was avoiding Sean's eyes and the blue shadows around his mouth were deepening.

"I told Randall about these advertisements as soon as I saw the first one. But he decided not to do anything about it." The faded eyes stared at an invisible humiliation.

"I put my own reply in then. I wish to God I'd done that immediately. By the time it went in he was dead, of course." He stopped, looked down at his hands, at the paper on his knee. "The police say they're satisfied. So does Randall. And so does— You'd better understand this, Sean—" His mouth worked, a faint flush of blood crept under his withered skin. "So does everyone else I've tried to talk to. They say that if it was Redwin who put these in—" He lifted his hand, let it fall on the paper, heavily, without any life or strength in the movement. Like a dead hand falling. "If it was, then it was just something—unbalanced—money trouble, he doesn't seem to have had anything like that, but of course you can never tell—some scheme to get money out of us, or just plain madness, just his mind working over the past until it drove him off the rails. I know these things can happen." He lifted his eyes to Sean's. "And the implication has rather been that I'm in the same way. Don't ever retire, Sean. Get them to put you down." He tried to smile. "You need to hear all this. If you want to say 'no'—" He looked away from Sean again, his face dark with humiliation.

"I don't want to say no," Sean said.

The major stiffened in his chair, put up one hand to his heart. His face turned from dark red to lead-gray, went rigid with an effort of control. His other hand felt in a waistcoat pocket. "Get me a glass of water," he whispered. "Don't call

—

31

that woman. There's a washroom off the hall with a glass—"

When Sean had found and filled the glass and brought it back, the major had two small white pills in the palm of his hand. He swallowed them and Sean held the glass for him to drink.

"Let me get a doctor," Sean said.

The major shook his head. "I'll be all right in a minute."

Sean waited. The leaden look went out of the major's face, a shadow of color came back. "I'll be all right," the major said again. "You'd better get on if—if you want to do this."

"I want to."

"I don't know what to tell you to look for. I'm not even sure it's there. But try and talk to the widow. Try and find out what he was doing just before—he died. What he was talking about—"

Half an hour later he'd been on his way down to Learham. A long way from certain that he wasn't wasting his time. And now? Nine hours later? Someone had been quite sure he wasn't wasting his time. What had they meant to do? Frighten him off? Or simply find out who he was? And where did Major Cannon fit in?

He hesitated over whether to ring Major Courtenay from another road house or wait till he reached his flat. But an hour wouldn't make much difference and he didn't fancy going into another pub with his face and clothes looking the way they did. He didn't let himself think of the other reasons. He was on the outskirts of London before he admitted to himself that he was afraid. He would have stopped then and telephoned from the next box, but there was no point in it.

And when he reached his flat he found there was no point in telephoning at all, wouldn't have been any time in the past hour. "The major's had a dreadfu' bad turn," the housekeeper told him, her voice filled with the morbid pride of an often disregarded and now justified prophet. "I had to call

—

32

the doctor to him juist before his tea. He's in the nursing home the noo and not to be having calls or veesitors of any kind. That's the strict orders from the doctor himsel'. No, no, no, I couldna' reach him. No, I'm no even givin' ye the doctor's name if that's what ye're thinking of. The major's no conscious. I'm tellin' ye, he's under sedation. No, it'll be several days the doctor says."

Sean put the phone down. Ring Randall? He ought to. He ran a bath and lay in it, letting the heat soak into his bruises, the torn muscles of his stomach, holding the sponge against his face in a slow luxury of pain. He ought to. But tell him what? Major Cannon. Two men in a lavatory stealing his wallet. He imagined the curved gray eyebrow lifting, the slow, malicious smile. "In a *lavatory?*" He thought of the major's face, darkening even at the memory of his humiliation. If Randall didn't want to be convinced by the major, he'd hardly be moved by what happened today. Unless he could get more.

"Try and find out what he was doing just before he died —what he was talking about." Where he worked. Midlands Television. If there was something there that he could tell Randall. Something. He found he was half asleep in the bath, and dragged himself to bed. He dreamed of two men with huge ginger mustaches, forcing him to drink, holding him down and forcing something vile into his mouth, down his throat. And when he tried to fight, tried to scream, he was suddenly alone, in the dark, closed in. And he knew in a paralysis of horror that he was in a coffin, that the coffin was moving, moving, sliding on rollers into the throat of the fire.

He tried to scream, tried to move his hands, screamed for Margaret, the major, beat his head against the padded side of the coffin. Heard the mourners praying, the priest saying, "We do now commit—" And the heat of the flames burned the coffin, reached into him with burning tongues— ahhhaahhhhhh.

—

33

He woke drenched in sweat, a tight knot of sheet and blanket twisted around him; fought his hand out to turn on the light. He lay awake for an hour after that, unable to sleep, his whole body aching from the bruises. It was almost daylight before he slept.

4

IN THE morning Sean tried to get through to the major again, and got as far as the doctor's telephone number and the name of the nursing home. The doctor had already left on his rounds. The matron of the home said that the major couldn't see anyone, and couldn't talk to them if he did. "He's very poorly, I'm afraid, sir. No visitors at all, not even close family."

Sean went back into the bathroom to shave. A bruise had spread over his right cheekbone up to the corner of his eye, turning greenish black in the night. His nose was swollen and one of his teeth was loose. He put talcum powder on the bruise to disguise it, but it made it look worse instead of better.

As he shaved he stared out of the bathroom window, not really looking at the street below, trying to think what he ought to do, what the major would want him to do. Across the road a man was leaning against the wall, reading a newspaper. He'd been there ten minutes earlier. Before Sean had made the phone call. Why not? It was a pleasant day, a reasonable thing to do. But he couldn't remember anyone doing it exactly there on other pleasant days. It was quite a narrow

—

pavement. And a hundred yards down the street there was a square with trees and public benches and a stretch of grass.

Sean tightened his tie, went down the one flight of stairs to the street and turned right, away from the square. When he reached the next corner he looked back. The man was walking slowly along the far side of the road, his newspaper folded under his arm, his eyes now on a shop front, now staring up at the sky with the air of a man with time to kill. Sean went into the chemist's shop on the corner. The man strolled past on the far side of the road, stopped a few shops farther along, stared into a toy-shop window, pursed his lips as if he were whistling a tune, and strolled back.

"Yes?" the girl was saying.

Sean touched the bruise on his cheek. "Make me beautiful again." He bought his razor blades and toothpaste here whenever he was in London, and for months had carried on a mock flirtation with the assistant. Once or twice he had almost thought of becoming serious about it. She was thin and dark and Italian, with languishing eyes and cool, beautiful hands. She spread make-up on his cheek with swift, professional movements and then smoothed it with a shade more than professional care.

"You should be more careful," she breathed. She smelled of the dozen perfumes she dabbed on her wrists each day for customers. It came to Sean that he wouldn't mind being more careful. Niccolò was right. It didn't do to think too much.

"Would you be more careful with me?"

"Don't be wicked," she said and tapped his other cheek very softly. The man across the street was reading his newspaper again. But he was holding it in such a way that he could see over the top of it by merely raising his eyes.

"Could I go out the back way?" Sean said. She looked at him in surprise. "I owe that man some money and I don't want to pay him. At least not today." He nodded at the door-

—

way and the distant newspaper reader framed in it. "Could I?"

She sighed, finishing the make-up, lingering over it, finding a hand mirror to show him what she had done. "I suppose so. But you should pay your debts. Weren't you ever told that?"

"Yes," Sean said. "I was. And I will. But just for now?"

She sighed again, looked to see if there was an imminent customer and took him out through a frosted-glass door behind the counter, leading through a dispensary to a small courtyard. The backs of tall houses closed it in. "Go down that passage and you're in Verreker Street," she said.

He caught her wrist. "If that man comes in to ask where I've gone—tell him I went out the front way ages ago. You don't know anything about me."

"That's true," she said. He lifted her wrist, kissed the palm of her hand with mock-gallantry. When he glanced back from the mouth of the passage she was still watching him. It made him feel slightly ashamed. And then pleased. It might do no harm to write to Niccolò. Just to keep in touch.

Halfway down Verreker Street he took a taxi. No one was following. He paid it off at Lancaster Gate and took the underground for Piccadilly Circus. Midlands Television occupied an Aztec temple just off Soho Square, five minutes north of the Circus. A vast reception area. A reception desk like a raft on a marble sea.

A woman with bleached hair and a lifted face was monopolizing the receptionist, introducing her to a six-foot snake draped around her neck like a scarf. "Right down the bloody W with just his poor tail sticking out of the S bend. I thought I'd never get him out. Toto darling, was it horrible? Was Muzzer's scrumptious nearly drownded den? And all the stupid sod of a plumber said on the phone was, why don't you flush him down?"

"Excuse me," Sean said. The snake slithered half its length

—

36

down its "muzzer's" bosom onto the desk and rubbed its throat on the blotter. The receptionist looked very unhappy. Sean tried to explain to her what he wanted, but most of her attention was on the snake. The gilded bronze doors of the central lift opened and five young men came out. Their hair hung in shaggy masses to below the shoulders of their crimson velvet coats. Under the coats, cut in what some Carnaby Street genius imagined was an eighteenth-century style, with huge rolled lapels and enormous gold buttons, the broad blue ribbon of the Garter crossed the white ruffled lace of their shirt fronts. Black silk knee breeches and gold-buckled shoes completed the Regency effect. Only the twentieth-century brutality of the faces looked out of place.

Along the red leather couches by the far wall girls and young men waiting for auditions looked at the five with envy, whispered to each other.

"It must be Mr. Vining you want," the receptionist was saying. The snake was flowing over the edge of the desk into her lap.

"Toto!" the bleached woman was crooning. "Muzzer will be jealous." Her eyes in their wrinkled pockets of eyelid were measuring Sean for size. She wore a cross-over blouse that molded her bosom like an elastic bandage, and she lifted her shoulder a little, angling her left breast in Sean's direction like a gun.

"Mr. Vining? There's a gentleman here—" The receptionist looked at Sean.

"Inspector Ryan." As he said it he wished he'd given another name, but the woman's breast, the snake, the eighteenth-century dandies had distracted his mind. Out beyond the glass doors female voices were screaming, "It's Them, it's Them!"

"If you'd go up to the fifth floor, sir. Mr. Vining will meet the elevator."

The bleached woman hauled Toto back by his tail. "I suppose it's having him in the bath with me. He just thinks any water is bath time—"

The elevator purred upward. "Who were the boys in velvet?" Sean asked, for something to say. The elevator operator, old and wrinkled, like a tortoise in a bottle-green overcoat, looked at him in astonishment. "That's Them of course, the Them Group. Top of the charts nine weeks running. You must know Them." He sounded like a verger who had just been asked about God. "Fifth floor, sir." Sean wondered if Redwin had had to work with Them. And Toto. No wonder he'd shot himself.

The fat young man from the funeral was waiting as the gates opened, already smiling, hand lifting. It looked as though it would be damp, and it was.

"Inspector! Come along to my office. Didn't I see you at the funeral yesterday?" He steered Sean through a doorway into a large cool room with pastel walls and a secretary, and then through a farther doorway into a much larger room again. One black wall, with an orange and crimson abstract splashed on it; the other walls lime green and bare. All the furniture was low and black and pneumatic.

"My pad," Vining said. His eyes were quick and dark and didn't seem to belong to his face. Like eyes behind a mask: the mask fat, pasty, suet-pale and sluggish, but the eyes sharp as a ferret's, small and black, sliding away from Sean's. "Sit down, sit down." Sean sank into a chair like part of a black zeppelin, felt air gush out of the interior, the leather mold itself around him. Vining smiled at him across the black leather top of the metal desk, pulled a cord, and the angle of the Venetian blinds behind the desk altered, let sunlight in and turned his face into a mask of shadows.

"Can't bear the dark," he said. "One sees so little of the sun. In this dreadful climate." His hands caressed the top of the desk, ran on it like small fat animals.

38

"What can we do for you?" the hands scuttled, lay flat, waited.

Sean wanted to move his chair but it was too heavy and he was sitting too low down to get purchase. The sun was blinding. "I wanted to know exactly what Redwin was doing just before he died."

"Poor Olaf," the almost invisible mouth said. The little animals on the desk ran together, made a loving heap, separated. "A tragic thing. But—forgive me—one rather gathered after the inquest that—how shall I put it?—that the police had no further interest. Is one wrong about that?"

Sean hesitated. "Just a loose end or two. I believe he was making a film about colored immigrants—"

"Ah!" Vining said. "I see you've been talking to poor Mary Redwin. I hope you didn't take her *au pied de la lettre.* She's—well, one doesn't want to be unkind—"

"Of course not," Sean said. "But if I could see the files— there are files?"

"My dear Inspector! With pleasure." The pleasure seemed genuine. A change, a warmth had come into his voice, his manner. "I'll send for them." He touched a button on the intercom. "Eva? Bring me Olaf's files on the Britain 1970 series, will you? To my office." He leaned back and adjusted the Venetian blinds again. The glare eased "A tremendous undertaking. Tremendous. No wonder the poor devil cracked. Project the future of a country in a series of documentaries." He shook his head. "I don't know how we'll replace him."

"Was he doing the whole series by himself?"

Vining laughed. His eyes slid about. "Good heavens, no. There'll be a half dozen directors, myself as executive producer, a whole team of us, naturally. But he was preparing it, doing the donkey work."

"What's it about?" Sean said, not thinking of what Vining

was saying, but only of how he was saying it. Why had the atmosphere changed like that?

The fat white hands spread themselves. "Britain 1970, exactly that. Our Swinging Britain. Only—one doesn't have to approve of all the Swing, don't you agree?" He had picked up a pencil from somewhere on the desk and he leaned back, holding it between his two hands, delicately. "We're usually accused in TV of climbing on bandwagons, of debasing taste. It's not always true, you know. Some of us have a sense of responsibility. In this series we're rather aiming to prick the balloon. Show viewers the way things are going and ask them if they're quite sure this is the way they want them to go on."

He balanced the pencil upright on its point. "One may have an effect. One prays so. One can imagine sometimes what Lot felt like in Sodom." He smiled deprecatingly, his eyes almost disappearing. "But I'm being too serious, Inspector. Perhaps you're a devotee? A Swinger?"

"Not really," Sean said.

"The music has to stop sometime, you know." The pencil fell on its side with a sharp, small tap. "Like that. Then the hangover will start. And all of Carnaby Street and the Go-Go clubs and the Beautiful People won't be much good to us then. The photographer-earls and the fashion-princesses and the beat-millionaires. They won't pay our bills for us when our foreign creditors present them. I'm afraid we're in for a rather unpleasant time, Inspector, unless we stop swinging fairly soon." He smiled again.

"How do the immigrants fit in?"

"One has to ask oneself exactly that, Inspector. How *do* they fit in?" The eyes slid, then fixed themselves on Sean's. "Or do I shock you?"

"No," Sean said, lost for the moment.

"One doesn't say these things in public. But isn't it one of the symptoms of our death wish almost, that while our best

—

40

brains and bodies are emigrating—to America, Australia, South Africa—we're importing, how many is it to date, two million? three million? of the dregs of Asia and the West Indies? Illiterate, diseased, unskilled, most of them unable even to speak English—How much of your work as a policeman, Inspector, is a direct result of all this?" He raised his eyebrows, waited. Sean nodded knowingly. Vining and Mary Redwin together, seeing Chinese under the bed?

"I'm afraid I'm riding my hobby horse," Vining said. "Of course, one can't say these things bluntly on the screen. But one can present facts dispassionately, one can suggest and indicate. One hopes that one can even persuade."

The door had opened. "Ah, Eva, come in." The girl. She was wearing a peasant blouse and skirt, embroidered, the blouse cut very low, showing smooth, full shoulders, her neck beautifully set on them, beautifully molded. Sean stood as she turned toward him, her arms holding a sheaf of orange and purple folders. The green eyes recognizing him, widening for a second with shock, with fear, the full, dark mouth opening. He saw her bare arms tighten on the files, press them against her breast. One of the files slipped, began to fall. Sean caught it; his fingers brushed her arm, warm, smooth.

"Inspector Ryan is particularly interested in the program about immigrants," Vining was saying.

"That was the one I was looking for," the girl said. Her voice was low, almost a whisper. A slight accent. "That was why I was so long. It was not with the others." She went on looking at Sean while she was saying it.

Sean looked down at the file in his hands, the one that had been on top of the pile she was carrying. "Britain 1970—Immigrants." The telephone rang.

"Excuse me," Vining said. "Yes, Vining here."

Sean looked at the girl. Redwin's mistress? He had been lucky if she was. Not fashionably beautiful, but the kind a

—

41

man could drown in. Had he drowned? His fingers still felt the contact with her arm, a warmth, a richness that had tightened his nerves. He lifted his eyes from her hands, folded over the bright covers of the files, the fingers touching the smooth curve of flesh above the edge of the blouse, looked at her face. What was she afraid of? Him? And there was something else in her eyes.

"He's here now," Vining was saying, his voice starting sharply, then dropping to a low murmur. "How the hell could I know? Yes, yes, soon as you can." His hand on another phone. His voice still very low. "Send up Jenkins and Williams. Quickly, please. Yes. Trouble." And in an even lower voice, "Call one of the mechanics to see to the elevators immediately." Sean heard the conversations without translating them into meaning, his mind on the girl, her eyes. As if she was trying to tell him something. The sound of Vining's words came back to him like an echo, so that there was a long time lag between hearing and understanding.

"He's here now."

Vining crossing the floor, holding out his hand, smiling, his face very white. "Let me see if we can find what you want, Inspector." His voice not quite steady. Someone ringing up about—Sean Ryan? Being told, "He's here now." And then someone else—reception?—"Send up Jenkins and Williams." Security men?

Vining reaching out casually to the file in Sean's hand. "Let me take that from you. Eva, would you see about getting us some tea?" Smiling, his face white and sweating, the small eyes sliding, insect-dark and quick and frightened. His hand on the file. Eva half turning, looking in surprise, as if she too caught the sound of fear in his voice. Sean put the flat of his hand against Vining's chest, pushed. His hand seemed to go in a long way, into a cushion, a rubber mattress of fat. Vining staggered, tottered backward, taking little

—

42

mincing steps, was caught across the back of his thighs by the desk, fell backward over it.

Sean reached past the girl, thought for a fraction of a second of taking more of the files and rejected it, found the handle of the door.

"Stop him," Vining shouted. Sean's arm against the girl's shoulder, pushing past her, her eyes wide. He was in the corridor, running for the elevators, the stairs. No elevator. He started down the narrow starcase, stone, used only for service, fourth floor, third. Men were coming up toward him, running. They only needed to have stopped the elevators, blocked the staircase. He made the second floor as they reached it, two men in uniform, a man in overalls behind them, carrying a monkey wrench. Sean swung right, down a long corridor, rubber-floored, endless. Vining shouted behind him, "Thief! Thief!" There was an opening to the right and Sean threw himself into it, opened one of three doors and was on a narrow catwalk, metal, a thin rail, a forest of metal rods, full of shadows. All the light came from underneath, through the expanded metal of the catwalk, up through the gratings among the rods.

As Sean ran he saw a studio under him, huge, empty, infinitely far down. Screens, scenery, cameras, like toys on the floor. And the rods hanging below the gratings, ending in huge spotlights, the square frames of monitors. The men were on the catwalk behind him and he felt it sway under their feet, shake him as he ran. The catwalk branched, turned right and left among the lighting controls, lost itself in the shadows. They were close behind. Sean turned, gripped the rails on either side of him with both hands and swung both feet, up and out. The man closest behind him tried to stop, to throw himself sideways, half fell, and the man on his heels tripped over him, came sprawling forward. The flat of Sean's kick caught him in the face, stood him up-

—

right until the third man crashed into his back and knocked him forward. Sean was already running. He heard the ring of metal falling, the wrench hitting the catwalk, sliding, ringing between the metal bars.

He was at the far side of the studio, saw an iron stairway, steep as a ladder, dropping down into nothing. He went down like a monkey, missing five steps at a time, the rails burning his hands, the cardboard file threatening to drop out of his coat pocket, where he had stuffed it, roughly folded, bulging. Two of them had reached the ladder, were coming down. Halfway. Near the bottom. Floor under his feet, soft, quiet, a great canvas screen beside him, a vast hanging curtain surrounding the studio, as high as the ladder. He found an opening, was in a narrow, stifling space between screen and wall, cables under his feet, the screen swaying and yielding at his shoulder. Voices behind him. The space opened, there were huge shapes, scenery, things covered in sheets—a fire engine, the front of a shop, a telephone kiosk, armchairs, the wall of a house, a lamppost, the wreckage of a car, a double bed.

He ran and the voices ran behind him, their feet almost silent on the rubber floor. Someone hit the lamppost and it fell softly, made of balsa wood and plastic foam. "There's the bastard. George! Bill!"

A man in an apron came out from behind a tree, holding a branch in one hand and a hammer in the other, his mouth full of nails. "Yer? Yer?" His eyes widened, seeing Sean coming; his mouth opened, let the nails fall.

"Stop him! Stop him!"

The man lifting the hammer, in self-defense rather than attack, falling back before Sean could reach him. But the branch of the tree caught between Sean's legs, tripped him, and he fell, sprawled, hit scenery, felt it sway, crash down. He was in a ruined kitchen, lying on the floor, a dresser falling, spilling plates, cups, saucers, pots, pans. He got to his

—

knees, saw a scatter of papers on the floor around him, from the file that had been thrown out of his pocket in the fall. He saw the corner of the file cover, an orange triangle sticking out from under the dresser, reached for it, realized it was empty and grabbed a handful of the papers. One of the searchers ran past the far side of a heap of scenery, bumped into something that fell.

"Which way did he go?"

"Over here."

"Where the hell are you?"

Feet crunching on broken glass, the side of a room swaying, collapsing on top of Sean's kneeling back. He stayed still, hidden in a cave of darkness. Feet stumbled a yard away, a voice cursed, another voice from much farther away yelled, "Jesus Christ, what's happening out there? Don't you know what a bloody red light means, you mucking nit?"

Voices explaining, moving off. Sean waited. The voices started to come nearer again. More of them. He crept on hands and knees around the edge of the dresser, squeezed between a penny-farthing bicycle and a roll-top desk—so like the major's old desk from the office that he felt a shock of recognition—more furniture, a heap of rocks made out of foam rubber. He put his hand through a rock as he tried to lean on it—soft, spongy, clinging. A long couch, screens, a flood of brilliant, blinding light.

He was in another studio, chairs set for a discussion group, cameras crawling on motor trolleys toward the woman with the snake, a man with platinum hair and a leopard cub in his lap on a silver chain, another man holding a hooded falcon on his gloved wrist. The fourth in the group was saying, "How does Toto look from up there, Jimmy? He looks bloody weird from here."

Sean half stopped, went on walking again. A man with headphones turned, saw him, looked unbelieving, lifted the papers in his hand and flung them on the floor. "Creeping

—

45

Jesus! They walk through the flaming studio now. Do you realize we're within forty seconds of VTR, you monkey's grunt? Look at that, curse you!" He pointed a quivering hand at a red warning sign which flared "On Air," gripped Sean's sleeve. "Get out of here before I kill you!" Pushed him toward an opening in the high canvas screen on the far side of the studio. "All right, Jimmy, twenty-five seconds, just mucking sightseers, oh Christ—twenty seconds, Paul—"

Sean was out through the opening in the screen, in the dark, saw the shadow of a heavy door, a handle. Behind him footsteps ran, voices shouted, the man with the headphones screamed in fury, "What in hell's name are *you* doing, we're ten seconds from VTR—Christ, stop it, stop it, Jimmy—"

Sean was through the door into a wide hallway crowded with people drinking coffee out of paper cups, eating sandwiches. Roman soldiers, senators, a girl in transparent draperies, a queue of early Christians at the coffee bar. "—if that bastard thinks I'm going to be crucified for Equity rates—" He was through the line of actors, down the stairs to a wide doorway leading out to a courtyard, in the open, running between high walls, past a lorry, down a long slope lined with parked cars, around a corner. A long way back he heard shouting, turned another corner and was in a public street. A taxi went past, and another, flag up for hire.

He flung himself in, said, "Marble Arch," and looked through the back window. No one. The taxi swung in a tight turn, made up Kerch Street past the Turk's Head, turned north. Sean lifted a hand to wipe the sweat from his face, found he was still gripping the papers he had picked up from the floor. Three sheets of paper. A copy of travel expenses—Manchester, Birmingham, Coventry. A copy of a letter booking hotel accommodation. And one copy from a memorandum. Page 2. "very much if we'll get the facts unless we're prepared to pay for them. I've one or two contacts who're eminently bribeable, but I think that our best bet is

—
46

still Bryce's contact, old man Akho at 118 Honeywell Road, because we'd have a double pull there. The others have the idea we're made of money—the man I mentioned to you on the phone yesterday, Khalil, was on to me again this morning saying that he'd tell me everything I wanted to know—for five thousand American dollars! I think a hundred pounds in two halves would loosen up Aziz. There's a very odd story about . . ."

Sean tapped on the glass. "Not Marble Arch," he said. "Honeywell Road."

5

MAJOR WILLIS swallowed his whiskey and held up the empty glass to catch the barman's eye. One more and he'd feel all right. Maybe two more. "Give me another double, Fred." He ran his finger around inside his collar. The bloody thing was choking him. It must have shrunk. He looked sideways quickly, undid the collar button, loosened his tie. Fred brought the whiskey, poised the water jug. Major Willis waved the jug away, swallowed, sucked in his breath, let it go in a long sigh of at least physical relief, swallowed again. It spread inside him, gave him strength. Everything'd be all right. It'd have to be. Christ, he didn't know a bloody thing about it. No one could say he did. No one. "Give me another one," he said huskily. "Small one this time." And as Fred turned away, "No—better make it a double." But he'd have water with it. He pulled out his handkerchief, mopped his face. Why had he got into it? Why? Why?

Shadow Force. "Cromwell." A bloody nonsense if there ever was one. A resistance army set up in peacetime and then put in bloody mothballs till war broke out and the poor old UK was occupied by the bloody Reds. The officers recruiting their own men without having to tell anyone who the hell they had on the jolly old swindle sheet, and even most of the sodding officers kept dead secret from the War House in case there might be some kind of leak if it ever came to the real push. He'd smelled it was wrong from the beginning. Christ, you couldn't be as old a dog as he was in Intelligence and not smell that kind of stink. For a moment he felt irrationally better, remembering how easily he had guessed the wrongness. From the beginning, the bloody beginning. The kind of thing that was likely to happen to an exercise like that. Outside all official control. Bloody well built to be uncontrollable, unfindable once the painter had been cut. Well, so what? All he'd wanted was his little whack out of it. Why not, for God's sake? Like the answer to a maiden's bloody prayer. Retire on full pension. Take on a cover job as sales manager for an electronics firm, and start building up the North London section of Shadow Force, at a bloody sight better screw than he'd been getting inside the pukka Service.

Who the hell could have refused it? And when the extra money started coming in as well, who'd have refused that? Fifty quid a week, over and above his pension and his "sales manager's" salary. Paid into his account from a "trust fund." No message, nothing. Six weeks running. How the hell could he have sent it back even if he'd wanted to? There wasn't anywhere to send it.

And finally the message. Over the telephone. No name. Disguised voice. "If you would like the trust fund to continue, just obey orders. Telephone messages like this preceded by the code word Trust Fund. Or memoranda with the same heading. You will destroy such memoranda immediately you have memorized them. Do you understand and accept?"

And even then what could he have done? Refused a buck-shee fifty quid a week? How did he know it wasn't still on the level? Part of a test? "I accept," he'd said. Even when the orders started coming—it could still have been on the level. He had known it wasn't, but it could have been. They were the sort of orders they should have been. About selection of personnel, communications, letter drops, training, safe dumps for weapons, ammo, materials, objectives for demoli-tion, warning codes.

It was all rational enough, at least by bloody W/O stand-ards, so that we wouldn't be caught with our nappies down when the bloody Russkies or the Chinks started dropping out of flying saucers onto the poor old Smoke. By any other standards, of course, the whole mucking exercise was a load of coswallop. Because the next war wasn't going to be like that. But who the hell was Tommy Willis to argue with a full pension, plus full pay, and then Trust Fund's fifty a week on top of that? Even when Bryce and his horrible little lot were brought into it.

Except that it was all too good to be bloody true, it *could* still have been on the level. Only he had known that it wasn't, smelled it wasn't. That the man at the top, "General Cromwell," or the men around him, had a lot of other fish to fry besides the Russians or the Chinese in a World War III that might never come off. They weren't worrying about ten years' time. They were worrying about tomorrow.

He had started to burrow then, and got almost nowhere. Except to become certain that whatever they were they weren't Reds. And to realize that whatever Shadow Force could do in a war against an army of occupation, it could do a perfect job in peacetime against its own government. As-suming the whole country was covered with sections like his own, it could be paralyzed inside a week. It was then he had

—

begun to get frightened. And the first and only time he'd queried an order, he had been a lot more frightened. The telephone at three in the morning.

"If you go into your bathroom and turn on the hot-water tap, there will be a most unpleasant explosion. You may care to spend the next hour or so looking for the explosive and rendering it harmless. We still feel very friendly toward you but please do what you're told in future. And don't try to find out what doesn't concern you." The telephone had been put down and he had lain for a long time before he could make himself get up, open the bathroom door. The explosive had been there all right. Half a pound of it, wedged on the underside of the bath. It wouldn't have left much of the bathroom. Or anyone in it.

That little incident had taken a hell of a lot of gilt off the bloody gingerbread. And Redwin and the whisper about Crystal Night. Not that he was shedding any tears over Redwin. If ever a stupid bastard asked for it, he did. But if that little exercise came unstuck, who was going to bloody well pay for it? Trust Fund? He tried to smile sardonically and found that his mouth was shaking, wouldn't twist itself even into a caricature of a smile. The bastards. The bloody bastards. Whoever got dropped in the dung, it wouldn't be them.

He had a dreadful vision of standing in the dock, trying to explain to prosecuting counsel that he hadn't known anything about Redwin, hadn't had anything to do with it. And an even more dreadful vision of that gray slab of plastic explosive stuck under the bath, and the wires, and the battery, and the detonator. The memory of that early morning search had stopped him asking even himself unnecessary questions about Crystal Night, let alone anyone else. Some sort of a stage-managed pogrom—Jesus, he didn't know anything about it—nothing—never heard of it, never would hear of it if he could bloody well help it. It had been a very impressive

—

lesson. He mopped his face again with the sodden handkerchief, ran it around his bull neck. The barman came back
with his whiskey.

"Telephone, Major."

"Who—?"

"Couldn't say, sir."

He took the glass with him to the phone booth in the passage, drank half of it on the way. Bloody stupid to ask who.
His nerves were going, he ought to get away for a bit, take a
woman somewhere, Monte. Christ, Monte. A few quid on
the tables, a bit of sex. Instead of this. "Willis here."

"Randall speaking." The voice thin, the undertone of sarcasm there even when it couldn't be meant—there was nothing in the bloody universe to be sarcastic about, damn him.
"There's a tiny emergency—"

He felt his heart swell, fill his chest until it hurt. He
couldn't breathe. "What is it?" He heard his voice crack in
the phone, coughed to cover it, took a hasty swallow from
the glass in his hand, sucked it in. "Emergency?"

"A tiny one. Meet us as soon as you can, will you? Edward's place. Don't be long." The phone clicked. Major Willis stared at it, anger rising in him like water boiling in a ket-
tle, feeling the top of his head lift up and down like a lid,
feeling the pressure of anger, of blood behind his eyes, bursting them outward. To put the blasted phone down on him
like that, cut him off. "A tiny emergency." The sodding
pansy. And then the terror gripped him, paralyzed him.

He dropped the phone back onto the cradle from short,
stubby fingers that were no longer strong enough to hold it,
looked into the spotted, peeling mirror with its cigarette advertisement on a level with his eyes. His eyes stared back at
him out of the mirror, veined, yellow, his face dark with too
much blood, the cheeks purple, the lumpish nose thickening
over the scrubby gray mustache, sweat running down his
forehead from the edge of his gray, damply curling hair. A

small stuffed bullock of a man, squat with flesh. But all he saw in the mirror was terror staring at him. He felt for the glass, found it was empty and left it there, stumbled out of the booth into the passage. They'd found out. Reopened the case. He tried to pray, couldn't think of any words. "A tiny emergency." Oh God, oh God.

6

THE ROOM was full of shadows and smells: garlic, rancid butter, too many people too close together, boiled rice, the acrid, throat-catching smell of incense. A stick of it was burning in front of a small shrine set up on top of a chest of drawers—a plaster statue of Siva, brilliantly and hideously painted in reds and whites and yellows, decorated with dead flowers, a brass cup to hold the incense stick, a little brass figure of Ganesha arranged in front of it.

The only light was a naked fifteen-watt bulb hanging in the center of the room from a stiffened, rotting rope. The men around the table whispered quietly, because other men were asleep, two to a bedstead, three bedsteads filling three sides of the room. The fourth side was occupied by the shrine and the chest of drawers, and two doorways, one on either side of it. There was no door in the right-hand doorway, only a curtain made of flowered cotton, very dirty down one edge where greasy hands had pulled it aside in passing through. Behind the curtain women were talking, louder than the men, laughing, saying "Sshhhh," laughing again. And there was the sound of cooking, of pots rattling,

—

the smell of food. Curry, garlic, boiled rice, adding fresh fla-
vors to the smells already in the front room. Ten people ac-
tually lived in the two rooms. The others were visitors, or
daytime lodgers, men on night shift who slept in the beds by
day and paid a daily rent to the old man sitting at the table
He was small and bearded, his lips and teeth and the upper
edge of his beard stained bright red by betel-nut juice, the
rest of his beard a ragged, yellowing white. His fingers
played all the time with a circlet of beads, and his eyes slid
about as if they were searching for someone in the shadows.

"They say He has been born already. In Karachi."

The younger man beside him laughed in frustration, exas-
perated out of all tact, patience, respect for his father-in-law.
Every time he tried to pin them down they slid away from
the subject like water off a stone. "We are not here to talk of
imaginary saviors being born in stupid places, but of what
we are to do now." His face might have been handsome but
for the pockmarks. They were like deep depressions made in
leather by the round head of a nail. "What are we going to
do? I ask you, and you start talking like children."

Everyone answered him at once. They were speaking
Gujarati and the words fell tumblingly, at once liquid and
guttural, as if they were spitting out of the back of their
throats. A boy with wild eyes and a pale face said, "It is true.
He is born. But not in Karachi. He is born among the Baluchi. I have seen His horoscope."

The pockmarked man put his head in both hands with a
dramatic gesture of despair-driven-ot-the-edge-of-madness.
"Karachi! Baluchi! Horoscope! Am I hearing what you say or
have I got voices in my ears? We are civilized people living
in a big city, working in factories, trying to secure our demo-
cratic rights as citizens and human beings, to secure justice
—justice, do you understand such a word?—and you begin
to talk of Krishna coming again, of Siva, of a new messiah, of
a new Jenghis Khan. What do you think the white people

—

will believe if they hear such talk? They will believe that we are not fit to share their justice, and they will be right."

"They will be afraid," the boy said softly. "They will be very afraid. Not at first, it may be, but soon. When He grows up. When He begins to gather His followers. It is written. I have been told by those who have read it in ancient prophecies. And now He is come."

"He is come," several men said. One of the sleepers in the beds woke up, rolled out of his blankets and joined in the conversation as if he had already been taking part in it in his sleep.

"He is come," he said. "There will be Holy War. Then all will be solved."

The man with the pockmarks thumped his two fists on the table and raised his voice. "I won't listen, you are raving madmen, like peasants at a bazaar listening to a fortune-teller, giving him your money that was meant to buy seed. War. Kill the white men. Fairy tales, when we should act like rational people. It is not Krishna who will protect us, it is Mr. Singh, it is the law."

More of the men sleeping in the beds woke up, protested at being awakened, and then threw themselves into the argument. The noise became deafening. The old man took out an empty soup tin from under his clothes and spat a great jet of scarlet betel juice into it. Some of it dribbled down his beard.

"You are a child, Shankar," he said tiredly. "How can we appeal to Christians against Christians? To white men against white men?"

"They are not all the same!" Shankar screamed. "Some are bad, yes, Here in Honeywell, some men, some landlords, this organization. Yes, yes, yes. But also there is justice, there is law. No no, let me speak, let me say out what is the true position. Mr. Singh tells us he will speak for us, asks us to give the right evidence to the police. And what do we do?

—

54

Do we go like men to tell the truth—no, be quiet, I *will* speak, hear me out—" The shouting had become almost deafening. Women's faces were at the curtain, listening, the small faces of children below their elbows, small, drained faces pale with exhaustion, violet shadows under the liquid brown eyes, oil-dark and soft and bewildered by the noise their parents were making.

"Hear me! Do we go there to tell the truth? Not at all. We sit here and argue about Krishna, about Siva, about a Jihad, about hatred for white men who are willing to help us, who have given us work and permission to come to their country. And why? I will tell you why!" He thumped on the table with his fist and the light above his head seemed to sway and dance. "Because this old villain is afraid the police will also find out that he has brought in relatives who are not his relatives at all, but strangers who have paid him one, two, three hundred pounds each for his help in getting them into this country against the law. And so he talks and talks in order that we shall do nothing. And when he is rich enough he will buy two, three old rotting houses like this and *he* will be a landlord like Mr. Bryce and squeeze even more blood out of people like us."

The old man looked shocked, and at the same time resigned, like a saint being tied to the stake. His fingers flickered over the beads and his lips moved. The young man, who was his grandson, leaned over the table and waved his fist under the nose of the pockmarked man. "Has this family not enough misfortunes that you should be married to my aunt? Do we ask you for more than your share of the rent, and the expenses? Who is it that pays these dues you are so noisy about? Is it you? Out of your miserable wages?" He spat contempt, sprayed Shankar's face with it. "Who asks you for anything? If my grandfather pays these people, what is it to you? Can you not shut your mouth? Who asked you to go to Mr. Singh?"

—

"It is justice," Shankar shouted. "Do you know what that means? You are like a worm, without a spine, without courage, without stomach except to eat! How much rent do I pay? How much expenses? Ten families could live on what I pay your grandfather, that old villain, that heap of cowardice. Why must I pay it? Because he must pay Mr. Albert, Mr. Bryce, the organization, pay and pay and pay. So that he must squeeze us." He stabbed his fingers at the men who had been sleeping. "What do they pay? Just for a dirty bed during the day while we work? At home they could buy a house for what they pay. Squeeze and squeeze, until we have no blood, no bones left, nothing. And you say we do not pay these dues."

"Then go away!" screamed the grandson. "Take my aunt, your thieving children, take them away and find your justice somewhere else. Must we be killed for your justice? Must we be beaten in the dark street and left like dead for dogs to lick us?"

"The police—"

The boy spat full on the table, dribbled saliva in his fury. "Police! Are you mad? And our passports? Our permits? Are you a child?"

Everyone was shouting. The noise was so ferocious that for more than a minute no one saw, no heard the newcomers, until the little fat white man in the billycock hat came forward and thumped the table with a stick. It was a loaded stick and the table sagged and shook under the weight of the blow. The noise in the room stopped like a dozen competing radios being switched off at once.

The old man with the beard lifted his watery eyes to the white man and his face seemed to turn gray, leaden under the brown surface of the wrinkled skin. All the men around the table sat very quiet, frozen into the attitudes of quarrel and separation. Behind the little man in the hat stood two other men. And two dogs, Alsatians, held on short, powerful leather straps. The dogs whined, their mouths red, teeth and lips were wet with saliva, tongues hanging a little. They strained forward at their collars. The men holding them wore reefer jackets, stained jeans, elastic-sided boots with chisel toes. One had a fat, meaty face and a cap with a shiny, broken peak. The other was bare-headed; long, curly, bleached hair brushed back, falling onto his collar. His face was small, ferret-sharp and scarred with acne. They looked at the little fat man in the hat, waiting for their orders.

"Well, well, well," the fat man said. "What a hubbub. What a hurly-burly. I wouldn't like to be your neighbor, I reelly wouldn't. And the pong, pooh." He held his nose delicately between finger and thumb of his left hand. "I'm disappointed in you, Akho, I reelly am. I thought we was friends, I thought we had a nice relationship, and look what you've gone and done. Telling such lies to Mr. Singh. Mr. Bryce is disappointed too, he truly is. 'Albert,' he said to me, 'I'm disappointed, Albert. My faith in 'uman nature 'as taken another knock.' Those are 'is very words, weren't they, Sid?"

The boy with spots nodded, smiling a tucked-in, expectant smile, his little mouth like a knife hole under his nose.

"I have done nothing, Mr. Albert," the old man said. "Nothing at all, I do not understand what you say, why you think it necessary—" He fluttered his hands at the dogs, at the two young men, lowered his watering eyes to look at the loaded stick which still lay across the table, one end of it in Mr. Albert's small, plump fist. "I have the agreed rental ready, just one moment, I will—"

"It was him," whispered the old man's grandson, his voice hissing with venom, and also with fear. "My grandfather had nothing to do with it. *He* went to Mr. Singh—" He glared at his uncle. No one else spoke a word. The room became quieter still, until the panting of the Alsatians seemed loud and they could hear the noise of traffic in the main road, fifty yards away.

—

Albert turned his small eyes like weapons, like the beams of torches, onto the pockmarked Indian's face. "That was very wrong of you, Shankar," he breathed. "It is Shankar, isn't it? I'll have to go and tell them where you're working, Shankar, that you're a troublemaker, that you don't appreciate things. Won't I?" He lifted the loaded stick very slowly, held it close to the pockmarked face. With a sharp flicking movement he brought it up under the fleshy nose. Shankar's head went back and his eyes filled suddenly with uncontrollable tears of pain. He put his hands up to his face and Albert lifted the stick sideways and slammed it into his stomach. Twice. Three times. Shankar opened his mouth to scream, but no scream came. Only a gagging, retching sound, a struggle for breath, his mouth open like a black wound, hands rigid in the air, until he sagged forward, arms clenched across his stomach, head between his knees.

Albert looked at him, sniggered, fished under his nose with the end of the stick, levered the stick across Shankar's knee so that his head came up, the mouth still open, dragging in air, going "Ah ah ah ah" like a broken gramophone. Albert aimed the stick delicately, like a billiard cue, against the tip of Shankar's nose, poked his head gently backward, until his body was upright again, his hands lifting to scrabble at the stick, his throat stretched.

"What an ungrateful little wog you are," Albert said. The stick swung away, poised, whipped down across the brown, naked throat. Shankar's arms, hands flung up wide, like broken sticks, leaves. The chair fell backward, crashed onto the floor. Shankar fell out of it, sprawled sideways, legs thrashing like a dying rabbit's, heels scraping on the wooden boards. He made dreadful broken sounds in his throat, his body arched, blood came gently out of his mouth in tiny threads. For what seemed a very long time there was no sound in the room except Shankar struggling to breathe, the echo of his heels on the boards. His knees clenched themselves up convulsively against his stomach, straightened again. He lay on his back, his hands at his throat, his eyes wide open, staring at the ceiling, showing too much white, as if the eyeballs were rolled back into his skull.

"He is dead," whispered one of the day-sleepers, and one of the others slipped down onto his knees beside Shankar, felt his heart.

"E'll be all right," said Mr. Albert. "But next time 'e may not be, savvy? We've 'ad a very nice little relationship for a very long time. A proper dialogue, as they say. We don't say nothing to your little bits of 'ilarity, Akho, and we expects you to reciprocate. Live an' let live, that's what we say, isn't it, Sid?"

"Yerss," said the boy with spots. His Alsatian scraped his claws on the naked floor, panted softly.

"Oh, I do appreciate that so much," Akho said. His face was mud-colored and his hand shook as he lifted it toward his trembling mouth.

"Then give me the rent," Albert said. Akho got up, opened one of the drawers of the chest, took out a cash box, felt under his many clothes for the key.

"It is just ready, Mr. Albert," he whispered, "absolutely ready. This stupid fellow, he does not understand English ways, does not understand what a good place we have here, how good Mr. Bryce has been to us." He unlocked the cash box and the two boys holding the dogs crowded closer to him. The dogs mouthed against his legs and he shrank away from them. "Good fellows, oh yes, I am most fond of animals, such handsome dogs, but if they would not stand so close—" He fumbled money out of the cash box, tried not to let Albert see what more was inside it.

Albert tapped the lid with his stick. "If we was villains," said Albert, "we would take the whole bloody box. 'Ow much you got in there, Akho? A couple of thousand?"

"You are such a joker, Mr. Albert," the old man said, try-

—

ing to smile, hurriedly relocking the box. "Always such jokes and laughter when you come to see us. I appreciate it very much. I have included something for you"—he pushed a wad of money into Albert's fist, as if begging him to take it—" for you and your friends to take some much needed refreshment on your way home. Rest assured about this foolish matter of Mr. Singh, I did not know." He spread his hands, clasped them quickly on the cash box again and held it to his stomach. "Shankar is so headstrong, we will explain to him, please do not worry, or allow the good Mr. Bryce to feel the least concern. All will be as before, I assure you."

"That's what I like to hear," Albert said. Shankar had crawled onto his hands and knees, was leaning his forehead on the seat of a chair. Mr. Albert took the chair away and Shankar fell down again. The two boys with the Alsatians laughed. Mr. Akho gave a wan smile. "Well, cheerio, till next time," Albert said. The two boys, the two dogs followed him out of the room. The Indians sat listening to the sounds of their footsteps on the stone stairs leading up to the street.

Ten minutes later Sean knocked at the door of the flat. He had wasted nearly an hour on the way, telephoning the nursing home, trying to persuade a nurse to let him speak to the major, trying to persuade her to bring the matron to the phone, trying to persuade the matron.

"But it's no good, I keep telling you. If you were here and I let you into his room, which I wouldn't, he couldn't talk to you, he couldn't understand whatever it is you want to tell him."

After that he'd tried to reach the major's doctor at half a dozen different numbers. At each of them the doctor had either just left, or not yet arrived. In Honeywell Road he told the taxi to stop outside number 20 and walked the rest of the way. The houses were Victorian genteel, decayed into tenements; built in the 1850s for small businessmen and successful shopkeepers, with basement areas and bow windows at ground level. The windows hadn't been painted since 1939 and some of the panes were missing and patched with plywood. Clusters of dirty milk bottles stood outside the scarred front doors and on the stone steps leading up to them. Most of the children playing in the road and on the steps were colored and all of them were noisy. The adults looked at him sideways as if they thought he was a plain-clothes policeman or a debt collector for the installment sellers.

He went up the steps of number 118 and looked for Akho's name beside any of the row of a dozen bell pushes. Miss Grumman. Miss Fox. Mr. Polyanski. Mr. Khalil Jinnah and Mr. Jam Mehta. Miss Porson. Miss Treblinka. The others were blank or too weathered to be legible. A lot of the bells looked as though they were broken. He rang "Jinnah" and "Mehta" and waited. A small girl came up the steps, stared at him, and ran away. He rang again, and then rang "Polyanski." A Negro bus conductor trudged past. "Akho? No, sir, I don't know any Akho." He ran all the bells. After a minute or two he heard footsteps, heels clacking on bare wooden stairs.

The door opened and a sleepy-looking colored woman in a black kimono stared at him in surprise, yawned and smiled. "You come for a massage?" She let the kimono fall aside, show her naked breasts. "Five pounds."

"I'm looking for someone called Akho," he said. She let herself look tired and half asleep again, pointed down the area steps. "Down there. Come back sometime."

He went down the area steps, squeezed past a garbage can, rang the bell. Nothing happened, but through the curtained window he could hear the murmur of voices, a woman crying. He rang again and then knocked, hard. Slippers dragged softly on stone, the door opened. A boy with hair like midnight, blue-black, oiled and shining, looked at him out of flat, hostile eyes.

"Mr. Akho?" Sean said.

61

"Who is it?" an old man's voice called out. "Is it my good friend Mr. Albert come back again?" Other slippers flapped and shuffled on wood, and then on the stone flags of the passage. The boy said something over his shoulder.

The old man came into the narrow doorway, faces peering out of the shadows behind him. The boy slithered two or three steps back along the wall, stayed looking at Sean. Hatred reached out of him like a smell.

"I am Mr. Akho," the old man said. His mouth smiled, his hands pressed bonelessly together. "In what way can I be of service to you?" His eyes examined Sean, probed, apologized for probing, tried to smile.

"You knew a Mr. Olaf Redwin," Sean said.

The old man's eyes faded, seemed to become opaque, sightless. His mouth looked bewildered, as if he could not understand the words. His hands fluttered, expressed helpless anxiety to please, infinite regret at being helpless.

"He was making a television film," Sean said.

"Television? Film?" The beard wagged from side to side, slowly, in baffled ignorance.

"A Mr. Bryce sent him to you."

The name fell into the passage like a stone. The faces seemed to draw back into the shadows, become shadows. The old man's head stopped shaking, the smile vanished. "You know Mr. Bryce?"

Sean hesitated. "Yes."

The old man had caught the hesitation. "Then he will doubtless know of this film, this Mr.—"

"Olaf Redwin. You were going to tell him things for his film—" He knew that he had handled it wrong, that he was wasting his time. Had there been a right way to handle it? It didn't seem likely. "He was going to pay you a hundred pounds."

The wrinkled, crumpled leather face in front of him

—

62

creased into new folds of sudden pain. "I am so sorry. It is some other Mr. Akho no doubt."

"One hundred pounds!" a voice said in English, from the shadows. Someone else drew in breath sharply, with a small hissing sound, like a snake. The old man seemed to want to look over his shoulder. His head moved, as if it were loose on his neck. His eyes filled with hatred, with agony. His smile widened, contorted his face, his fingers pressed together, bending so far back from the palms that the knuckles cracked, softly, like tiny sticks.

"There was a story about a conspiracy," Sean said, "of all the colored people in this country." He smiled to show that he realized it had all been a joke, someone pulling a solemn inquirer's leg. "Did you tell him that?" Among these shadows, these hatreds, it didn't seem like a joke.

The old face looked sightless. No one moved. No one seemed to breathe. He had the feeling that there were listeners behind him as well as in the stone passage in front of him. It was hard not to look round.

"I tell you it is all a most absolute error, all this TV, this story, I do not know anything of it, I am so sorry." The eyes rolled up into the skull, showed their whites, the bent fingers worked, pressed. The boy who had let Sean in slid forward again.

"I think you should go away now. My grandfather is sick, he is very busy just now and cannot be worried with this kind of questioning. He has told you he knows nothing."

"Then you tell me," Sean said. But tell me what? he thought. "Where will I find Mr. Bryce?"

"Please go," the boy said. "We do not know any such person. You are in our private premises, for which we pay the rent. We do not wish you to stay any longer."

The old man nodded his head like a doll, smiled. The boy smiled, his eyes venomous.

—

"Why don't you want to answer?"

"Please." The boy smiled

Sean went back up the stone area steps. People melted away from the top of the steps, the railings, as he turned. Dark faces, a sari, a black woman with a pram, black children. It wasn't London. Wasn't England. Faces watched him from the dirty windows across the street, from behind torn gray net curtains. The street smelled of dust, of boiled cabbage, bad drains, of rotting wood and bricks, of decay. Old Victorian houses turned into tenements. He walked away. The taxi had gone and he wasn't likely to get another one in a street like this. Who was Mr. Bryce?

He turned the corner. An Indian was leaning against the railings of another area, breathing hard as if he had been running and was not used to running. As Sean passed him he held up a cigarette. "If the gentleman would give me a light?"

Sean gave him one. The Indian cupped the flame in both hands. His eyes slid up to Sean's, over his shoulder, seemed to take in the windows, the street. "I heard you just now, sir, and have run very quickly to meet you. If we might perhaps talk? You can be asking me the way to the underground station perhaps and I can be showing you?"

His face was thin and shadowed, middle-aged before its time, as if he had never slept or eaten enough. His eyes never stopped moving, like frightened animals behind glass, dark and soft and terrified. He took two quick, boneless paces to Sean's one. "Perhaps the gentleman is from the organization?" His eyes looked away from Sean to the left, to a Jamaican leaning against a lamppost, to a child playing with a worn-out motor tire, to an Indian woman trudging toward them, weighed down by a stuffed basket of washing from the launderette.

"Yes," Sean said.

The face at his shoulder turned gray, died. "The gentleman must not believe—Mr. Akho—he is an old foolish man —for one hundred pounds he would tell lies on the Holy Books. This foolish story—conspiracies, a new redeemer out of the East—all lies, women's stories. Conspiracies! Such wicked lies. We are happy people, so happy to be here in this good country. So fond of the good organization that looks after us and protects us. My family are slaves of the gentleman, they kiss his feet. Do not believe Mr. Akho, sir, I beg of you, there is not one of us that would lift his little finger against the organization. We pay our rent, we pay our dues, we do not breathe one word to anyone—"

Ahead of them three men turned into the street from an alleyway, two of them holding Alsatian dogs by short, heavy leashes. The third man was small and fat, walking a pace ahead of them, his billycock hat pushed far back on a round pink forehead, a stick slanting under his arm like a farmer's at a fair.

"Who collects the dues in this street?" Sean said. But the Indian was gone. The three men passed him, the little fat man staring at him out of hot blue eyes, questioning. One of the dogs brushed its damp muzzle against Sean's hand. The boys holding the leashes looked at him, their eyes flat, contemptuous, the eyes of men who owned the street they walked on.

Three of the collectors? Sean wondered, and looked back over his shoulder. The small fat man was doing the same thing.

"I wonder who that is?" Mr. Albert was saying thoughtfully. "You see the way that little nignog scarpered when he saw us coming? I'll bet that was one of old Akho's lot. Go an' arsk the ol' bastard, Sid. Arsk 'im if 'e knows that bloke."

7

SHE LAY on the white couch like a splash of blood, the red housecoat trailing its wide skirt down to the floor, covering her from throat to ankle. Her hair flowed over the white velvet cushion in a gold embroidery of pale, shining silk, softly shimmering, a river, a waterfall of gold. Her doll-blue eyes stared at the ceiling, her mouth sullen, poutingly babyish, half formed in the rounded, adolescent cheeks, the jawline soft and smooth, running down without a bone visible into the full-throated immaturity of the neck.

She heard him pacing, saw his shadow.

"Why don't you stop walking about?" she said. Her accent was flat, neither educated nor uneducated; neither London nor Provincial. As if she had bought it in some tasteless shop along with her make-up. The man with the seaweed hair, limp and thin and colorless, spread up and over his bald skull, went on walking, not looking at her, not seeming even to hear her. Out of habit more than desire she let the edge of the housecoat fall away onto the floor, leaving her right leg naked to the hipbone. A long leg, beautifully molded, shaped, tapered, the knee smooth and dimpled, the foot small and fat. Her ankles were thicker than they might have been, but neither Mr. Edward Bryce, her present lover, nor any of the other men she had known intimately were purists about ankles.

"I might as well not be here," she said.

"Yes, yes," Mr. Bryce said. He turned, saw the naked leg, stared at it for a second as though he was not sure what it was and then put out a distracted hand to touch it. The knee swayed toward him, the doll's head rolled on the cushion, looked at him with opaque contempt. He ran his fingers absently down the inside of her thigh and she reached up her hands to take hold of him.

"No," he said, "they'll be here any minute. D'you want them to find us—?"

"What do you think they think we do here when we're alone? Play chess?" Her hands wound into his clothes. "Can I have it?"

He was baffled for the moment, his mind a thousand subjects away from what they had recently been arguing about. "I told you they—" He remembered then that it was the coat. "I told you I can't. Four thousand—it's—it's not rational—"

"You've got it, haven't you?"

"That's not the point."

She had his shirt undone, was at his trousers. "What is the point?" She pushed her hand inside the fly, was gripping him. Her eyes had lost their sullen vacancy and were alive, full of malice and a narrowed pleasure.

"Goddammit!" he said. His voice broke, squeaked in rage. He struck at her wrist and the result hurt him very much. "You dirty little rutting bitch."

"Suppose I tore it off?" she said. Her smile had turned thin and hard and her eyes were no longer china-blue but steel. He let himself be pulled down on top of her. Her other arm went around his neck, her mouth was on his, hot and soft and moist, the lips full again, pouting, formlessly hungry.

"If you don't want me, I know those that do."

"I want you," he mumbled.

She took him like an animal and the brutality woke him. He gripped her face with his spread hands, smearing her mouth with his two thumbs dragging the corners, rocking his little body in a quick frenzy of passion that lifted him up like a wave and dropped him across her in almost the same second.

"You need a pill," she said viciously.

He didn't hear her. He lay spent, a pain in his groin, feeling sick and dizzy and victorious, and then weakly angry. The bitch, the bitch. As if he hadn't enough today without that. She rolled him off her and he lay against the back of the enormous couch, half wedged between the expensively padded back and the great down cushions. She got up and he heard her go out to the bathroom, heard water running. Don't let them come just yet. Not just yet.

It wasn't fair. A man fought all his life for something, for a bit of security, a bit of luxury, and what happened? People came and took it away. Just took it away. As if there wasn't any law, wasn't anything in the world to stop them. Just took it away. Just rang up one night—just like a wrong number ringing up.

"We've been admiring you, Mr. Bryce. And your organization." He'd thought it was the police, his blood had run like ice water, thinking something had gone wrong, there'd been a foul-up in Honeywell. "So we're going to take you over." Just like that.

"Take—?"

"We don't expect you to say yes at once. Tomorrow morning will do. We'll ring again at ten."

He hadn't meant even to take the call only he'd lain awake so long that he overslept. In the four-poster bed, Nellie beside him, the park outside. He hadn't known he was happy. The finest Elizabethan dower house within forty miles of London. A little gem of a dairy farm; seventy Jerseys and two first prizes in the last county show, Lord Brampton himself had spoken to him about them. "You're becoming quite a farmer, Bryce. Showing us old fogies up with your new methods." He hadn't known what the new methods were, the manager saw to all that, but it meant he was in. There'd be invitations next.

And how long he'd fought for it. More than twenty years.

Starting with one house, the one he and Nellie got married in, and realizing like a revelation that it'd be cheaper to buy the whole bloody rattrap than rent three rooms in it. If he could raise the deposit. Nellie's uncle had done that for them, he'd never forget it, even if he'd never done another thing for them before or since. But that five hundred quid—

It had transformed a chemist's assistant into a property-owner, a tenant into a landlord. They had started with students and found that the colored ones were willing to pay double. But even then it had been slow. He'd been slow. Still hadn't seen. He'd saved the money to buy his own chemist's shop instead of another house. It was six years before they bought the second house, ten years before they bought the third. And then suddenly, like a dam bursting, he had realized what property was, how it ought to be used.

The three houses he had bought already were in reasonable condition, elderly Victorian terrace houses on the edge of Honeywell that were dilapidated but a long way from the end of their lives. Two coats of paint and a few new floor boards and they looked almost worth the money they had cost him. But the next houses were different. Houses with ten, five years left in them before they fell down of their own accord, already condemned by the local authority. He got the leases for a few hundred pounds apiece because they carried the obligation to repair or demolish, and to repair houses like that would cost more than building new ones.

But he repaired nothing and demolished nothing. The court cases cost him hundreds until he found the right way to shut the local officials up, but in the meantime he had the houses stuffed from cellars to attics with Pakistanis and Jamaicans. He made more money in that first year of the new-style operation than he had thought existed outside the Bank of England. He had bought a Rolls Royce, and then the dower house, and started taking on a new kind of staff. The kind that wouldn't let the rents be taken off them by local thugs on a Friday night. At least, that had been the first consideration. And he'd found that the simplest way to make sure of that was to employ the local thugs. Mr. Albert Fetter was one of the earliest and most valuable of his finds. When rents got difficult to collect, or existing tenants in houses he bought turned obstinate and refused either to pay the new rents or to make room for those who would, it was Albert who showed him how to solve that kind of problem.

Not that he wanted to hear the details. "I hate anything sordid," he told Albert very early on. He hated it so much that nowadays he never so much as saw most of the houses that he bought. Never even lent his name to the transactions, which were carried out through a web of companies and holding companies that would have taken a tax expert five years to disentangle. Most of his tenants had no idea that he existed. It was only the older ones, like Mr. Akho, still surviving in the first of the "demolish or restore" houses, who knew and referred to him by name. In law their rents were paid to Manor Estates, or Lucinda Holdings, or Welfare Garden Housing Corporation, but being for the most part poor and ignorant men they still talked about Mr. Bryce as the Landlord.

If it ever came to law-court matters, of course it would be quite simple to prove that they were entirely mistaken, and so long as it didn't there was no point in objecting. Once or twice reporters on the make had tried to dig up scandal and make something out of nothing. But the libel laws were a very fine protection and so was money. It was amazing what a few well-placed thousands could do in the way of preserving privacy. Like a nice thick hedge.

He had been happy. He had been really happy. A year ago he'd have said his cup was full. Really full. Nellie over her operation. This flat. He'd set it up originally for Queenie. And when Queenie went off with Benjamin he'd found Charlene, and then her friend Marna, and then—Babette. He ran his tongue slowly over his dry, slightly scummy lips and stared at the satin wallpaper above the back of the couch. Twenty-seven pounds ten a roll wholesale. He wouldn't spend that on his own bedroom. Nellie would have a fit if she thought he spent that much papering a whole room, let alone on one roll.

Twenty-seven pounds ten. Four thousand for a coat. On top of the Alfa Romeo. Like a sponge. Like a bottomless hole in the ground. You threw money in and it vanished. Why didn't he just put her out? Like he'd done with Marna? He'd only to tell Albert—one of the others—

His mind circled around the money she spent like a talisman, to keep away from the other thing—the other—

They had rung back at ten and he'd laughed into the telephone, the way a man does at ten in the morning with the sun shining on his thirty-acre park and his lawns, and with a hundred thousand pounds in a Swiss account and another hundred thousand in Canada just for safety, and—

He'd put the phone down and gone out to the garage, because it was Samuels' day off, and started the Rolls. The front end had seemed to lift off the ground, quite slowly, everything in slow motion. Then the sound hit him, shock waves of sound slamming in against his eardrums, flattening his skull like giant clappers, dislocating his eyesight, wrenching him up out of the leather seats, beating him from side to side. He heard himself yelling, and the yelling went on even after he stopped knowing who was yelling, stopped knowing anything. Cartwheels of scarlet revolving slowly in his head as his little neat body in its neat gray suit collapsed on the upholstery, his fish mouth open, gasping for air, his little manicured hands fluttering, fluttering.

It was not a very large explosion, and it had been carefully shielded to wreck the car and not the driver. He hardly lost consciousness; heard them shouting outside the timbered, rose-grown garage; heard Matthews the head gardener run-

—

71

ning in shouting, "Fire! Fire!" Then the butler. And one of the housemaids. And then Nellie, last as usual. Out of breath, sobbing with fright, trying to drag him out of the seat. The fool. The clumsy fool. Suppose his back had been broken? Suppose it was broken? But he let her take him inside and put him to bed. And call the doctor. But not the police. And when they rang back at eleven o'clock he listened very carefully and did what they told him to do. Then and after.

He still didn't really understand what they wanted. "We have a big organization. You have a small one. We want to incorporate you. It's as simple as that. We will increase your revenue and take a share of the increase. That is all. And quite frankly the revenue is not important to us. Obedience is. And secrecy. Don't question orders and don't discuss them. We'd hate to have to replace you."

He sweated even to think of that voice. To be controlled by people he'd never seen, didn't even know the names of, nothing. What did they want? What the hell did they want?

"You will become a member of an area committee of our organization. You will co-operate with it in every way. The other members will make themselves known to you shortly. In future you will receive your instructions through them. But we'll still be able to get in touch with you directly—if that seems necessary."

He heard her coming back from the bathroom. Heard her pour herself a drink. "I'll have one," he said. He meant to sound curt, imperative. When he spoke like that to Nellie she came to him like a fat old spaniel, practically thumping her arse on the floor.

"Are you paralyzed?" Babette said. "Why can't I have that coat?" But she gave him the drink she had poured for herself, putting the cold ring of the glass down on his stomach where his shirt had opened, smiling down at him from her narrowed, humorless eyes. She had taken off the housecoat and put on a Chinese dress, heavy silk, gold and old rose, a dragon embroidered on it, climbing up toward her throat like a lizard on a sinuous tree. The dress was split to the waist on both sides and she was wearing nothing underneath.

"Who's Babette's teddy bear?" she whispered, sitting down by his knees, sliding her hand up where the glass had been, kneading the soft flesh of his chest. "There's only three like it in the whole world, Steiny says. And we could go away together. You need a holiday." Her voice flat and irritating, like the slight rasp of her fingernails on his skin. "You could hire a yacht—"

He began to be terrified that she was going to start again. He'd die. "They'll be here," he whispered.

"Why are you so afraid of them?"

"I'm not afraid." He felt his mouth shaking, remembering. Even her hand there on his chest was a comfort, the weight of her body across his legs. It was madness, she'd turn on him like a snake, he ought to have got rid of her after the first month, but in spite of reason, common sense, every alarm bell of instinct in his head, he felt as if she were some kind of protection, some kind of barrier between him and them. He held her wrist, massaged the inside of it with his fingers. Why was he afraid? Who the hell wouldn't be? The four of them in this room. Robertson going out to the kitchen to help Babette, bringing back the drinks. And Redwin swallowing his, saying, "See you tomorrow," and trying to stand up. The look on his face. His mouth opening to shout. Trying to move. Half up. And then not making it.

He felt his forehead sweating. To see it, like that, in front of his eyes. Robertson looking down at Redwin, pushing his eyelid up with a thumb. And the man still alive.

—

73

"We could get away somewhere," she was whispering. And never come back. Never. The doorbell rang.

8

The third telephone booth he found was working. Someone had been sick on the floor and most of the telephone books were missing, but he got a dial tone. And then Margaret's voice. "Sheila," he said, and she switched him through onto the closed line, which couldn't be picked up by outside listeners.

"Yes?" Her voice very cool and detached. As if there had never been anything between them except their work.

"Something very odd has been happening—I think Randall ought to know about it."

"He knows already." Like ice.

"He—"

"You were at a cremation service yesterday. And afterward there was an incident at a roadhouse? Not a very edifying one apparently." Her tone cut like a razor.

"And today," he said, clenching his hand on the receiver. "Have you also heard about that?"

"Yes. We've just had a complaint from the Special Branch about impersonation. They're extremely displeased. So is Oliver. He would like to see you on Monday morning at nine-thirty to explain exactly what you've been doing."

He could see her face as if she were in front of him, outside the phone box. Savagely controlled. Savagely angry.

—

74

The anger of five months forcing its way up, threatening to break the mask, the smooth, cold surface.

"Until then, he asked me to tell you if you did happen to phone in"—her voice shook for a second, descended into sarcasm—" you're suspended. You will do nothing, talk to no one about anything that's happened yesterday or today. You will not ring this office again until Oliver has seen you on Monday. Is that clear?"

He didn't answer. The phone went down at her end. He took the receiver slowly away from his ear, put it back on the cradle. Outside, a white woman with two colored children in a pram went by, a worn cloth coat half-buttoned over her swollen six-month stomach.

"Where would I get a taxi or a bus?" he said. She looked at him out of drained eyes as if she wasn't sure what he had said, what a taxi was, or a bus. A child came from nowhere, from behind the telephone booth, a thin, knowing face, black crinkled hair, eyes like puddles of dark oil.

"Bus, mister? You wanta bus?"

Sean nodded.

"Which one you want, mister?"

"Or a taxi?" Sean said. His mind still on Margaret's voice, what she had said, what it meant.

"This way, mister. Down Honeywell Road—down the bottom there's buses and taxis—" He might have been eleven, twelve. His legs were like sticks and his fingers like a bird's claws. His eyes looked as though they knew everything that had ever happened in the street.

"There was a man going to make a television film round here," Sean said absently, almost automatically, while most of his mind was still with Margaret.

The boy looked up at him out of eyes that were suddenly not childish at all. "You a policeman?"

"No," Sean said. "Why do you ask me that?"

—

75

"Because he's dead."

"Suppose we went and had an ice cream somewhere?"

All the eagerness to please had vanished out of the boy's face. The street itself looked at Sean out of the deep-set, oil-dark eyes.

"Suppose I gave you half a crown?"

The boy hesitated, still moving slowly backward, almost on the point of turning and running.

"It might even be worth five shillings. If you knew a lot about him. Did he talk to lots of people here?"

The boy nodded, his eyes searching Sean's.

"Where could we find some ice cream?"

The boy jerked his head sideways, too large a head for the thin neck, the twig body. "Up the cut," he said. He half turned and led the way, walking sideways up the gutter, his feet scuffing the torn paper, the orange peels, the dusty litter of the street. Sean followed him, conscious of being watched. From windows, doorways, area railings. Women in curlers and torn jerseys, nursing half-naked babies on the steps of the tenement houses, their faces exhausted. A girl leaning out of a first-floor window, combing her black hair, smiling down at him as she caught his eye. Her blouse seemed to have been made out of a Union Jack, and it showed most of her breast. She nodded very slightly at the room behind her, beckoning.

The tone of Margaret's voice came back to Sean and hit him again in the face like an insult out of nowhere, like stepping on a rake in the dark. It would be a pleasure to see Randall on Monday morning. To tell him what he could do with his job and his Service and his complaints from the Special Branch. He stood still, and the boy stopped, watching him, watching his face.

Why go on with it? What was the point? He thought of the major, lying in a nursing home, dying. It was very sad. But did that give it a point? To run and tell him, "Good dog

—

76

Sean has found the ball"? Lay it at his master's feet? Suppose the ball belonged to Randall all along? It would explain a great deal. How else could he have known about the Coach Inn? Had he walked into someone else's exercise? And they'd beaten him up because they didn't know who he was or why he was there? Until they got his wallet and found out?

And Randall was livid because he was trespassing? Then what was Redwin's news, that he wanted the major to know? Something that he'd found in this street? He stared at the small boy, his trousers and shoes too big, his shirt torn, his eyes fifty years old. At the dirt in the gutter, the women on the steps, a black bus conductor trudging past them. Thought of Akho and the Indian boy in the basement of number 118 around the corner; the hatred and the fear; the woman with the pram. What in the name of God could he have found here that was worth telling to anyone?

He had started walking again, not really thinking of where he was going, almost forgetting the boy, the promise of the ice cream, the reason he was there. The boy stayed two paces ahead of him, watchful, puzzled by his change of expression, trying to read it for danger.

Hatred and dirt and fear. And the major dreaming of his forty years of service, of the England he had served. This? Had he ever walked down this kind of street, would he recognize it as England?

What did he see when he dreamed of the ideal he'd worked for all his life? The Sussex downs? The Changing of the Guard? And Margaret following him. Were they blind? He stopped again and smacked his fist into his palm, sending the small boy skittering three steps further away from him. Were they raving mad? Had he been mad, hypnotized by them? To work for this?

Redwin's widow and mother in their mock-Elizabethan house-agent's advertisement, with central heating and all

—

mod. cons. and their dreams of a world conspiracy. Had that
been Redwin's frightening news? Some rubbish he'd picked
up along these gutters, from a boy like this, an old man like
Akho?

And he thought suddenly of Venice, of Niccolò, of the sun
on the worn stones and the dirty, lapping water of the ca-
nals. At least the Venetians knew they were dead, that they
lived in a museum. They didn't look for conspiracies to explain it, or pretend that they still ruled the world. Sun and
wine and women and a knowing smile. Just to get out of
here. On Monday, I will give him a small, small surprise, he
thought. Like a swift kick between the legs. And send a
cable to Niccolò. "Arrive tomorrow. Provide girl." Something like the girl in the television office.

He looked at the small boy. They had reached a corner.
The road turned left along a railway embankment: a vast
barrier of soot-encrusted stone, weeping with a chill wet
even in the sun, weeds growing out of the joins between the
courses, here and there a minute blue flower. Someone had
painted a swastika high up on the wall and some words that
a later hand had almost painted out. "Niggers" showed
faintly through the second coat.

"Up here," the boy said. He looked afraid of Sean, afraid
even to run away. Sean smiled at him, feeling as if ten years
of his age had fallen off his back, a huge weight. He was
free. Of the major, Margaret, Randall, Redwin, the job, London, the lot. He'd sell the car, he had a month's pay coming
—if he didn't kick Randall, there ought to be leave money as
well. For a second he weighed up the money against the
pleasure. Be rational, he thought. Smile, be a gentleman, say
goodbye, buy them all a drink.

"I'll buy you the biggest ice cream you ever saw," he told
the boy. "What's your name?"

"Wilfrid." He kept out of reach. "It's up here." His eyes

calculated the danger against the possibility of the five shillings, the ice cream.

Fifty yards up the cut a Nissen hut had been stuffed into a tunnel under the railway lines, turned into a café. They went up the wooden steps into a smell of fish frying and old cooking and a chill, clinging damp. There were rows of tables and benches set with sauce bottles, and a counter to one side of the door. A blonde leaned on the counter, using the tea urn as a mirror to squeeze a pimple. When she saw Sean come in she smiled, leaned further forward, her breast full and soft inside the greasy nylon coat. The coat had once been white and the brassiere under it was black. She put up a hand to adjust the coat, opening it a little over her cleavage.

"Ice cream," Sean said, and hoped that it was wrapped.

They sat facing each other across one of the tables, and the blonde brought the ice cream and a wet cloth to smear over the table top. The boy ate with a quick nervousness, as if he was afraid Sean might not let him finish. The blonde hung around them, cleaning the far end of the table.

"He give me ice cream too," the boy said suddenly.

I ought to ask him something, Sean thought. But what was the point? "How did you know he was dead?"

"My daddy told me." The boy's eyes slid toward the waitress, the door. A man came in, whistling casually, leather jacket open over a checked shirt, heavy belt tight over narrow hips, a square brass buckle fastening it. He looked at Sean and Wilfrid sideways, under the peak of his leather cap, picked a table further into the shadows of the hut, snapped his fingers for the blonde.

"Did he talk to your daddy?"

"Uhuh." The boy looked over his shoulder at the man who had come in. "I think I better go now."

Sean slid two half-crowns across the table. He didn't know

why he was bothering. Habit. Obstinacy. "Tell me what he talked about," he said. "Tell me what he wanted to know. Could you tell me that?"

The boy looked at the half-crowns as if hypnotized, sank down again onto the bench. "Maybe I could," he whispered.

9

BRYCE opened and shut his mouth like a fish, stared at Randall as if he were something hideous that had reared out of the dark in front of him. "But we can't," he whispered. "Not —not just like—perhaps he'll—"

Randall lifted his narrow, serpent head, smiled gently at Bryce. "Perhaps he'll just forget about it and go away? Was that what you were going to say?"

Robertson sat quiet between them, looking down at the brandy glass suspended between his two hands, his two thumbs revolving it. Round and round. Bryce found himself looking at the movement, at the thumbs, broad, powerful. It was like a nightmare. He felt sweat oozing on his skin, cold and sickly. He couldn't stand any more of it. Get out. Anywhere. Escape. They wouldn't touch Nellie if he was gone, she'd be all right, she'd have the dower house, the farm, Albert—Albert would look after her, would see to the rents. Send him money. They wouldn't follow him if he stayed quiet, didn't talk. They couldn't—

He thought of the front of the car lifting, the slam of sound against his ears. He closed his eyes against Randall, as if he could close him out of his mind, his life.

—

"Well?" Randall said. "Need I remind you that a great deal of this is for your benefit? As Vining has just told us, it is your name that Ryan succeeded in finding. And it was here"—he paused, waited until Bryce by sheer force of mental pressure opened his eyes, let himself be fixed, hypnotized—"that Redwin's"—the sculptured eyebrows lifting, the thin, curving lips tasting the words, the thought—"that Redwin's final exercise began. Or have you forgotten?"

It gave him intense pleasure to torture Bryce. To torture anyone. But Bryce was so helpless, and at the same time so rich—had his small, soft, unpleasant hands on so much power without the knowledge of how to use it that to torture him was like a work of art, a beautiful liqueur. To take that small, squashy, greedy mind and apply pressure. Like gently pressing his sharp heel onto a fat and helpless toad. Harder and harder, until the toad mouth gasped in agony and the toad eyes filled with tears. It was one of the several reasons he had arranged for the emergency meeting to take place in the flat. That, and Babette. And Bryce's future usefulness. Or lack of it. He wondered with a delicate curving of his mouth how Bryce would look when at last he knew what they really wanted him for, along with his revolting, squalid little organization. He looked forward to explaining Crystal Night to Bryce almost as much as he looked forward to taking over Babette.

"If I was to hazard a guess," he said, "I would say that at this moment Ryan is in one of two places. Either in Honeywell, investigating your activities there, or in Richmond, discussing them with Major Courtenay. Does that hasten your agreement?" It amused him to pretend that Bryce's agreement mattered. And in a sense it did. There must be no possibility at all of Bryce's turning against them, either over this or anything else. As long as they still needed him.

Bryce slid his eyes away, avoiding Robertson, looking at Major Willis for help, for a sign of protest. But the major

—
81

was sunk deep into his chair, his eyes staring resolutely at
the wall above Randall's head, like a man determined to
hear and see nothing that he didn't want to. Vining sat next
to him, his face still white with shock from the way Randall
had spoken to him five minutes earlier. And the thought of
what Vining had done to him, the sheer imbecility, the wick-
edness of it rose up in Bryce's mind and threatened to stran-
gle him. A film. Making a film about Honeywell. Going to
Akho—getting Akho's name out of him by a trick—sending
that vicious fool Redwin—

How could he have done it? How could they have let him
do it? Propaganda. Were they mad? He wanted to spit in
Vining's face, scream at him. But he sat trapped on the
couch, twisting his mind this way and that, hunting for a
way out.

His eyes were caught again by Robertson's hands, the
thumbs pressing gently, delicately on the fragile balloon of
glass. The voice saying, "You will do exactly as Captain Robertson tells you." Why hadn't he run then, got away before—? But he hadn't known, how could he have guessed?
Even when—when it happened he hadn't known—even
driving the car down that night. Christ, how could anyone
—how could he have thought—they'd just carried him out
—he'd still been—been alive? Even waiting for them to
come out of the field, the gateway—all he'd thought of was
to stop Redwin talking. He hadn't thought how, he hadn't
touched him, how could anyone—his whole business, his
whole life threatened—Nellie—Babette—just stop him talking. And now—now this. He writhed on the soft swan's-
down cushions of the couch, smelled his own terror, sour,
acid.

"I want a clear yes," Randall was saying. "From each of
you. We want to have no doubt afterward that this was a
unanimous decision. Do we, Edward?"

Bryce stared at him, helpless, one little soft hand lifted to the level of his heart, palm outward, as if it could protect him. Supposing he went without telling even Albert, just cleared out with Babette, left everything? There was enough in Canada, in Switzerland—they couldn't find him then—

"Edward?" The voice like a razor touching skin.

"I—"

"Yes. Or—no?"

"Yes," Bryce whispered, felt the sweat pour down his chest, under his arms. Like tapwater.

"And you, Major?"

Major Willis tried to think, a gentle veil of brandy and whiskies between his mind and the room, the sound of what Randall had just said and the reality of what it meant. Yes or no. That was the bloody question. Yes or no. A straight answer to a straight bloody question. He had stopped the taxi on the way from the Turk's Head and had another quick couple of stiffeners. He'd felt a lot better even before he arrived. A bloody sight better, and sitting on the down cushions of Bryce's armchair, drinking Bryce's bloody fine brandy, he had felt better again.

Robby there. Robby'd fix it. Fix that bastard the way he'd fixed Redwin. Didn't know how. Didn't want to know how. Fellow shot himself. All Vining's fault. Like a slug. He had sat listening to Randall tearing strips off Vining's skin with a warm glow of righteousness and disengagement, Bryce's brandy floating down inside him to join the whiskey.

The smell of Babette was in the chair, in the room, and it came to him like spring, like the scent of April flowers. What a little smasher. He wished Bryce hadn't sent her away. Better, of course. Couldn't have the ladies mixed up in a thing like this. But what a smasher. That dress. Like a bloody apron, fore and aft, and not a stitch under it. Just her. See her leg damn near up to her bottom when she turned around.

His mind wandered away from the room, the voices, the

sound of Randall's cold destruction of Aubrey Vining. He imagined taking her to Monte. By God, you wouldn't get much of the old Chemmy in with her around. He swallowed the rest of his brandy and looked vaguely for more.

This was what a man needed. This was what life was about. A tart like Babette, a flat like this with a few bottles of the old Napoleon tucked away in the sideboard. Vining. Ryan. The names reached him out of the fog, irritated him like flies buzzing. Randall talking. Questions, questions about Ryan. They'd fix the bastard. Robby'd fix him. Interfering sod. If he got it where the soldier got the bloody bayonet, bloody good riddance to him. Robby'd fix it.

He peered across the room, searching for Robby. Two of a kind. Himself and Robby. Old sweats. Square bashers. Real soldiers. That's what mattered, being a soldier, bloody comrades. Shadow Force, Trust Fund, all that codswallop, none of that mattered. What counted was comradeship, loyalty, men shoulder to bloody shoulder. The thin red line. The Empire. A picture floated into his mind, bright-colored, beautiful. Hanging on the classroom wall. Sunlight through the window. Trees outside. Picture on the wall. The Fuzzies charging. Black faces screaming hatred, devilish, hideous. A line of clean English boys, pith helmets, rifles, mowing them down. The Square. The British Square. Two officers, spotless khaki, swagger sticks under their arms, curled mustaches, fearless. By God, that was soldiering. The picture floated, came closer. Himself and Robby. Shoulder to shoulder, fearless. Mowing them down.

It had been one of a set of patriotic prints decorating the classrooms of his preparatory school. Not a very good school, although one boy, long before Willis's time, had gone from there to Eton. But a very patriotic school. The set of prints had engraved themselves on Willis's mind far more deeply than anything else he had learned there. "The Charge of the Light Brigade." The lone survivor from Kabul, riding toward the little frontier fort, blood streaming from his wounds. The death of Nelson. Gordon at Khartoum. The Zulu *impis* charging at Isandhlwana, falling in black heaps and walls of blood-crimsoned corpses. For Major Willis those pictures and the others in the set contained all that was of value in British history and the Empire.

He became aware of silence, started awake. Randall staring at him. "Wha'? What?"

"I'm waiting for your answer, Major."

"Yes, yes, of course—"

The telephone rang in the bedroom, very shrill in the quiet. Bryce started, looked around, looked at Randall helplessly. Randall nodded, and Bryce went into the bedroom, hesitating about closing the door and finally left it ajar. No one said anything. Randall waited, his head a little to one side, almost theatrically listening for whatever they would hear.

"Yes, yes, Albert, Mr. Bryce here." His voice breathless, frightened. Dirty little bastard, Willis thought. Scared of his bloody shadow. He reached out for the brandy bottle on the low table, tilted a good stiffener into his glass.

"What does he look like? Tall— Has he—has he got an Irish accent? No, no, of course not—"

Randall shut his eyes in dramatized impatience, got up and went into the bedroom. "I'll talk to him," he said. "Major Cannon here, Albert. What is it?" He listened to Albert describing Sean Ryan, the call to Akho's flat. In the other room Major Willis was on the Afghan frontier, riding through a hail of bullets toward the distant fort. Beside him Vining sat rigid, fear and a savage, almost hysterical anger coming now one now the other upmost in his mind, his eyes looking at Robertson across the room from him. His head cocked, listening to Randall's occasional voice almost in a parody of the way that Randall had listened to Bryce. But it didn't give, wasn't meant to give, that half-amused, contemptuous effect. A mad dog. Vining's mind shuddered away from what had happened, what was going to happen, the reality of what he was involved in. Men like these. Murder. He stared at the bronzed, mindless face in front of him, the black mustache like a huge caterpillar, something vile and alive, barely moving, seeming to creep above the stained, gap teeth as Robertson listened and smiled, absorbed in his own thoughts.

Randall was saying, "Where is he now?"

"I've had an eye kep' on him," Albert said proudly. " 'E's in a caff with a nigger kid just now. Name of Wilfrid. Arsking undesirable questions, I 'ave no doubt." For Albert the supreme crime, worse even than non-payment of rent, was either to ask or answer undesirable questions.

"Now that's very interesting," Randall said slowly. "Very interesting." He smiled at Bryce, willing for the moment to allow Bryce to share the smile, the thought behind it, since there was no one else there to share it instantly. Bryce twitched his mouth nervously in answer, wanted to sit down on the edge of the bed, wondered if he dared. If he could only lie down, put out the lights and lie quietly in the dark.

"Just a moment, Albert, while I think this out." He still looked at Bryce, fixed him with his bright eyes, smiled. "I think we can make use of this. It fits in very well." He turned back to the telephone. "I think he's after that little boy, Albert, I really do. And you ought to show some vigorous disapproval. Have you got two or three of your lads on hand?" He sat down on the bed, stretched himself out, his shoes elegantly crossed on the ivory satin spread. "No, not the dogs. That might complicate things afterward. But as vigorous as you like. Short of complete finality of course. And when you've disapproved of him I'd like you to bring him to 37 Portman Road. It's his own flat, just behind Marble Arch. He'll have the keys in his pocket, and you can leave him

—

86

there. You've got a car you can use? In case anyone sees you bringing him up to the flat you can pour some whiskey over him. But I'd rather you weren't seen. Is that all clear? Thirty-seven Portman Road. Good, off you go, Albert. And report progress to Mr. Bryce. He'll be waiting by the phone."

10

THE CHILD stopped talking, abruptly, as if he had run out of words, was suddenly emptied. He looked frightened, glanced sideways from under his eyebrows at the waitress, leaning now by the tea urn, picking her teeth slowly and methodically with a matchstick.

"Go on," Sean prompted.

Wilfrid shook his head, slid sideways along the bench. "I got to go," he whispered. "My ma'll kill me, I got to mind my brother."

The café door swung open and Albert came in, followed by the two strong-arm boys who had been collecting rents with him. Wilfrid saw him coming in and turned gray with terror. He froze on the end of the wooden bench, stared at Albert with his mouth slowly opening and twisting, ready to howl. Although he knew that howling would be useless. Albert smiled at him.

Sean saw Wilfrid's face changing, heard the door swinging. "There he is," Albert said. Sean swung around on the bench, his shoulders tightening and then loosening. Out of the corner of his eye he saw the man at the far end of the café getting up, his hands on the heavy, square brass buckle of his belt. The two boys behind Albert were solidly across the door.

"What is it?" the waitress breathed. She looked at Albert and then at Sean. "Not in here."

"What's he been doing to you, eh?" Albert took Wilfrid by the back of the neck, half lifted him off his feet and pinched heavily, still smiling down at him with a kindness that Wilfrid found more terrifying than ferocity. He didn't know, didn't even try to guess how Mr. Albert had known that he'd been talking. He knew, and he was going to kill him, and he opened his mouth and screamed in terror, his bird fingers knotting together. "Did he hurt you, the bastard?" Albert said, and Wilfrid screamed again, feeling the stubby fingers dig into his neck, grind on his neckbone. Albert let him go and turned to Sean. "After little boys, eh? I know how to treat your kind." He beckoned the three men forward, keeping his eyes on Sean. "You're going to be mucking sorry you ever set foot in Honeywell, Mr. Bloody Bugger Ryan." Sean went back until his shoulders were against the wall of the café, the edge of a bench against his right knee, a long table hard against the wall preventing him from stepping over the bench to his right. The two boys brushed past Mr. Albert. The man with the belt closed in along the far side of the table.

Sean reached down, felt for the near end of the bench, pulled and lifted. The two boys in front of him crouched for a second, thinking he was going to try and throw it. Instead he lunged forward, holding the end of it, pushing it like a swinging gate. It caught them across the body, swept them backward into Mr. Albert. Sean felt them stagger, begin to go down, and lunged harder. They fell, and he let the bench fall on top of them, tangling their arms and legs. Mr. Albert shot back behind them like a cork out of a bottle, hit the counter and the tea urn swayed forward, huge, leaning above him, the lid lifting like the jaws of a grotesque chromium shark. He had his shoulders against the counter, his face upward, saw the round mass of the urn falling, the steaming fountain of tea spurt up and out and over him, a brown tidal wave, ten gallons of boiling tea in a solid wall, falling, steaming, hitting him like a belch of flame out of the door of a furnace, tearing hair, skin, eyes out of his head, breaking, running, filling his clothes, his mouth, so that his shriek of fear turned into a choked nothingness, his hands clawing at his face, trying to shield it, the skin of his hands blistering to the wrists, to the bone. He writhed and twisted on the floor and the tea ran out of his clothes in a sour smoking tide, like brown lava.

Sean heard him screaming as he reached the door, heard the scream cut off as he wrenched the door open. He looked back and saw him arching up from the floor in agony, saw the man with the belt buckle coming across the table in a scrambling jump, throwing himself forward. Sean swayed backward, pulled the opening door with him. The edge of the door took the running man full in the middle of his face, split his forehead, nose, mouth, shocked him upright. He stood for almost a second, his eyes open, no blood coming, a huge, opening wound in the middle of his forehead. Then he fell on the floor and a sheet of blood seemed to appear quite suddenly, cover his face.

The waitress was crouched in terror behind the counter, her hands over her face, moaning, "No no no no," over and over. Wilfrid was still standing where the fat man had dropped him, like a thin piece of refuse, his eyes huge, blind with terror, his mouth working. Not looking at anything. Sean moved and he seemed to come awake, to see the fat man at his feet, his face scarlet, like raw meat, the skin lifting off it, a flap of skin, boiled flesh, peeling away from his jawbone, hanging down on his steaming collar.

Wilfrid cried in his throat, a little, weeping shudder of

fear, of horror. He looked at Sean, tried to say something. His legs began to shake, almost as if he were running while his feet still stayed where they were. Then he ran, stumbling, slipping on the wooden floor, his too-large boots skidding like roller skates. Slid through the door, down the two cement steps, ran, crying with terror.

The two men who had gone down under the bench were still struggling clear. One of them on hands and knees, looking at the clawing, twisting figure of his master, his eyes wide, not taking it in, not realizing what had happened. Sean stepped toward him, slowly, as if he were not in control of his own movements, his mind beginning to shudder, in horror, in disgust at what had happened, what he had done, the suddenness, the completeness of the destruction. He saw his own foot swing, saw the point of his shoe swing in a long, smooth arc, kick the man in the side of the head, saw the head slam sideways and back, the hands leave the floor, the body fall. He looked down at him. Like a man who has half killed an animal by mistake.

The waitress screamed, "Jesus! No!" The other boy looked at Sean from the floor, crouching, toad-helpless, frightened, looking at Sean's foot. And Sean knew that he was going to kick him and tried to stop himself. Knew that he was kicking him out of terror, was sick with fear. Saw the boy's face, white with shock, spots like points of fire on the thick, unwholesome skin. Swung his foot in a dream of disgusted, shuddering terror. The boy threw himself sideways, crawled, scrambled, the bench still across the calves of his legs, like a toad half crushed by a piece of fallen wood. His mouth slobbered, grunted in panic, twisted his face sideways.

Sean bent and caught him by the coat, lifted him, slack folds of cloth in his two hands, jerked him upright. The boy gibbered, lifted his hands, tried to use his knee as he came up, and Sean felt better seeing the resistance. He let go of him with one hand and hit him across the face, his own

—

mouth twisting. If he could obliterate him, smash him out of sight, out of hearing. The head fell back and he hit the boy in the throat, with his closed fist, driving his knuckles into the Adam's apple. Felt the weight of the body sag and thrash, slip out of his hold.

The boy spun around on the floor. Sean poised his foot, wanting to drive his heel down into the gasping face. Something a long way back in his mind said, "No, no, no." It was the waitress, still moaning like a broken record player, but the word penetrated. Why not? If he killed he wouldn't be frightened, there would be quiet, he could walk away. Walk away very slowly and quietly. The body was twisted around his feet, his legs, arms holding his legs, he couldn't move, and the panic lifted in him like mercury, filled him, blinded him. He lunged away with one foot, got it free, got the second foot free, dropped on the body with one knee and hit it three times, once with the edge of one hand and twice with the other. It lay completely still, and he stayed beside it, half kneeling, breathing in shallow, quick gasps, his heart pounding.

The waitress was hidden behind the counter, crying. He listened to her, not knowing what the sound was. It was half a minute before he stood up. The four bodies lay where they had fallen. He knelt down beside the fat man. "Search him" his mind ordered. He ran his hands over the sodden clothes. There was a roll of notes in one hip pocket. A greasy wallet in the other. A silver turnip watch in a waistcoat pocket, a fob, keys, a dog-eared notebook in a brown paper cover in the inside pocket of the coat. Steam rose out of the cloth as he moved it, it was hot to the touch. Sean pushed the things into his own pockets, except for the watch and fob. Stood up.

He wanted to run but he made himself walk. Out of the café, turn right, walk alongside the gray, weed-flowered stone of the railway embankment. The back gardens of de-

—

pressed small houses across the road. A lane more than a road. The sun was shining. He walked quite slowly. A green trail of weed hung down in front of him, specked with the minute blue flowers. He pulled at it as he passed, and the whole weed came away, out of the shallow soil between the stones, cement dust falling in a dry, ugly shower behind it. The dust fell on his clothes and he shuddered, let the weed fall.

He stopped and leaned against the wall, coldly damp even in the sunlight, as if it lived in shadow. He shut his eyes and wanted to get sick. "I know how to treat your kind." "After little boys." Margaret's voice on the telephone. "A not very edifying one, apparently." What were they trying to do, they, they, they? The men in the Coach Inn. He saw the fists coming, felt them in his stomach, saw the flesh hanging from the side of the fat man's jaw, the gray boiled strip of flesh like pig boiled to strip the skin and bristles.

Wilfrid talking about Black Jesus. The bird voice whispering. "My daddy a preacher every Sunday. He says the Black Jesus coming." The claw fingers, the chopstick arms surrounding his ice cream as if Sean were threatening to take it from him, the eyes like wells, wide with belief in the Jesus child, small and black, born far away, far, far away in a cave in the mountains, high, high up to the sky and the green trees hiding it. From the soldiers, from the Europeans. My daddy knows. He preaches and he knows.

And Mr. Bryce the landlord, the eyes clouding, the voice whispering, my daddy say never to talk about the landlord, never to talk to anyone. But one day Jesus come and then there won't be no more landlords, no more ever. Small, small Jesus with his mother, smaller than the smallest baby and the soldiers looking to kill him. White men killed the last Jesus on the cross, but this one—they'll never find him, the black people hide him till he's grown big and strong.

Mr. Redwin, yes, yes, my daddy talk to him, he was talk-

—

ing to everyone up and down the street, I don't know what they tell him. And then the little whispering river of talk drying up abruptly in frightened silence, the ice cream plate empty, a speck of ice cream at one corner of the brown, childish mouth, the eyes cloudy with fear. The door swinging open, the voice shouting, "What's he been doing to you?"

The fight began to unroll again in his mind like a film, like a tape recording. He put his hands over his eyes to blot out the look of the fat man's face, the blind eyes, took them away because that made it worse. A woman was in a garden across the narrow road, hanging out clothes to dry. Dusty garden. Gray cement walls. A bush, leaves black, flowered with soot. White cloth. She looked at him suspiciously, her mouth full of clothes pins, her hair in curlers. A small child came out and hung on her skirt, a yellow and white pacifier stuck in its mouth like a cork. She pushed it away with her knee, must have mumbled through the clothes pins, "Go inside quick." It took the pacifier out of its mouth and began to cry.

Sean pushed himself away from the wall, went on walking. Twenty yards more and there was a tunnel under the embankment, smelling of soot, of wet; someone had used it for making love, draping their french letter on a rusty nail sticking out from the stones.

He went through the tunnel, and on the far side of the embankment there was a different world: a wide suburban road with new street lamps and semidetached houses, a bus shelter. He went and stood in the shelter and a bus came. He got onto it and gave the conductor a shilling. "Where does this go?" he said, and the conductor looked at him as if he was out of his mind. There were only three other people downstairs on the bus, three women with shopping baskets, all sitting together, making an outing of their shopping day.

"Finchley," the conductor said.

—

Sean nodded, took his ticket and his change, let the bus take him to Finchley. "Four and eleven a yard," one of the women said. "I told her I could get better than that in Oxford Street for three and eleven and she said saucy as you like, 'Why don't you go to Oxford Street then?' I could have slapped her face."

The women got out and schoolchildren got on, school caps and pink faces, shouting at the conductor, at each other. He thought of the major lying in the nursing home, his face the way it had been yesterday morning, gray, haggard, the head trembling with a kind of palsy. What was he going to do, what was he going to do? The bus stopping and starting, stopping and starting. Niccolò. Italy. Margaret. The major. The blind eyes staring up at the ceiling of the café, the flesh hanging. "We know your kind." "Peter, you see what he did?"

Why? So that if he talked, no one would listen. He was after a small boy. He exposed himself. He's that kind. Who'd listen? Like Redwin. It's a world conspiracy. A world conspiracy of colored people to destroy us. If his widow, his mother talked, who'd listen? He hadn't listened. Had left them and gone away. If they hadn't followed him, attacked him he'd have gone away for good. Was that why Vining had been relieved? That he was on this safe, wrong track? Why hadn't he left him on it? And this time. If they hadn't come to the café. He might have gone away. To Italy. Left it. What could he do by staying? It was very strange. Twice. As if they didn't want him to go. The major didn't want him to go.

"Don't leave. The job's still worth doing."

"We don't go any further. Come on, mate. This is the terminus." The conductor shaking him by the arm. He was deathly tired. If he could go somewhere to sleep. Go back to his flat. It was only then that he realized that he couldn't go back to it. That they'd be waiting for him outside.

—

11

THEY broke up after the phone call from Albert. "I think we can safely leave him to Albert and his little friends for an hour or so," Randall said, his hand on Bryce's arm, steering him back into the living room. Bryce sweated, dried his face with a silk handkerchief, sweated again. The thin mouth smiled down at him, the eyes fixed on him like cold glass. "Telephone me as soon as you hear from Albert."

Major Willis and Captain Robertson went together. The love nest was the top half of a mews house within a stone's throw of Hyde Park, with garages below and a very good public house on the corner of the cobbled yard. "Let's stop for a freshener," Willis said. Now that the threat of having to do anything unpleasant himself had vanished he was feeling full of comradeship. He linked arms with Robertson, forced him toward the door.

"You've had enough, and anyway they're shut," Robertson said. He didn't like Willis nearly as much as Willis liked him, and he had a lot of organizing to do before he went to Ryan's flat.

"Bloody country," Willis said. "Can't get a drink. Can't get a woman. The place is run by homosexuals, Robby, did you know that? Foreign Office is stinking with them. Catholics and homos. So's the BBC. D'you know you can't get on the telly if you haven't got a funny accent or a rosary? Honor bright, Robby. Bloody country's creeping with it."

A taxi swung around the Crescent. Robertson hailed it. Willis clung to his arm. "But we'll fix them, won't we, Robby? Fix the sods."

Robertson shook him off, got into the cab. "Sorry I can't offer you a lift, Tommy, not going your way." The taxi ground away, left Willis standing, small and squat, like a

—

fleshy pillar box, his hand still extended, in protest, in rejected friendship. And not a bloody drink in sight. He half thought of going back to Bryce's flat. Make the little bastard give him a freshener. And the tart might come back. Little smasher. Given him the eye, too, when she let him in. Looked as if she could do with a real man after that flabby piss-quick.

But Randall hadn't left yet and he didn't want to run into him again. If he'd thought being called GSO—second in command—meant working under a swine like that—who did he think he was, for God's sake? Commander Bloody Rat Randall R.N., Retired. It was a bloody wonder someone hadn't drowned him the first time he went to sea. If he'd ever been to sea. Couldn't be a day over forty-five. Still wet behind the sodding ears. Retired, his arse. They'd chucked the bastard out.

GSO. He wasn't GSO. Wasn't bloody well allowed to be. A bloody training manual, that's all. Did Trust Fund know what was going on? The man was just bloody well empire building. A filthy little office politician. Empire building. Office politician. He rolled the phrases on his tongue, his short fat legs taking him toward the park. Got to fill in an hour or two before they were open again, damn them. Sit in the park. Look at the kiddies, the ducks. Some of the nurses were still damned good-looking wenches, even these days. A bloody wonder anyone could afford them. Jews probably. Jews and wogs and City shits. A bloody nigger the other day moving into the flats. Got the flat right underneath him. The ambassador of some bloody God-forsaken arsehole in West Africa if you don't bloody well mind. Ambassador! Have to wind his tail around his bloody waist before he presented his credentials.

He found a bench in the sun and sat on it, waiting for a good-looking nurse to pass. The uniform did it. The starched apron and those little collars and cuffs. He'd had a nurse

once. Hospital nurse during the war. Hadn't let her take a
bloody stitch off. Collar, cuffs, apron, black shoes, lisle stockings, the lot. Just her knickers. God, she'd been something.
He wet his lips. The war. Battle of Britain. Alamein. Eighth
Army. Slogging through the desert. Young chaps going up.
Just out of school. Spitfires. God, those were the days. Cairo.
Shepheards. The Long Bar. Coming out of the damned
office, sodden with sweat, going back to the flat to change.
Nice crisp drills laid out, starched and ironed. Abdul polishing his Sam Browne while he showered. He couldn't ever
think of the war without smelling polish and starch. Good
old Abdul. A bloody good wog and he didn't care who heard
him say it. Worshiped the ground his master trod on. God
that was the life. Down to Shepheards. A couple of Tom Col-
lins to set him up. A nice bottle of Hock with dinner, or a
spot of Tokay. And then up the Quarter for some fun. God, it
had been a war. A real man's war.

His mind drifted, looking down at the dusty ground under
his small, dumpy shoes. The desert. Alamein. Monty and
him. I know I can rely on you, Tommy. You can, sir. Call me
Monty, man, there's no one listening. All right, Monty. Get
these dispatches through for me, Tommy, they're vital. Not
Alamein. It was Tobruk. Get these dispatches through to
Tobruk for me, Tommy. Tell them to hold on. There isn't
another officer in the Eighth Army I'd ask to do this,
Tommy. But I don't mind asking you. Hands clasped. I'll get
through, sir. Or die in the attempt. You're a bloody brave
chap, Tommy. And I don't say that often.

Sand and darkness. No stars. Mine fields. Christ, put a foot
wrong and that'd be the end. His sergeant sweating bricks.
Teeth chattering. Come on, sergeant, you sound like a Span-
ish whore with castanets in her Micky—next step the damn
fellow puts his foot on a bloody mine and it's raining mince
meat. Corporal and three men gone with him. Just Tommy
Willis left. His right leg blown off at the knee. Tie up the

—

stump with his handkerchief. Jesus, the blood. God, his left hand gone too. Tie the knot with his teeth. Dispatches soaked in blood. Jerry putting down tracers, star shells, bangalore torpedoes, four-pounders, the bloody kitchen sink.

The wire. Get the cutters out. Bloody near fainting with the pain in his stumps. Crawl through. Into the perimeter. Aussie soldier. Sentry. Who goes there? Dispatches. From Monty. About all in, cobber. Christ, cobber, you look bad. Jesus, your leg. Never mind the bloody leg, cobber. Take— these—dispatches—to your—C.O.—tell him—Tommy W— A nurse went by. Christ all bloody mighty, the kid in the pram was black. What had they fought for? Make England safe for the wogs. Jews and wogs. He was half asleep in the sun; his mouth hung open and he began to snore. The nurse hurried on. Bottom wagging under the tight blue uniform. What the hell was she doing on the Somme? Mud and blood and corpses on the wire. Robby beside him on the firing step. It looks damn bad, Tommy. If the Huns attack again we're bloody near out of ammo. But I can't send a man through that hell for more supplies. I'll go, Robby. It's a bloody thin chance but I'll try it. England expects and all that rot. By God you're a game 'un, Tommy—

The phone rang in Bryce's flat. Bryce came out of the bathroom, holding his trousers up with both hands. "Yes?" It'd be Albert. His hand shook, he almost dropped the receiver. Babette's voice. Purring, wheedling. "I'm in Steiny's place, Teddy darling. Give you three guesses what I'm doing." He didn't say anything. His face, his whole body shook with rage, fear turning into anger, hatred of her greed, her senseless blind selfishness. "Well, if you won't guess, I've got it on. And Steiny says we can have it for three five. We don't even need to pay cash—" He put the phone down on her, imagined hitting her across the face, slamming her stupid, vicious little face with both hands, from side to side, hitting her with his fists, kicking her. The phone rang again. He picked it up, started to scream, "No, no, no, no," into it. When he stopped for breath a man's voice whispered, "Listen, for God's sake, Albert's in hospital, the ambulance is taking him to hospital, I got to tell you what happened, hadn't I?"

He listened, not taking it in, the voice buzzing in his ear. When the voice stopped he didn't say anything. "What'll I do?" the voice said.

"I don't know," Bryce said. "What did you say?"

The voice blasphemed, told him again. "Albert didn't tell us what he was like. Just said he was a nosy needed doing. Jesus, you should see Albert. He's got no face left, and Sid —we left the mucking dogs behind so we wouldn't kill him—Christ, when I get him I'll—"

Bryce put the phone down again. He'd known it'd be like this. He tried to think. He ought to phone Randall. Damn them. Damn them. His bowels trembled, shook with warning, and he ran for the bathroom, reached it just in time. He sat on the padded seat and doubled over with weakness, felt his forehead cold and wet, his head dizzy, empty of blood. Get out of here. Pack and run for it. But when he got up to go into the bedroom and start packing he had to sit down again. "Nellie," he called in a weak voice before he remembered that he wasn't at home, he was in the flat. If that bitch came back with the coat—He tried to straighten up to curse her properly, but he had to double over again. He was fainting.

His shirt felt sodden with sweat and his head was going around. He pulled himself off the lavatory, got a towel and buried his face in it. He pulled off most of his clothes, left them in a heap on the bathroom floor, tottered into the bedroom, his underpants clinging and flapping against his shrunken little legs like the skin of a small elephant. His

—

stomach bulged under his silk undershirt, shaping his bosoms, and the mirrors tilted his reflection at him from a dozen angles, walking down, up, left, right, showing his drooping buttocks, his bald skull through the seaweed strands of hair. The pathos of his aloneness, his unlovedness struck him like a wound in the heart. Nellie. Babette. He'd given them his heart, his soul, the dower house, the Alfa Romeo, this flat, God, the bed alone had cost four hundred and sixty pounds not counting the hangings, and all she could think about was that coat. What had he done, dear God, what had he done to bring such a girl into his life? And Nellie, saying she was lonely, sniveling half the night. Wasn't he lonely? Did she ever think of him? Working, working, working, trying to build up a business, trying to put together a bit of capital, having to worry about staff, about tenants, about the Rent Act. He paid more to solicitors than most men paid in income tax, and who thought about him?

His mind hunted for futile things to occupy it to keep the big fears out. Babette, the coat, Nellie, an argument he'd been having for the past eight months with the Appleford council about building a cottage for his head gardener. They were all against him. Everyone. But the real fears crept up to his shoulder, leaned over him like the dark when the lights fail, were suddenly there. Redwin. The thumb pushing at his eye. Waiting in the dark.

He made himself move, look for a case. Where did she keep her cases? Wardrobe. He couldn't reach the cupboard above the hanging space and had to drag a chair over. Don't thing of anything. Just pack. Making a film. Dear heaven, Akho talking on a film. How mad could anyone be? Three thousand five hundred for a coat. How many coats could she wear? Look at them, a rack, racks of coats, suits, dresses, how much money was in this one cupboard? Three, four thousand pounds? Her mink. A sable. And the things he'd bought her. Fifty guineas for a housecoat, one hundred and

twenty for a suit that she didn't like. You could dress a
chorus out of this cupboard, send them to the North Pole in
fur coats. He found an aluminium airweight case and
dragged it down, bringing half a dozen feathery, gauzy,
senseless hats along with it. Passport. For days he'd carried
his passport around with him, not admitting even in his
thoughts way he was doing it. Money. How much money
had he got with him? And the wound in his heart opened
again. It was rent day. And Albert had been collecting rents.
The hospital—He started for the telephone and realized
halfway that he didn't know which hospital. Tears began to
run down his gray, flabby cheeks. He stood in the middle of
the room and wept.

12

SEAN got off the bus as if he were leaving the only familiar
place he knew. He turned a corner and was in a shopping
street, a Wimpy Bar beside him. He went in and took a table
as far away from the door as possible. It was stupid and he
knew it was stupid, but he couldn't help it. As if somehow
going into the furthest corner was a protection. The place
was empty after the lunch-hour rush. Two Italian cooks
stood half asleep behind the wide service counter, checkered
blue and white cloths tied around their necks, white chef's
hats tilted forward over their eyes.

"Give me a Wimpy and some salad and some milk," Sean
said, and one of the cooks put himself into reluctant motion.
Sean sat trying to think. But nothing happened. All he could

see was the man's face, scarlet, flayed, the fat body heaving in agony, trying to breathe, to scream. He felt the hot, steaming cloth against his hands, the greasiness of the wallet. He felt in his pocket, took the wallet out, looked at it under the edge of the table. Not here. He looked up at the service counter but both cooks had their backs to him, one cooking, one talking. Italian words came to him above the hiss of the chopped beef on the stove. Talking about a girl. Niccolò's voice. "You and me together, Giovanni mio, we could do something. Can you guess what a man I know made in one week, just one week, doing one simple little job for a chemical firm? Twenty-five million lira—thirty-five thousand dollars. To get three files of papers from a rival chemical firm in Paris—some formula they wanted, details. So he went to Paris and found the girl who worked with those files—"

He opened the wallet. More money, a driving license in the name of Albert Fetter with an address in Paddington, a photograph of a woman in glasses, of two children wearing glasses who might be the woman's daughters. All three of them plain. A football coupon, long out of date. A raffle ticket. The Convent of the Holy Rosary. First prize a TV set. Sixpence a ticket. He shuffled the wallet back inside his coat, and the cook put a tray in front of him.

When he smelled the food he found he was starving, but the first mouthful choked him and he pushed the tray away and drank the milk. The roll of notes was heavy in his coat pocket and he pushed his hand down onto it, rubbing his thumb across the edges. Even in singles it must be a lot of money. "You just need enough money to keep you one month," Niccolò had said. "We need to hire a villa—you got no idea how much a villa impresses people—flat, apartment, anyone can have an apartment, but a villa, that's really something, these people are big operators, they think, and the price goes up like a gas balloon, voom. And for girls, too—"

He pulled the roll out carefully, looking down at it sideways. They weren't singles. Fivers. In the center a wad of tens and twenties, folded small and square, the fivers rolled round them. He tried to count. Five hundred? "And we need a car too. A good one. We go in evens, eh, Giovanni? Everything split half and half. Even the girls—" Slapping him on the knee.

"I tell you what life is about. Life is about pleasure." The round brown face creased with laughter, bitterness behind the laughter, behind the bright greediness of the eyes. "Belief? Ideals? Pardon me while I laugh myself sick, Giovanni. You see that old woman begging there? She believe in something, God, Christ, the Pope, the Pearly Gates, she believe in everything. And look how thin she is. Did you ever see a thin bishop? I believed in something once. Oh yes, I believed. Democracy. After the Fascists a new heaven. And then I went to Sicily for four long years, Giovanni, and I didn't believe in democracy any more. The democrats and the priests. They carve up the people like salami. Who do you think makes the Mafia possible? *Che coglioni.*" Spitting on the sunny stones, laughing to take the taste out of thinking. "Pleasure, Giovanni. And lots of money."

"The job's still worth doing." Did the major know what life was about? He took out the red notebook. A boy and a girl came into the café, holding hands. The girl had a black and white plastic skirt six inches above her knees and the boy's hair was cut in a thick bob. His eyes peered under his fringe and his mouth was soft and babyish and gentle. He sat down with the girl and held her hand under the table.

The major's dying just in time, Sean thought. He leafed through the notebook. Columns of addresses. Amounts listed against them that must be the weekly rents, mostly between

—

twelve and twenty pounds. A second figure had been squeezed in against some of the addresses, alongside the first, in red ink. Plus ten, plus seven, plus eight. The dues? Rack rents and protection. 118 Honeywell Road was on the fourth page. There were eight rent entries against it, some of them apparently for single rooms. Basement, eighteen pounds and fourteen pounds. Thirty-two pounds out of that basement? He felt the roll again. There must be five hundred pounds in it. One week's rents? Not even that. Democracy. Flourishing behind the major's wall.

"I always think of our job as something like Hadrian's Wall, Sean. One side of it there's civilization. The other side —chaos. It's worth defending the wall."

Pardon me while I laugh myself sick. He looked at the notebook again. On the first page there were three telephone numbers. Paddington. Knightsbridge. Appleford. A small cold voice in the back of his brain said, "If you've got any sense at all you'll throw this notebook and the wallet in the nearest dustbin and get the hell out of it." He could be in Dublin tonight. Get an Irish passport again. Be in Italy inside a week. He needn't even throw these away. Send them to the major. Write to him. What else could he do? Randall didn't want to know about it. No one did. Except the major.

The telephone numbers looked at him from the page. The time to go is now, the voice said. He felt for pennies. Four. There was a coin-box telephone on the wall. He could make one call. If it didn't answer—Appleford? Knightsbridge? Honeywell? He chose the Knightsbridge number because it seemed the least likely.

It rang and rang. Twelve, fourteen times. He was putting the phone down when a voice answered. A man's voice, but high-pitched like a woman's, frightened. "Yes? Mr. Bryce speaking."

"This is the North Thames Gas Board," Sean said tiredly,

cursing under his breath. "You reported a gas leak and we've—"

"No, no you've got the wrong number, I don't—" Mr. Bryce stood by the telephone, holding the packed airweight case in his left hand, too nervous even to put it down on the floor, too nervous to hang up. His hand shook, tapped the receiver against his cheek.

"But we've got your telephone number. You're Mr. Edward Bryce, aren't you?"

"No, no, I mean yes, but I haven't got gas, just electricity—"

"If you wouldn't mind telling me your address, Mr. Bryce —I'll have to follow this up."

"Seventeen Cranleigh Mews." Answering automatically, his ears listening for the door, his eyes sliding about the room. Gas. Complaint. The words pattered against his ear, meaning nothing, not touching his mind. He had forty-eight minutes to get to the airport.

"Thank you very much, Mr. Bryce. I'd like to come and see you about this complaint—"

"Damn you," Mr. Bryce said, his voice rising, cracking, "damn your complaint. I'm going away, going out. I have to catch a plane. We have no gas." He put the phone down, felt for a handkerchief to dry his face.

In the café Sean paid for his meal. The boy and girl were still holding hands, their coffee getting cold between them. The girl might have been seventeen, her face thin and tired, her hair hanging in an untidy curtain to her shoulders. It wasn't as pretty as the boy's, or as thick, or as well kept. She looked at the boy with adoration.

Why? Sean wondered vaguely, passing their table, cursing his luck, his stupidity, the major, Mr. Bryce, who hadn't had the sense to leave his phone unanswered. The girl looked up, glanced at Sean, not really seeing him. Just a shadow, an adult, someone out of the dead world, who didn't know what life was about, how wonderful it was going to be. Her eyes were sorry for him and for half a second it was as if he were the boy and saw her as the boy saw her, and she was beautiful and a grown woman and held the future in her hands. Then it was gone and he was out of the café.

He crossed the street and found a taxi outside the underground. At almost the same moment Edward Bryce was climbing into a taxi in Cranleigh Crescent, looking over his shoulder, both hands gripping the handle of the silvery airweight case. Inside it along with a handful of his own clothes he had Babette's sable jacket, her sapphire mink stole, and all of her jewelry that he could lay his hands on. It wasn't much but it was something.

"London airport," he wheezed. "I haven't much time."

13

SEAN paid his taxi off in Cranleigh Crescent and walked up the cobbled yard past a Bentley, a Jaguar, an elderly Maserati and a Mini-Minor before reaching number 17. The houses leaned over the yards, painted bright blues and pinks and yellows, window boxes outside the upper windows, an aura of happy wealth surrounding cars, courtyard, houses, breathing off the car-washed cobblestones. The door of number 17 was painted scarlet and fastened with a snap lock. Sean rang the bell and waited. When no one came he leaned against the door and slid a strip of mica into the small gap

—

he had created between door and doorjamb, level with the lock. The mica bent as it met the jamb, fed itself around the corner of the door, found the curved surface of the lock's tongue, pressed it back into the lock. He let himself in and closed the door gently behind him.

Narrow heavily carpeted stairs led up to the right, ended on a small landing. He didn't need the mica strip there because Mr. Bryce had left the flat door open. A smell of brandy, cigarette smoke, expensive scent; heavy green-velvet-covered chairs, a white velvet couch, glasses, stuffed ash trays, a delicately useless writing desk on curved, fragile legs.

He stood listening. Gradually, out of the silence, distant traffic shaped itself into a murmur, an almost featureless whisper of sound. He went to the desk and opened it. Papers fell out like snowflakes. Bills. For flowers. Clothes. Wines and spirits. Telephone. Rates. Bank overdraft. He sifted through them quickly, not expecting to find anything. A letter without a sender's address signed "Teddy Bear." "Teddy Bear's scrumptious lickle pot of honey." A jar of hand cream. A gold fountain pen. An envelope postmarked "Appleford." The drawers and pigeonholes were empty. The desk of a woman who used it as a rubbish dump, only opening the lid to throw in another unpaid bill. Presumably Teddy Bear dealt with the bills periodically.

He went into the bedroom and for a second as his reflections advanced on him from half a dozen directions his heart jumped in his chest and his hands lifted. Then he saw what it was and tried to laugh. A bed surrounded by mirrors. Even the bathroom door was a mirror. He sat on the bed, telling himself that he was simply tired, that he just wanted to sit, that it was nothing to do with his nerves. The scent came up to him from the pillows, the pastel silk sheets, like chloroform, made him feel dizzy. Whoever lived in this bed must be quite something. Lucky Teddy Bear. He hoped it wasn't the man with the bald head and the sagging cheeks. But it probably was.

He looked around the room. Even the padded seat for the dressing table was a piece of equipment out of a fantasy-brothel, a swan with half-spread wings. Only Leda sat on it instead of lying under it. The top of the dressing table was another mirror, laid flat, scattered with powder, cigarette ash, jars, tubes, gold crystal, silver, combs, hairbrushes, sprays, bead necklaces, ring boxes, vitamin creams, pills in bottles, reflected and re-reflected from the mirror top into the facing mirror, into the mirrors on the walls. Underwear lay across the swan, stockings trailed on the corner of the mirror, some kind of dress was heaped on the floor: heavy silk, pale rose and gold, so stiff with gold thread that it seemed to be trying to stand up.

Sean thought of Margaret's bedroom, cool and tidy. Like her love-making. "What more do you want?" Was it this? Niccolò's face seemed to smile at him out of the mirror. "This is the life, Giovanni mio. Everything else is a damn fraud."

Beside him the telephone rang. He stiffened where he sat, felt his mouth open, his body lock in panic. The telephone. His nerve was going. He stared at it. It went on ringing. He put his hand out to it very slowly, trying to think whether he should answer it or not. He lifted the receiver, didn't say anything. A voice said sharply, "Edward? Edward?"

He tried to copy the voice he had heard on the telephone when he called this number. Whispered, keeping his mouth away from the speaker. "Yes, yes." It wasn't difficult to sound as frightened as Bryce had been.

"Well? Edward! Are you there?"

He recognized the voice. It was absurd. He couldn't. It sounded exactly like Randall.

"Edward, dear boy, this is Oliver Randall. Do you mind answering?" The voice thin with anger. "Has Albert rung yet?"

"No," Sean whispered.

"Ring me as soon as he does." The phone went down at the other end. Sean stayed holding the receiver, his hand shaking. When he put the receiver down he saw that where he had been holding it, it was wet. He looked at his hand and the sweat stood on it. Randall. He tried to feel relief. It was a department exercise that he didn't know about. He'd got in the way. That was all. But even while he was trying to think it, he knew that it wasn't true, couldn't conceivably be true. All Randall would have needed to do was to tell him, warn him off. But he had warned him off.

And also sent Albert after him. The telephone rang again. He picked it up, expected to hear Randall again. A different voice, an Indian accent. "Mr. Edward Bryce? I understand you employ a Mr. Albert Fetter?" "Yes," Sean said. "I'm very sorry to have to give you bad news, Mr. Bryce, but I'm afraid Mr. Fetter died a few minutes ago. I'm still trying to get in touch with Mrs. Fetter—" The woman with glasses. The two girls.

"Thank you," Sean said. He put the phone down. The Indian doctor at the other end looked at his own telephone with cold distaste. He was a socialist and disliked all employers on principle. But this one had sounded worse even than most of them. As if he didn't care that a man who worked for him, had probably given the best years of his life to him for a slave-wage, had died. And the English tried to read lessons to India on social justice.

In the Duke of Marlborough public house on the corner of Cranleigh and Mews and Cranleigh Crescent, Major Willis slid off his barstool, folded his evening paper with a flourish and headed for the door. See if she was in. See if the little love bird had flown back to the old love nest. Left me umbrella behind, me dear. Or his cigarette case. That'd be better. Could be anywhere. Down the back of a chair. Get her over the chair, eh, feel her behind. Attack, that was the word, toujours le jolly old attack. What a smasher. Too bloody good for Eddy Bryce, and that was certain.

He trotted up the cobbled yard past the Bentley and the Jaguar, felt the cool breeze like a lover's kiss on his sweating forehead, sang in his heart, "Tralala trala." He'd show her what a real man was like. Get her onto that couch and she wouldn't get off in a hurry. Ahead of him he saw a tall, broad-shouldered man coming out of one of the doorways, squinting his eyes. Bloody like her door. By God it was. So that was her game, eh?

He smiled, felt himself folded in cunning, in mastery, saluted with the paper. "Bryce in?"

"No," Sean said, taken by surprise. A short thickset, beetroot-colored man, swaying slightly in front of him, his face twisted with drunken cunning, his eyes screwed up until they seemed on the point of disappearing.

"Then the little lady's alone, eh?" Willis said. His eyes, his face, his tone wrapped Sean in a man's conspiracy. He had had four swift stiffeners in the Duke of Marlborough and he felt like an army. A bloody one-man army. All the fears were defeated, taken prisoner, buried in POW camps far back behind the lines, in the furthest recesses of his dazed frightened mind.

"She's out too," Sean said. "I was just locking up for Bryce. He's gone to the airport." He started to move past the fat man, get away from his questions.

"The airport?" Willis said. He put his hand on Sean's arm. "Not so bloody fast, chummy. What's he doing at the airport?"

Sean hesitated, on the point of shaking him off. But something in the man's voice, an air of ownership, of indignation and suspicion, told him not to, that this must be more than just someone calling. He let himself be held. "It is a bit of a surprise, isn't it? Randall doesn't know about it yet."

Willis peered at him. "Are you from Randall's lot?" Sean

—

nodded. "I'm Willis. Major Willis to the bloody scruff. Tommy to a pal. What's your name?" His eyes drilled into Sean as if they were lie detectors, his hand heavy on Sean's arm. More than half his modest success in Intelligence had depended on that trick of suddenly piercing anyone he was talking to with a hot, challenging stare that seemed to say "Liar!"

He did it because he was near-sighted, but it had made him deeply feared in Intelligence circles in Cairo during the war, where he had been concerned with checking agents' pay and allowances. Men trying to put one over on him about their expenses had found themselves reduced by that angry, myopic stare to scarlet stammering, and the then Lieutenant Willis had acquired a reputation for shrewdness that had survived twenty-odd years of masterly peacetime inactivity. He had been chosen for Shadow Force on the strength of it. He peered at Sean, trying to bring him into focus. Whiskey vapor came out of his mouth like ectoplasm.

"What's *your* bloody name?"

"Captain Nicholas," Sean said. "Did you know that Albert was dead?"

"Albert? Christ! What happened?" Some of the whiskey-imprisoned fears broke out, crept forward through the darkness, into the front of his mind. His face sobered for a moment. "How did—who—?"

"I don't know yet," Sean said. "The hospital just rang up. That swine Ryan, I think."

The major's hand shook, lifted from Sean's arm to his own trembling mouth, plucked at the scrubby mustache. "What do we do now?"

"We could go and have a drink," Sean said.

"The bloody bastard," the major whispered. He looked around, as if he expected to find Ryan at his back, hiding in a doorway, creeping up on him. Sean took his arm, guided him back along the courtyard past the Bentley. The major

—

let himself be guided, turning the information over in his mind. Albert dead. Bryce gone. Airport. Damned odd.

"It's damned odd," he said. Something else in his mind came forward, penetrated the fog. He stopped short, fixing Sean with his little, ferocious eyes, wet and savage under the thick gray eyebrows, the damp curls of his hair like a bull's fringe. "Are you Irish?"

"I am," Sean said. "But there's good and bad even with us."

"Ha," the major said. "I knew it. The bloody second you opened your mouth I knew it. That chap's Irish, I said. And I was damned right." His face cleared. The fears were back under control. They couldn't fool Tommy Willis. By God no. A chap opened his mouth and he was onto him like a damned flash. "You're Irish." And by God he was Irish. He was filled with a shallow gratitude to Sean for giving him the opportunity. He could have thrown his arms around him. Poor bastard. He couldn't help where he was born.

"A chap can't help where he's born," he said largely. "Knew a damn fine Irish chap once. Quartermaster at GHQ Cairo in '43. Name of Wilson. Ever meet him?"

"No, but the name is familiar."

Willis leaned forward on his stumpy legs, almost doubled up with a sudden, barking paroxysm of laughter. If he was laughing, there was nothing to be afraid of, everything was going to be all right. Bloody good. "Bloody good" he said. "The name is familiar! Bloody good, Nicholas. But he wasn't like that bastard. He was a man. Drink! Two bottles of whiskey for breakfast. God, he was a man. A bloody Irishman, but he was a man. I'd have gone to hell with that chap, Nicholas, d'you know that?"

They had reached the door of the Duke of Marlborough and Willis' feet turned in of their own accord. He seemed quite surprised to find himself back in the bar. Old time-blackened oak and beer handles and leaded windows. There

—

was no one there except the barman. "I'll have a pint," Sean said, "and—?"

"The same as before," the major said. "A double."

They took the drinks to an alcove. The major emptied his glass, felt the glow of all-rightness again. "Wait till Robby catches up with that swine. He'll fix him."

"How?" Sean said casually, pushing his tankard gently about the smooth oak table, spreading the moisture ring into patterns.

"Ha," Willis said. He laid a thick, stumpy forefinger alongside his bottle nose. "No names, no pack drill, eh?"

"That's right," Sean said. "Careless talk—"

Willis glared at him, suddenly enraged at the hint of patronage in Sean's approval. "You're too bloody right I'm right," he said. "You don't need to teach me about careless talk. Keep your bowels open and your mouth shut. That's my motto."

"And a very good motto," Sean said soothingly. "Have another."

Willis looked in surprise at his empty glass, and then at Sean, trying to focus him. Bloody pup of an Irishman trying to teach his grandmother to suck eggs. "You're damn right it's a good motto." Careless talk. Chaps popping off gossip in the Gezira club. Not Tommy Willis. Security Willis. "Used to call me Security Willis," he said.

"I know," Sean said.

"You knew?" Willis peered at him. If only the blighter's edges would stay together.

"Randall told me. 'You can trust Major Willis with your life,' he said. 'He's known as Security Willis.' "

"He said that?"

Sean nodded. The major beamed down at his empty glass. Trust Major Willis with your life. By God you could. By God you could trust him, Security Willis. The barman gave him another whiskey and he smiled down at that with the

—

same warm approval. Everything would be all right. Robby would fix that bastard. Then it would be over. He wouldn't know a thing about it, and it'd be over. Redwin. Ryan. R and R. That was damned funny. He peered at Sean. Nicholas. Don't be ridickolus, Nicholas. He started to laugh. Don't be ridickolus, Nicholas. Christ, that was funny. It was all over. He wouldn't have to worry about a bloody thing. Go on leave. Not a care in the world. And the old balance mounting up in the bank.

"Come on," he said, "drink up, man. This is on me."

He had another double before he thought of Bryce again. Sean cradled his fourth pint in his hands. The other three, still full, were under the bench.

"Bryce," Willis said. "Eddy Bryce. There's a damned unnecessary swine for you. What did you say he was doing?"

"Going away. I hoped you'd know where."

"I don't know and I don't care." Willis held himself stiff. If he didn't hold himself stiff the table was inclined to lift up toward him. And the bench was bloody unsteady too. "Good riddance," he said. "A bloody brothel keeper." If he put his elbows on the table very carefully he could hold the table down. He wasn't drunk. God, a few whiskies? Who the hell thought Tommy Willis was drunk? "Do you think I'm drunk?" he said challengingly.

"I'd say you were comfortable," Sean said.

"You're too bloody right I'm comfortable. And I'm going to stay that way. Look after number one and the country'll look after itself, that's my motto." He tried to lay a finger alongside his nose and missed it. The finger waved in front of his eyes, momentarily lost. "Don't get me wrong. I love this damn country. Love it. Bloody best country on God's earth, bar none. Bar bloody none. But it's finished. Kaput."

His face was purple, swollen, his neck garroted by his collar, the veins standing out dark and knotted against the damp mauve skin. "It's a bloody tragedy but it's the truth.

—

114

Empire gone. Everything gone. No guts any more. No respect. Boys like bloody tarts all over the place. Girls like bloody boys. Di' I tell you 'bout BBC? Can't get a job on BBC 'less you're a homo. True. God-awful but true's I'm sitting here."

He waved his finger uncertainly at Sean, turned the gesture into a summons for the barman. "Same again, Ridickolus." He choked with laughter. "Ridickolus. Nicholas. Your name. Get it?"

"That's damn funny," Sean said. "It rhymes."

"Of course it bloody well rhymes," Willis snarled. "That's the bloody point." He didn't like this chap very much. A bloody Irishman. Teaching his grandmother to suck eggs. A bloody know-all. "You think you know so blasted much," he said. "You don't know anything."

"Not as much as you do."

"Too bloody right you don't." He fixed Sean with his pay-and-allowances stare, drilled holes in the wavering target in front of him. "You think you know what Shadow Force is for, eh? Next war. Fight the Russkies. Occupied Britain and all that crap? That's all Randall's ever told you, eh?"

"Something like that," Sean said carefully, looking down at his glass.

"Bullshit," Willis said. "Knew from the start, right from the ruddy start. First I ever heard of it I said—d'you know what I said?"

"Bullshit?"

"Goddammit," Willis snarled, "who's telling this blasted story?"

"You are."

"I am." Willis gathered himself, loosened his collar and wrenched the knot of his tie down onto his sweating chest. He looked as if he were going to burst with blood, spout it over the table from his little crimson eyes, his purple cheeks. "Minute I heard about this Shadow Force crap I said—" He

—

waited threateningly for half a second in case Sean was tempted to interrupt again. Sean waited. "That's a load of codswallop I said. Next bloody war's not going to be like that. Maquis. Resistance. Chaps with gelignite blowing up other chaps. Codswallop. Russkies drop 'tomic bombs on us. Voom. End of bloody story."

He began to cry. Vague pictures floated in his dazed brain. The Coronation. Trafalgar. The Queen, God Bless her. Little Lady on a horse. Regular ripper. Zulus charging. Mow them down. The map colored red. Everything colored red. 'Tomic bombs. Voom.

"Give my life for the old country," he whispered.

"But Shadow Force," Sean said. "There's more to it than that—"

Willis squinted at him. He didn't feel well. If he lay down, felt the cool wood against his face. Floating. Sean pushed him upright. "You can't go to sleep yet. Party's not over."

"Who said I was asleep?" He stared around, his eyes so bloodshot they were almost blind—like eyes behind crimson glass, gorged with blood. "Never welshed on a bloody party in my life. Gimme a drink and see if I'm a welsher. Walk a bloody tightrope if they ask me. Gimme a damn drink an' I'll show you." The room was so bloody dark he couldn't see. Hear but not see. And out of the back of his mind the shadows swarmed, sudden and terrifying. "Don't leave me alone," he whimpered. Robby. Where was Robby? Robby'd fix things. Fix that bastard.

"What about Shadow Force?"

Who was saying that? Shadow Force.

"Isn't it for the next war?"

"Don't be bloody stupid," the major said. "First minute I heard 'bout it, knew that was all crap. No good. 'Tomic bombs. Then Trust Fund—"

"Tell me about Trust Fund—"

"Too late. Trust Fund's too late. Whole bloody country

—

116

sold up the creek. Jews and homos and bloody Yanks. Country's finished. Cromwell!" He squinted into the dark. "Take more than Crom'ell put this dungheap straight again." Saying too much. Trust Fund. PE under the bath. Voom. "Don't get me wrong. Every respect. Every respect in bloody worl' for Gen'al Crom'ell. Trust Fund. Marv'lous. But too late. Too bloody late." Bowels open and mouth shut. That was him. Trus' Tommy Willis. Like a flash.

"Onto it like a flash. Too late I said. Soon's I knew what Trust Fund doing, take over Shadow Force—I said, too bloody late I said. Jews and niggers got the place rotted. Di' I tell you 'bout the BBC. Lesbians too. Homos 'n' lesbians. True."

"Trust Fund won't be too late."

"Will. Country's finished. South Africa all right. Kith an' kin. Niggers start trouble 'n' those bastards in Whitehall start helping them—'Nited Nations start helping them—Trust Fund fix it, fix our bastards—Crystal Night—you know about Crystal Night?" Careless talk. Security Willis. "Mum's the bloody word, eh? Crystal Night—"

"Of course I know about Crystal Night."

"You do?" He peered into the dark. "Serve 'em right. Too many niggers. Voom. Country finished. Help South Africa bu' this country finished—"

He swayed on his seat, glassy, rigid. Don't think about Crystal Night. Get out before it happens. "Gerrout 'fore it happens—ge' to S'th Africa—only place left—" He thought he was talking to Robby. The only bloody man he wanted to talk to, Robby. Why Robby keep running away? Not bloody fair. Robby running away. He began to cry.

"Crystal night—you were telling me about it."

Robby knew about Crystal Night. "Robby knows. Kill the niggers. Voom. Hundreds of niggers. Bryce's niggers. Gerrout first. Going to be bloody murder af'wards—" Too old for it. All he wanted was a bit of cash, a bit of skirt. Monte.

—

And a cottage somewhere. Roses. Apple tree. The tears ran down his face. Apple tree. England. It wasn't much to ask. Old soldier fade away.

"Old soldier. Thassall I am. Jus' an ol' sweat. Desert rat. Seen it all. S'all too bloody late now." He fell forward, stiffly, face onto the table. Dark. Robby! Someone shaking him. Robby shaking him. No man's land. Shell hole. Killed thirty Huns before they got him.

Sean dragged at him, got a stubby arm over his own shoulder, heaved him up off the bench. "Upsadaisy," Sean said. "Home to byebyes. Where d'you live?"

"Killed thirty Huns," Willis mumbled. The barman laughed, gave Sean a hand with him to the door.

"I'll be all right," Sean said. "I can manage him." He balanced the major upright on the cobbles outside the pub. "C'mon, Major. Charge!"

"Charge!" Willis shouted. Whiskey came out of his mouth like yellow blood. "Guns!" Guns to the left of 'em, guns to the right of 'em. Christ, look at that fellow Willis. Out in front of 'em. God, what guts. Charge the six hundred. Blood coming out of his mouth. Shot. Dying. "I'm dying," he wept. Robby holding him up. "Kiss me, Robby."   ,

Sean pushed him. The stumpy legs moved like scissors, folded, collapsed behind the Bentley. Sean looked around. The barman had gone back inside. The bright-curtained windows with their colored window boxes were blind. He ran his fingers through Willis's pockets. Keys. Wallet. Folded newspaper. "Where do you live?"

Someone shaking him, shaking him. "Live." "Where live? Dying. Leave 'lone."

The shaking went on, a hand smacked his face, hard. "Live?" staring up at a shadow. Policeman. Drunk. Take me home. "Live Chel'sford Gardens. Eighty-eight. Take me home again, Kathleen."

Sean dropped his head back against the cobbles, left him

lying between the Bentley and the garage doors of number
12. There was no one in sight. He walked quickly down the
yard, past the Duke of Marlborough into Cranleigh Crescent. Babette's taxi passed him on the way through the narrow entry to the mews yard.

14

SHE CAME back to the flat like a tigress. To put the phone
down on her, cut her off. In front of Steiny. She paid the taxi
driver with a snarl of fury, under-tipped him, and when he
started to protest, gave him a look of such barely suppressed
violence that he crashed his gears and drove a safe fifty yards
before he cursed her for the nastly little whore that he could
see she was. She went up the stairs two at a time, split the
seam of her skirt, kicked the door open and prayed that his
filthy friends were there to see.

"Where are you?" she shouted, flung her parcels across the
room and slammed into the bedroom and then the bathroom.
So he hadn't dared stay and face her. She took the shower
curtain in both hands, wrenched it down off the rail, tried to
tear it, threw it in the bath. Looked for his electric razor to
smash it into the bath after the curtain. Stayed still with her
hand lifted. It wasn't there. But it was always there. With
his toothbrush and his pills. None of them were there.

A faint chill touched her. They had to be there. She
looked in the medicine cupboard that was too crammed with
her own bottles to have room for his. No razor. No Seconal.
At least, not his. He was playing a joke. She ran into the bed-

—

room, tore open the drawer where he kept his spare under-clothes and clean shirts for when he stayed all night. All gone. She looked at the wardrobe, its doors pushed back, clothes spilling out, a colored mist of hats fallen on the floor. She hadn't touched those hats— She threw herself at the rack, hunted for his dark suit, the one he always kept there. Gone.

She stood in the middle of the floor, staring down at the hats, her face tightened like a ferret's. So. That was the way he wanted to play it. Her eyes narrowed, her mouth became a knife slit. If he thought it was going to be as simple as that, then he had a huge surprise coming. Yes. She looked at the telephone. How long before he'd be back in Appleford? Not till six, probably. Perhaps she'd give the house a ring first, leave a message. Such as "Olaf sends his kind regards"? That ought to set him up for the evening.

She might also ring Steiny and tell him to send the coat around, that Mr. Bryce would be paying for it tomorrow. In full. Steiny could give her the five hundred as a kickback. And that'd be only the beginning of the lesson. She might start working on Randall to begin the take-over sooner than they'd planned.

She sat on the bed and phoned Steiny and thought of Randall. And Robertson. "Steiny? Is that you, darling? Babette. Don't you recognize my voice?"

She lay down, cradling the telephone, stretched her legs, crossed them, almost exactly as Randall had done two hours earlier, squeezed them together with the sudden thought of Randall, his hands touching her. She wanted someone. She wanted someone so badly that it was like a pain. Christ, how had she stood it, month after month, that little paddler? Afraid to do anything in case Albert, one of the others saw her, told him. But not any more. By Christ, not any more.

She finished the conversation with Steiny, kissed into the

—

telephone, put it down. "Bloody yid," she said, and swung off the bed, pulled her split skirt off, her blouse, stood in her cobweb girdle and new-moon brassiere, put her hands up to touch her breasts, looked at herself from a dozen angles in the mirrors. By Christ, not any more. The front doorbell rang. So he'd come back. She touched the points of her nails to her skin, dug them in far enough to feel the beginning of pain. Imagined raking them across that pallid, flabby, rabbit face. The bell rang again, went on ringing.

She crossed the bedroom and the lounge almost at a run, threw herself down the stairs. She was halfway down before she wondered why he was ringing, why he hadn't used his key. But who else could it be? She hesitated, slowed. The bell went on ringing. She opened the door, meant to open it an inch to see if it was him. A shoulder crashed against it, flung her back so hard that she fell on the stairs.

Major Willis stumbled in. "It's me!" he cried, peering around for her. It didn't surprise him in the slightest that she was almost naked. He had expected it. "You little smasher!" He opened his arms, fell forward on top of her. She raked his face with her nails, half blinded him. "Firebrand, eh?" he gurgled, and buried his face against her shoulder, felt the delirium of her bosom against his mouth. He arms went around her, picked her up, crushed her against him. "Woops."

The little smasher. Blood ran down his face, she was trying to get at his eyes again. "Steady on!" he protested. Enough was bloody enough. Get her on the bed. Lie flat. That was the ticket. Stairs too bloody steep, too bloody narrow. Woops, nearly fell. Not a stitch on her. He nuzzled against her skin, nibbled her breast, nearly fell again. Landing. Door. Through door into room. Someone screaming. She was screaming. Enough was bloody enough. Wake the neighbors. Shouting about Eddy. "Eddy gone 'way. Poor li'l girly. Eddy gone 'way airport." He made flying motions with his stubby flipper arms. "I look after you—take over bid, eh? Tommy look after li'l Babette."

She hit him across the face and he laughed, caught her wrist, twisted it. Frog-march her. That was the ticket. Try to kick, eh? He let go of her with his other hand, twisted her wrist until she was facing away from him, crying with the pain in her arm, trying to lash out with her heel. He smacked her across the bottom, caught hold of the elastic of her girdle and pulled. It came a long way away from her bottom and he let go of it like a catapult. Bloody funny. He tried to do it again, and she broke away from him, grabbed a pint scent bottle in French crystal off the dressing table and smashed it across his head.

The crystal broke, gashed his temple. Scent ran into the cut, burned him like liquid fire, maddened him. "You bloody little whore!" he yelled. Play hard to get, eh? He'd teach her, teach her a lesson she wouldn't forget in a month of Sundays, wouldn't sit down for a week. He flung himself forward, tripped, skidded on his face on the carpet and came to rest in the cloud of chiffon hats. She knelt over him, hit him on the back of the head with another bottle.

He twitched, grunted, lay still. Scent. Flowers. Spring. Nurse with no clothes on in the spring. Chasing her across the grass. Voom.

She crouched by the bed, panting, her hair in strings, the bottle lying cold against her lap, ready to hit him again if he moved. She realized he wasn't going to, got up unsteadily and went into the bathroom. To be wanting a man and have that come in, blind drunk. He was another one Randall could fix very soon. She leaned against the basin, feeling it cold against her hips, her hands, her stomach wrenching with sickness. The smell of whiskey, the stench of it against her face. She got a sponge, held it filled with water against her mouth, let the water run down her breast, her stomach,

—

sponged herself slowly and completely, trying to sponge away the smell. Her father. Waking in the dark. That smell. She shut her eyes and vomited into the basin.

She took off her sodden brassiere and girdle, threw them on the floor and went back into the bedroom to find a house-coat. She made herself step over him, ran her hands along the clothes. She had a coat chosen and half on before she realized that the sapphire mink and the sable jacket were gone. It wasn't possible, they couldn't be gone, they were moved, they were under something else. She tore at the tight rows of dresses, coats, suits, the fox fur, the squirrel, flung them out and down; scrambled up to reach the cupboard, emptied it of the remaining hats, a hat box, tissue, half fell on top of the fallen major, kicked him in the head with her bare foot, and when it hurt her toe, stamped on him with her heel. Flung herself at the heap of clothes, shook them, tossed them up like a volcano, scattered them across the room, the major, the bed, the dressing table. They were gone.

She went to the dressing table then and with unsteady hands opened the jewel case, emptied it across the mirror top, the clothes. Looked for her pearls, the gold bracelet, the diamond earrings, the emerald ring, the rubies. All gone. All that was left was the rubbish. Costume jewelry, Venetian beads, a silver bangle, amethysts, cheap rings. She began to scream, picked up the scatter of cheap jewelry and flung bangle, earrings, necklaces against the glass. Picked up a gold and crystal scent spray and flung it after them, saw the huge mirror star, shatter, great cracks run to the edge of the frame, the beveling, scar her reflection into fragments. Behind her the telephone rang. She could smash that too, smash it against the mirror beside the bed. She picked it up, lifted it. Suppose it was him? Tell him first and then let him listen.

"Is that you, Bryce?" the voice said, coldly furious. "Randall here. Why exactly have you not telephoned?"

—

15

SEAN reached Chelmsford Gardens about ten minutes after Randall's phone call to the mews. It was a quarter to six. Number 88. A big, handsome house with mock-stone balconies and sun blinds, staring out over a scrubby rectangle of grass and soot-stricken plane trees. No one in the hall. A name board, a row of letter boxes. "Major Thomas Willis, 3rd floor, flat 8." Nothing in his letter box except some kind of trade paper. A slow Victorian elevator like a bird cage. No one on the third floor. It was the kind of house where people could live for ten years without knowing the other tenants except by sight. If that.

Sean sorted the keys in his hand, chose the likeliest one and walked along the corridor. Number 7. Number 8. The second key fitted. The elevator started down. A woman's voice floated up the shaft, the words indistinguishable against the noise of the machinery. He was inside the flat. There wasn't going to be anything here. A hall the size of a wardrobe, smelling of mackintosh. A shooting stick hanging on a coat rack beside a stained, ancient military trench coat, khaki, rubbery. A tweed cap.

A living room with a kitchenette visible through a half-open door. The remains of breakfast on a round table in the center of the room. Egg cup and toast rack and crumbs and teapot. Not a room to come home to. Had he been married? Divorced? Widowed? The room said nothing. A tiny bedroom beyond. Unmade bed, pajamas trailing out of it, silk dressing gown hung over the corner of the bathroom door.

A couple of books on a shelf by the bed, along with a telephone, a pipe and an ash tray full of cigarette stubs. *Justine* by de Sade. *Venus in Furs. Sin City.* A magazine called *Peep Show.* A drawer under the shelf held a pair of glasses, an upper set of false teeth and a packet of French letters. In a cupboard on the other side of the bed there was a bottle of whiskey, half-full, a soda syphon and two tumblers. Clothes in a cupboard, a lot of dirty shirts and underclothes in a scrambled pile at the bottom. A chest of drawers. Ties, socks, shirts. The second drawer down was heavier. Underclothes. And books. Sean pulled them out, expecting pornography.

They were sales manuals. Electronic equipment. A stick-on label inside the cover said "Sales manager's copy. Not for circulation." Pamphlets on radio equipment, intercom systems "for office and home." Closed circuit TV. Advertising leaflets headed "Communicimports Limited. Why pay more? Let us offer you the world's best electronic equipment at wholesale prices, direct from factory to user. We can offer you fantastic bargains, unbelievable discounts because we by-pass the retail distributor—"

So that was what the major did for a living. Whiskey. Pornography. Electronics. The full life. He was going to toss the bundle of glossy material and the sheaf of Xeroxed paper back into the drawer when he noticed the red corners. In each case the top right corner of each sales manual's cover was a red triangle. To the uninstructed it looked like an office method of identifying one manual from another at a glance. Perhaps it was, Sean thought. But he'd seen it before. In his own office. Where it meant "To be destroyed in Situation Red." Situation Red meant different things for different documents. The outbreak of war, or the danger of arrest; every exercise had its own rules, its own "Situation Red." But the red corners were a constant for one kind of document. The sort that meant one thing to the owner, and something quite different to the casual reader. So long as he was casual and not really looking for hidden meanings with a trained eye.

Sean spread the manuals on the bed. Three of them. "Sales

—

organization." "Sales methods." "Sales targets." Each had thirty or forty pages, Xeroxed from typescript. But as well as page numbers there were copy numbers. And interleaved between the pages there were blank "memo" sheets. At least they had been blank until someone—the major?—had written on them in a neat, cramped handwriting. Mostly addresses. But also sales figures. Some of the addresses were in Honeywell and they and the figures looked familiar. He pulled Albert's notebook out and compared them. About half of the Honeywell addresses were the same in each book, and so were the figures in the second of Albert's two columns and in Major Willis' single column.

Some of the addresses were underlined in red and marked "CR." There were other addresses as well, with no figures against them at all but also marked CR. A note on the first page said "CR—Creditworthy." On another page there was a sales organization chart for the "North London Area." Area manager, sales manager, senior sales executives, junior sales representatives, assistant representatives. It seemed to be a very big organization. On another page there was a specimen chart for a subarea under a senior sales executive, with a junior and five assistants under him, in charge of "delivery," "collection," "maintenance," "advertising," "door-to-door selling."

On the first memo page of the sales organization manual there was a list of ranks and names and phone numbers in the same handwriting. The first was "area manager—Major John Cannon." The number was almost the same as the one Sean used for ringing Randall. Only the last digit was different, a six instead of a two. Major Cannon. Who had called on Mrs. Redwin to tell her not to talk. Among the other numbers were the three from Albert's book. The Knightsbridge number was against "area correspondence secretary—Miss Barbara Gore."

He sat looking at it, and some of the pattern fell into

—

126

place. This was the blueprint of what the major had called Shadow Force, at least for the North London Area. A resistance army for the next war. He'd heard vague references to it around the office. One of the hidden elements underlying the reorganization of the Territorials and the Ever Readies, and explaining some of the oddities about the reorganization. All that was clear enough. Cromwell? The code name for the Shadow Force commander. Britain's Tito in embryo. Or de Gaulle.

But where did Trust Fund fit in? And Crystal Night? CR. Crystal? Rather than credit-worthy? What had the major said about Trust Fund? Trust Fund's too late. And then, "South Africa—niggers start trouble—Whitehall, United Nations start helping them—Trust Fund fix it." How? And Crystal Night. Too many niggers. Voom. But too late. It could help South Africa but this country was finished. What could help South Africa? Sending volunteers from Shadow Force?

Whatever it was it was obviously something that the government wouldn't like. And Redwin must have stumbled on it. How? In Honeywell? It didn't seem very likely. What could he have found in Honeywell, apart from Mr. Bryce's and Albert Fetter's operation? And all he needed to do about that was go to the police. Why hadn't he? Because he hadn't had time? Because his "frightening news" had made everything else unimportant?

He ran the thing through his mind again, putting what couldn't be solved on one side and testing the remainder. A secret army set up in peacetime to prepare for the next war. But according to Major Willis this was only the surface object. "A load of codswallop." Did he mean that the official purpose was a blind, or that it had been perverted? Into extortion and protection rackets, à la Honeywell? Or both? The one thing certain was that the extortion was going on. Was that really Redwin's discovery? And he couldn't go to

—

the police about it without blowing Shadow Force? Risking more harm than good? Trying to get to Major Courtenay so that it could be cleared up from inside, without any public fuss?

Sean lifted the telephone, hesitated, rang the "area manager's" number. A girl's voice answered. He thought he recognized it. "Major Cannon, please." He tried to copy Major Willis' gravelly snarl. "Sales manager here." It was twenty to one against that being the right phrase to use. But the girl seemed to accept it.

"The area manager is out at the moment. If you'll let me know where you're calling from, I'll ask him to call you back as soon as he returns."

He opened his mouth to give Willis' number and changed his mind. Better play safe. "I'm calling from Miss Gore's number."

"Very good sir, I'll tell him." The phone went down. Outside, a church clock gathered itself, struck the quarters, and after a long pause the hour. Six. Was Randall the "area manager"? He looked at the papers and books spread out across the unmade bed, gathered them into a sheaf. They made a heavy bundle. Were the advertising leaflets genuine? Just cover? He didn't know enough about electronics to tell. Better take them. But if he was going to, he needed something to carry them in. A briefcase. Surely the major had one? If he ever carried these around, he must have some kind of case.

He found it under the pile of dirty linen. Old, worn out, the stitching going at the corners, the handle cracked. Inside it there was half a stale bar of chocolate, some tote slips, a membership card in the Lulu Club, Kerch Street. It was out of date. Sean stuffed the papers into the case, snapped the lock.

He looked around. There was no point in trying to hide that someone had been there. But he closed the drawer the papers had been in, pushed the dirty clothes back into the wardrobe with his foot and shut the wardrobe door. He was halfway out of the room when he thought of the girl in Midlands Television. As if she had wanted to tell him something. Did she still want to, now that she must know he wasn't from the police? But if she wanted to tell the police something, why didn't she go to them? Why hadn't Redwin? She'd been his secretary, his assistant. Cried for him. She'd been in the back of his mind all day. Did she know what Redwin had found?

He sat down on the edge of the bed, looked at the telephone. Tilted his head and listened. An old house, thick walls, no sound from the other flats. How long before Willis got his senses back? He'd looked set for an hour at least. Three minutes past six. He lifted the telephone, dialed Information. "Midlands Television—" When he was finally through, it was five past six. She'd be gone. "Miss Eva Lund, please. I don't know her extension, she's on the—" What floor had it been? He found he couldn't remember. All he wanted was to hear them say, "She's gone home." That would be the end of it then, all he could do. Except take these papers somewhere, give them to—who could he give them to?

"You're through now, caller."

And the girl's voice "Yes?"

He found he wasn't ready to say anything. Why was she still there? Like something around his neck, that he couldn't get rid of, that tightened every time he tried to free himself. "Do you remember this morning?" he said. It sounded so stupid that he flushed, felt his face burn.

"Yes," she said again, but this time her voice sounded breathless, as if she'd been running, was looking over her shoulder, was frightened. Very frightened. And yet eager. "Yes, I do."

"Did you want to tell me something?" He made it sound flat, pointless. Say, "no." Why had he rung her?

"Yes—but not—not on the—"

—

"Then where?" He looked at the wall. Embossed wallpaper. Originally cream, turned yellow with age. A dark stain from the major's head as he lay in bed reading. The other major lying in the nursing home. In the fraction of a second as he waited for the girl's answer he seemed to see the two elderly, gray-headed men, one measured against the other, one a caricature of the other. Like the devil's gross and dreadful copy.

"Where are you now?" She was whispering.

"It doesn't matter," he said. He wanted to ring off.

"I'll be in the Regent Palace in ten minutes," she whispered. "I was just leaving. Could you meet me there? In the foyer?"

"It'll take me longer than that." Was it a trap?

"I'll wait," she said. And then, "I'm so frightened.",

Not only you, he thought. And the vision of Italy, of Niccolò and safety and easy living, came to him like a stab of homesickness, like a man lost in the desert, seeing trees and water and knowing it's a mirage, a trick of the sky. He put the phone back and went into the other room. He was halfway across it when the doorbell rang. Shrill, piercing. He stood holding his breath, hearing his heart beat. After a few seconds the bell rang again.

16

RANDALL reached Babette's flat at almost exactly the same moment Sean opened the door of Major Willis'. He had already made arrangements about Edward Bryce. Babette let him in, showed him the major still lying with his face

—

buried in chiffon hats, snoring. Randall turned him over, smacked him across the face. The major grunted, smiled, flung his arms around an invisible woman, pursed up his mouth for kissing.

"How did he know Bryce was gone?"

She shook her head. She had changed into slacks and a sweater and drunk two stiff gins since the phone call. She was no longer interested in the major. Only in Bryce. "What are you going to do?"

"Bring him round." He dragged the major by the heels into the bathroom. "Give me a hand." They half levered, half lifted the major over the low edge of the sunken bath, let him slide down into it. Randall turned on the shower. It ran for a full minute before the major reacted.

"Raining," he mumbled. He lay face up, his mouth open, the water running into it, almost choking him, his head blocking the plug hole and the bath beginning to fill around him. He sat up suddenly. "Christ, where am I?" Looked at the bath, the pouring curtain of water falling on his head and chest. Then Randall. His mouth hung open; he stared at him like an ox in a slaughterhouse. Randall leaned very close to him, fitted the long fingers of one hand around the flabby creases of the major's throat, tightened them, gathered a handful of skin and sagging flesh, shook the major slowly backward and forward, rocking him in the bath. The water went on running, soaked Randall's sleeve.

"Tell me what's happened," Randall whispered. The major goggled at him, lifted both hands to free his throat. He didn't know where he was, whose bath it was, how Randall was there. He hoped he was still asleep.

"Give a chap a bloody chance," he said hoarsely. Randall tightened his grip again, threw him backward so that his head hit the taps.

"You stupid, fat, drunken bastard," Randall said. "What did Bryce tell you?"

"Nothing," the major whimpered. "Chap told me—Bryce

—

gone. Airport. One of your chaps—Nicholas. Ridickolus." He started to laugh at the joke and thought better of it. "It's bloody wet in here," he said. "If you could turn it off—"

"There isn't anyone called Nicholas." He was going to kill him. He had to shut his eyes to stop himself killing him, beating his lumpish head off the wall, off the edge of the bath.

"Don't be bloody stupid," the major said. "Course there is. Saw him. Had a stiffener with him. Two stiffeners." He reached up, found the shower control and turned it off. With the water out of his eyes he could see Babette. He began to remember, and gave her a roguish smile. Dressed now. Bloody shame. And just when they were getting onto terms.

"What did he look like? Nicholas?" He didn't want to hear the answer.

"Tall, dark chap. Irish. Bloody decent feller. D'you know what he said about—?"

Randall hit him in the mouth with his closed fist. The major's head slammed back against the white tiles with their colored dolphins and sea horses, the crabs and sea anemones. His thick body slid down into the bath, stayed there. Randall looked at his knuckles, his mouth white with rage, a pulse beating in his forehead. He put his wet sleeve against his face, held it there. He had wanted to do that to the major for a long time.

He stayed kneeling by the bath, the cold wetness of the cloth against his face, breathing slowly and deeply. As if his nerves were stretching, stretching. As if he could feel, see, hear everything magnified a thousand times. He was afraid to open his eyes because of what he would see in the cloth of his sleeve—the threads like ropes, the weave gaping. Babette said something and the sound crashed in his ears. If he could think. If it was quiet. The water running out of the bath, the major breathing, the girl moving her foot.

"Be quiet," he whispered, and the whisper was too loud.

—

132

Ryan. Drinking with the major. He leaned over the edge of the bath, felt the major's pockets. There were no keys. He got up and went to the telephone. So long as he was doing something. He pulled off his coat and then unbuttoned the wet cuff of his shirt.

"Robby? I think he's gone to Chelmsford Gardens. Have it watched, will you? Don't touch him. Don't let him know. Just follow. Delay him if you can to give us more time, but don't touch him. It's too late for scenes in the street or anything like that. I don't want him to know this time. Use everyone you can get hold of. We've got to finish this soon."

He felt better. Dialed another number. Babette came and sat by him on the bed, took his shirt cuff and squeezed the water out of it. He let her, and she rolled up the cuff, bared his forearm. He smoothed his left hand up her back, under the loose angora sweater, caught the nape of her neck, held it. "Warehouse? I may be bringing a visitor tonight. I don't know what time. But I'd like the launch standing by. We'll be going for a trip. Tonight or tomorrow."

He was himself again. In action. He felt the power in himself like electric current turned on, in his voice, his hands. Conscious of himself like a man on a tightrope, walking smoothly, swiftly, delicately powerful, swaying, balanced. He had a trick of considering himself, his mind, his body, as a rider feels and sees the horse he rides on, feels one with it and yet detached. He had that detachment from himself that was at the same time a sensuous oneness. Even while he ran his hand on Babette's skin he considered not her, not her body, but himself feeling her body.

He made her turn her head toward him, looked at her, brought her head slowly closer. She expected him to kiss her and prepared her mouth. He looked at it, smiled and pushed her softly away, still listening to the voice at the far end of the line. When he was finished he dialed again, gave orders, spread his net, traced Albert to the hospital, heard that he

—

was dead, made more phone calls to make use of that fact, forestall any damage in Honeywell, head off any inquiries by the police into a suitable direction.

"Get hold of the little boy, see how reliable he is. We may need him. Ryan made him an indecent proposition and Albert interfered. Give the boy's mother five pounds and a couple of hints."

Babette lay beside him, listening. His free hand moved over her body, exploring, like a blind man's hand, like a man fondling a cat. She was afraid to react, afraid to guess wrong. But she began to stretch and shiver, close her eyes as the hand smoothed, fondled, stayed still, moved. They had met first in his office, months ago, where someone had brought her from the Lulu Club, and she still knew nothing about him, was not even sure that his name was really Cannon, was sure of nothing except that he was very powerful and very frightening. She would never in a lifetime have recognized Mr. Drybergh's or Ryan's or Major Courtenay's descriptions of him.

Major Cannon had had her introduced to Edward Bryce. "Forget about me until I get in touch with you again. But make friends with Bryce and stay friends with him. And find out everything you can about him." Someone she had never seen before and never heard of again had brought her to a party, introduced her to a small, fat, elderly man with a big bald head and a Rolls Royce. From then on it had been simple, and much better paid than the Lulu Club.

On his side, in their infrequent contacts, Randall had recognized much more in her than a piece of flesh. He put her on Trust Fund's payroll and began to look forward to the time when she was no longer needed for Edward Bryce.

His last phone call was to Trust Fund itself. He was the only member of the Section who could get in touch with it without being first instructed to, and then only by roundabout and oft changing methods.

—

He told the voice that answered what had happened, outlined what he had done. The voice said nothing. Randall sharpened his tone a fraction. "Do you approve?"

"If you succeed," the voice said mildly. "Was that all you wanted to tell us?"

"Yes," Randall said very carefully, and put the receiver down gently and accurately on its cradle. "One day," he murmured, "I will teach those bastards a tiny lesson."

At London airport Edward Bryce was sitting hunched behind a newspaper on one of the long couches, waiting for his flight to Zurich. Every half-minute or so he lowered the paper, looked gray-faced at the doorway. He didn't know who he was looking for. There couldn't be anybody, nobody knew, nobody could know. Not for hours, days. And by then—by then he could be anywhere, anywhere in the world. Start again. Two hundred thousand would start him again. He gripped his small fat hands on the newspaper, tried to stop them shaking, tried to make himself read something, anything, to take his mind off the thought that it might be that man coming in now. Or that one. Or the one behind him. He stared at the headlines, tried to make the letters stay still.

"Call for action in S.W. Africa." "The permanent representative at the UN of the Republic of Liemba has demanded . . . Mali . . . the Afro-Asian bloc . . . pressure . . . . UN presence . . . Security Council . . . the United States in an embarrassing position . . . it may be difficult to veto . . . if Russia . . ." The words shimmered in front of his eyes, meant nothing. "Star loses snake." "Java Dawn the film actress lost her pet snake Toto for the second time this week when the six-foot Indian python escaped from her in the studios of Midlands Television in London during a recording session this morning. Miss Dawn, who has been appearing in the Rorschach Cabaret Club with Toto, is offering a hundred pounds reward. "He is quite

—

harmless and most affectionate," she said at a press conference.

"BEA announce the departure of their flight—" He lifted his head, caught the word "Zurich," tried to find his boarding card. A young man sitting beside him saw it lying on the seat between them, gave it to him with a pleasant smile.

"Was—was that my flight?" Mr. Bryce said, showing him the card. He found that his legs were weak; he didn't think he could stand up. The young man said that it was his flight, helped him to gather up his spectacle case, his newspaper, make sure of his ticket. They walked to the exit bay together, Mr. Bryce looking back over his shoulder, his legs shaking. He dropped the paper and the young man picked it up.

"It doesn't matter," Mr. Bryce said.

"I'll read it on the flight," the young man said. He didn't intend to kill Mr. Bryce until they were in Zurich.

17

He stood in the center of the room, waiting for the caller to go away. Nothing happened. The bell didn't ring again. There were no footsteps. He tried to remember if there was carpet outside the flat. He couldn't remember anything. The major's case weighed on the end of his arm as if it were filled with lead. He was afraid to put it down, in case it creaked, fell over, made the kind of soft, direction-indicating sound that the man outside the door was listening for. If he was still there. If he was listening.

—

He tried to think how anyone could have known he was in the flat. They couldn't. Very slowly he knelt down, lowered the case inch by inch to the floor, then himself, lay flat. The narrow line of light under the hall door showed clear. No shoes. No one standing there. He let his breath out softly, stood up again, went to the door and opened it. A young man moved forward from where he had been standing, out of sight, a yard down the corridor. Sean stood very still, felt his breath turn solid in his chest.

"Major Willis!" the young man said, his voice slightly, pleasantly American. "I just had a feeling that you were hiding out on me in there." He smiled, held out his well-shaped, manicured hand. His hair was yellow and close-cut, his tie was dark blue and narrow and his suit was dark blue and broad. His shirt was as white as his smiling teeth. "I've got a message for you, Major."

"A message?" Sean said. He had the bag in his left hand. He was trying to measure distances, and at the same time wanting to look behind him. He remembered the Coach Inn and the muscles of his stomach tightened and shuddered.

"The most important message you'll ever hear," the young man said persuasively. "And the best news. I've come to tell you that the Lord Jesus Christ died to save your soul."

"I'm very glad to hear it," Sean said. He felt like falling down.

"If we could just step inside your apartment for a minute I'd be glad to tell you how this news can change your life."

Sean moved sideways. "I'm very sorry, I'd love to hear it, but I have an urgent appointment."

The young man moved in concert with Sean's move. "Major, there cannot be a more urgent appointment than the one we're keeping right this minute. This could change your whole life."

"That's what I was afraid of." He moved right and then left and was past the young man, who followed him, stayed at his shoulder. "Why don't you come back another time?"

"Many are called," the young man said sadly, "but few are chosen."

Sean went down the stairs two at a time. "When could I call back, Major?" the voice cried after him from the landing.

"Tonight. Late." He was on the ground floor, out of the front door into Chelmsford Gardens, on the pavement. He turned left toward the King's Road and signaled a crawling taxi. I'm getting old, he thought. And frightened. This was the last one. It never occurred to him to look out the back window of the cab. And there was really nothing to notice if he had.

In the Regent Palace he didn't see her at first. Until he moved further into the foyer and saw her standing by the bookstall, looking at magazines. He went up to the counter, asked for the evening paper. She stood beside him without looking round. "Is anyone watching you?" she said.

"No one. Would you like a drink through there?" Nothing could happen in the Regent Palace. And if she'd brought anyone with her he could still find out what she wanted to tell him. And perhaps guess why. They went into the bar and he chose a table from which he could watch the door. He waited until they had their drinks, trying to judge her face, her expression. A very beautiful woman. And very frightened. She didn't like sitting with her back to the bar, moved her chair around a little, looked over her shoulder.

"I'll tell you if there's anyone I don't like," he said. "What do you want to tell me?"

She looked at him, looked away quickly, tried to compose herself. "Who are you?" she said. "This morning—"

"It was almost true," he said. "A kind of policeman."

"Intelligence?"

"If you like."

She twisted her hands.

"If you don't want to tell me anything there wasn't much point in asking me to come here."

"I'm afraid," she said.

"Of what?"

"Of being killed."

"Was Olaf Redwin killed?" She nodded. He started to say, "Then why didn't you tell—?" and stopped himself from being stupid. "How do you know?"

"I knew him very well. It wasn't—he wouldn't—couldn't have killed himself. Not—when he did."

A man strolled past the door, looked in, hesitated as if deciding whether it was too early to have a drink, walked on. Young and clean and healthy and big. Sean wished he hadn't come. He wished he'd never heard of Olaf Redwin. He held the dilapidated briefcase between his ankles and tried to think.

"How well did you know him?"

She turned her head away. "Very well." He wondered if she was connected with Redwin's Norwegian days. But she couldn't be old enough. She said as if she had just read his thoughts, "Olaf asked me to be his assistant a year ago because my parents are Norwegian and I speak it, and so did he. He wasn't very happy at home." She said it slowly, remembering. "He used to dream about getting away, living on a farm somewhere in the Norwegian mountains—"

"With you?"

She had continued looking away from Sean. Now she turned her head to look at him, her face slightly flushed, slightly frowning. "Perhaps."

"I'm sorry," Sean said. "I saw you crying yesterday."

She nodded. "Not many people liked him. But they didn't know him very well. He didn't show—a good side to most people. He was very bitter sometimes."

"Why did they kill him?"

"He wrote a report. He was going to send it to—"

"Major Courtenay?"

She nodded, looked relieved, as if for the first time she completely believed that he was a potential friend.

"What happened to it?"

"I have it hidden," she whispered. "A copy. They got the original."

"Have you read it?"

She nodded again. "I didn't understand it all."

"You're lucky not to have been killed already."

"I know. I don't care very much. Just enough to be frightened."

"You must have loved him."

"I still do. I won't love anyone else like that."

"How did he get involved?"

"They recruited him. Aubrey did. They thought the way he did." She gave a half laugh without humor. All the time they were talking she looked not at him but to the right, at nothing, as if a long way away she could see something, someone else, Olaf Redwin, the farm in the Norwegian mountains. "At least he thought so. He had some strange ideas."

"What kind?" He wondered what there could have been in Olaf Redwin, forty-seven, bitter, married, with strange ideas, to make this woman love him. If she hadn't been frightened her face might have been too calm, too much the earth-mother. The smooth shoulders, the magnificence of breast, of throat, the broad cheekbones. The fear lay in the green eyes, like a shadow moving in a deep, still lake. "What kind of ideas?" Half his mind was on the young, big man who had passed the doorway, glanced at them; on the other young, big man who had tried to tell him about Jesus Christ. It had to have been true. No one could have thought of it. And yet didn't that kind of gospeler work in pairs, with a satchel of leaflets and magazines?

"He hated everything about modern England. I think

—

sometimes he hated everything that had happened since the sagas. He used to dream of what he called a cleansing, a Götterdämmerung. But it was only poetry. He couldn't have hurt anyone. Not even his wife." Her mouth hardened and her eyes didn't look frightened any more. They held instead a remote and immense cruelty, as impersonal and terrible as a glacier.

"His wife has strange ideas too."

Eva Lund smiled, shrugged her smooth and beautiful shoulders in the embroidered peasant blouse. "Her father was a sergeant-major in the Indian army. She pretends he was a colonel. And she and Olaf's mother spend their time boasting to one another about their families. I think they've driven each other mad."

"He can't have had an easy life with them." He wondered if she was telling the truth. Or all of it. She seemed to guess.

"You're Irish?" He nodded. "And Catholic?" He hesitated but she wasn't looking. "You think I took him away from his wife, broke his mind and his conscience? I'm not interested in your judgments."

"I haven't made one."

"He was a poet who had been stifled, crippled. His mind had been warped and twisted like a tree that has been crushed by the rocks. And yet it puts out green leaves. Even the twisting of the trunk is beautiful. And if he had come with me he would have written what he wanted to write. Strange and terrible things that would have given a meaning to all the years he had suffered. She and his mother emptied him, drained his life away."

He thought of the mock-Elizabethan house, the madness. "I didn't make any judgment."

"It doesn't matter. They talk about Fascists. They called him one. They called Knut Hamsun a Nazi. If a man has a different vision, an individual vision. If he doesn't believe in the mob. They cannot believe that anyone can be great.

—

They won't allow it. He wrote. But no one would publish it. They never said it was bad. They just said it didn't suit the times. God damn the times." She was crying. The barman was looking discreetly inquisitive. A couple were sitting at the next table, discussing their holiday in Majorca. The woman was looking at Eva out of the corner of her eye.

"Could we go somewhere else?" Sean said. "There are a lot of things I want to ask you."

"All right."

"Where have you hidden the report?"

"In my flat."

He sat very still. "That was—a bit obvious."

"Then don't come." She had a disconcerting habit of reading his thoughts. "If you don't trust me. I've almost stopped being afraid. What can they do to me?"

"Quite a lot."

"I know." She sighed. Picked up her unfinished drink and put it down again. "One goes on living, wanting to live. I don't know why."

"I wish I'd met him. Major Courtenay liked him."

"He wasn't a Fascist. He wasn't any kind of a wholesale man. He was an individual. He dreamed that one day individuals could—come into their own."

"It got him into strange company."

"He wasn't clever. Only wise and good. And bitter. Aubrey can be a convincing talker. And they both hated the same things. He didn't realize it was for different reasons." She stood up. "Do you want to come?"

He lifted the briefcase, felt the weight of it. "Yes," he said. It wasn't true but there wasn't anything else he could say or do. They walked out of the bar. One or two men looked at Eva but only with a normal interest. He couldn't see the big young man. Or anyone else who looked as if he might be watching them. And yet he felt they were being watched.

"You know this can turn out very badly for you?"

—

She shrugged. "I'm sick of being a coward."

He wanted to say, "I'm sick of being a hero," but she wouldn't have understood. He wished there was a simple way of looking at anything. They went out into the summer evening; no dusk as yet, only a cooling of the daylight. He let two taxis go by and took the third. Although what difference could it make? I'm a swine to have let her do this, he thought. I will get myself killed and I will get her killed and even the major won't hear about it. He'll think I've gone to Italy. He wondered how they would arrange it.

There had been a man found almost naked in a cupboard, tied up and strangled with a woman's stocking. The only other thing he had been wearing was a black lace corset, and nobody had minded very much when his murderer wasn't caught. Which was the intention. Sean had known all the people concerned and had felt very sorry for the man. He had only tried to sell the same thing twice. Once to the British, and once to the French. Who after all were allies. But it had been a very important thing.

In the taxi he took out Albert's papers and added them to the contents of the briefcase. He had torn out a blank page from the notebook first and scribbled two lines on it to Major Courtenay. If he could ever read it. "This is the first installment," he wrote. "I hope there'll be a second." She sat in the far corner of the cab and didn't ask him what he was doing. He wrote the address of the nursing home and the major's name on the other side of the page.

The cab drove north and east, past Bloomsbury, and he kept looking out of the back. No one seemed to be following. After a mile or so he told the driver to turn back south toward Holborn and the Gray's Inn Road. They got down a hundred yards from her flat and he left the briefcase in the back of the cab. "I'll be with you in a second," he told her and made a business of hunting for change.

He gave the scribbled note to the driver with two pounds

—

and some silver. The silver was for Eva's benefit, or anyone else's who might be watching. "Don't look at it now," he said. "But there's an address on that note and I've left a briefcase in the back. Deliver it there and don't say anything to me now."

The driver nodded, the money and the paper disappeared into a pocket. "Good night," Sean said, and followed Eva up the pavement. She turned down a narrow side road of featureless, run-down houses. Bed-sitters and respectable flats for office girls. He looked over his shoulder. If they noticed he no longer had the briefcase. If there was anyone to notice. His mouth felt dry and he seemed to have been walking forever. A man was washing a Cortina. A small girl was trying to help him.

Eva let herself into one of the houses, waited for him inside the hall. "I live on the top floor. I'm afraid there isn't an elevator." It was eight flights. When he got to the top he leaned against the wall while she opened the front door. He expected someone to be there. When there was no one it was almost like an anticlimax.

There was no hall. Just a big bed-sitting-room and a cubbyhole kitchenette and an old-fashioned bathroom. He looked in all of them without making a pretense about why. She put on a kittle in the kitchenette. "I'll make coffee." He looked around the main room. A couch bed. A bookcase. *Doctor Zhivago. War and Peace.* Len Deighton. *The Managerial Revolution. Njalssaga. Gunnlaugssaga ormstungu. The Heimskringla* in English. *The Prose Edda.* The two or three he opened had the same inscription: "To Eva from her fellow exile Olaf."

"He taught me about Norway," she said. She gave him the coffee and touched a photograph in a leather frame. He wouldn't have recognized it as the man of the wedding photograph in the house in Learham. A dark, savagely intellectual face. The face of a martyr or a persecutor, of a tortured inquisitor. Not a comfortable man to fall in love with.

"Where is the report?" All the time he was listening. He went to the window and looked out, but it gave onto the back of the house, a scrubby garden, other gardens dwarfed by their houses. The flat roof of an added-on bathroom below the window. Across two gardens a woman was undressing by her window, a man with his braces hanging down was shaving. From an open window somewhere there was pop music. It faded and a voice said, "All the way up from number eighteen to number two. And now, still heading the charts after eleven weeks, the Them Group's Pomp and Circus—yow yow, you ziggytails, get loaded with the real noise, *Them Them Them.*"

The music snarled and wept. The beat version of "Pomp and Circumstance" assaulted the windows. The man shaving beat time with his razor. Sean turned back to the room. For some odd reason he was remembering the boy and girl in the café—the girl's tired, maternal face, pitying him. Did she worship Them? Am I defending her against Aubrey Vining? he wondered. Against Trust Fund and Major Willis? And Randall? It was very odd. How would Major Courtenay explain it?

"Where is the report?" he said again. He didn't believe there was any report. She took the *Njalssaga* off the shelf and gave it to him. He opened it and leafed through. There were no loose pages. Passages here and there were underlined, and there were manuscript notes in some of the margins. Like a lecturer's copy, or a university student's. He tried to read the notes but they were in Norwegian, like the text.

"They're in Old Norse," she said.

"And this is the report?"

She shrugged again. "In code. He scribbled notes in that when he was getting the facts together. If they were facts."

—

She went to the window and stared out and down. Perhaps she was listening to Them. Her shoulders and hips were too broad and her legs too thick. In a few years she would be fat, Sean thought. As if he needed to diminish the fact that she had loved a failed, middle-aged poet. He tried to guess if she was telling the truth.

"If you don't believe me—" She said it without turning round. "It won't bring him back whether you believe me or not. There is the book if you want it."

"And the report they found?"

"He made it look like a long report to the Norwegian Television service. It was in his pending tray until—he got an address he wanted. They found it there. The—day after."

"Major Courtenay put a number in the *Times* Personal Column. Why didn't you ring it?"

She still didn't turn round. "The Personal Column?"

"Were you afraid?"

She turned then. "Yes," she said softly. "I was afraid." Her body looked clumsy and her face plain. She sat down in the one armchair in the room and it creaked under her weight. He could see in her face what she would be in ten years' time. Already middle-aged. She will be my age, he thought.

"Tell me something," she said. She was looking down at her hands. Peasant's hands, big and square and strong. But she held them as if they would never have anything worth while to do. She turned them over and looked at their backs. "What went wrong for Olaf—in Norway, during the war?"

"Nothing," Sean said. "Except that people he trusted let him down."

She let her breath out in a small sigh. "You're kind to put it like that," she said. "Can you understand why I've been afraid—for him as well as for me? About that?" She looked at the book still open in his hands.

"I don't know."

"All I cared about in the world was that he should be happy."

He wondered if Olaf Redwin had cared as much. In the same way. He hoped that he had.

"I didn't have any illusions," she said. "I didn't want any. I just loved him. I wanted to hold him and keep him safe. I wanted to watch over him." Her face was beautiful again, her hands held something, protected it. "I don't want his memory hurt." She looked at Sean and the same icy cruelty was in her eyes, raised to such a power of hatred that it had nobility. "But I don't want his murderers to go free."

He didn't say anything.

"I don't care why he wrote that," she said. "I don't care what his motive was. I only know that it was good because it was his. I don't want anyone saying that he did it to be on the winning side—or on both sides—or to make up for some failure God knows how long ago. I don't want anyone to make his memory cheap."

She had let her shoulders sag again, heavy and ugly in the cheap, unpleasant armchair, with its worn and dirty upholstery, its suggestion of broken springs. Will any woman look ugly for me? he wondered. He looked down at the writing in the margins of the book. Minute. Angular. A contemptuous bitterness, a savagery even in the sharp accuracy of the letters, the pressure of the pen.

"Did he never tell you why he changed his mind? About this?"

"We were in Honeywell," she said. "Researching. It was pretty grim. Although he didn't like colored people." She looked at him, twisting her mouth into an odd, malicious smile. "You can't say that, can you? Everyone likes colored people. But he didn't. It wasn't personal. He didn't know any of them personally. He just believed that one day they were going to cut our throats. That that was what the next world war was going to be about."

She gripped her hands together, laughed in a kind of fierce frustration, like a mother consumed with both pride and anger at the doings of her child. "He'd say that kind of thing

—

at a party, in a room full of Negro diplomats and students. He'd get into ghastly arguments, and with him it would be all intellect and geopolitics and Götterdämmerung, and he'd have black third secretaries and Chinese law students jumping up and down and wanting to kill him, and then he'd offer them a lift home so that he could go on arguing, and wonder why they wouldn't go with him. I said he didn't like colored people. He didn't like the idea of colored people. He saw these things as a series of historical maps with population movements marked with big bulging lines. He saw their lines bulging over Europe, taking us over. He never thought of them as individuals."

She tried to laugh again, leaning back in the chair, letting her body go slack. She put her hands up to her face. "I didn't care what he thought. What he said. Only to hear him say it. Hear his voice." She was crying, not moving her eyes, not closing them. The tears ran down and she slowly pushed them away with her fingers and more tears came. "He used to come back with me here when we'd finished work and we'd close that door and make supper and there wasn't anyone else in the world, only the two of us. I don't want to go on living any more. It's just that I'm afraid of dying. If I could shut my eyes and that would be all of it."

"What happened in Honeywell to make him change?"

"He saw that they were individuals. And what was happening to them. And he heard something—from a man called Willis—it seemed to shock him out of everything—he wouldn't tell me about it. He just said, 'They won't have any Crystal Night if I can help it,' and it was the day after that that he started making those notes." She moved her hand toward the book without looking at it, or at Sean. It seemed as if every word she was saying hurt her. "He was like a child. He'd been playing a game and suddenly all the rules changed and he was playing a different game. But it was still a game. And then they killed him."

She put her hands over her eyes and held them there. He

saw her mouth open as if she were screaming without any sound coming. He put the book in his pocket. "Did they never try and find this?"

She nodded without opening her eyes or taking her hands away from them. "They searched here twice. But they were looking for a carbon copy. They never thought of the books. They just shook them out the way you did. I know because I put bits of thread between some of the pages. And it was gone."

"Didn't the police question you? After—he was found?"

"Oh yes. In front of Aubrey. I think he'd told them I was the cause of it. They were very understanding in a disapproving sort of way." She felt for a handkerchief in the sleeve of her peasant blouse, dried her face. "And someone from Military Intelligence—at least Aubrey said he was—a Major Cannon—"

"Was he tall and thin, gray hair, eyes a bit close together, very pale blue and small?"

"Yes, he was. Do you know him? Is he really—?"

"I don't know him as Major Cannon. What did he want?"

"He said it was about the Official Secrets Act. In case Olaf had written any memoirs about Norway and the war. I was certain he really wanted that book. Olaf said there were some of the police and intelligence people in this business, as well as people like Aubrey."

"He was right."

"Are you in it?" She was looking at him from a great distance, like a suicide on a window sill, or the top of a cliff.

"No. But if they saw you with me just now—"

"I couldn't go on being afraid," she said. "Either for him or for myself. I had to do something. I've sat looking at that book on that shelf for hours at a time, remembering him writing in it, trying to think what I ought to do. Oh God, not ought, ought, like a Girl Guide, like a citizen. But for him." She looked at Sean. "Will you protect him?"

"I don't think he'll need protecting. But I'll remember."

—

"You have a look of him."

"I hope I find someone like you."

She didn't answer. He tried to think of what he could suggest to protect her. He wished he could think of something to protect himself. "Is there anyone you could stay with?"

"I'll be all right," she said tiredly. "I won't answer the door. How long will it be before—before you finish?"

He thought of the major in the nursing home. "He may last the night," the doctor had said. "He may not."

"I don't know how long," he said. "You could—" What could she do? He tried to think they wouldn't bother about her, that all they'd be interested in was the book, what she had told him. He imagined them trying to find out what she had told him. And her "not answering the door."

He went back to the window and looked down. The flat roof. Heavy drain pipes angled at intervals to break the fall of the water in them. Even a girl could do it. "Would you go to an address I'd give you? With this book?" She looked at him, and at the window. She opened her mouth a little, and her face lost color. As if being asked to do something moved the whole affair onto a different level, made it no longer a private grief and problem.

"I—"

Below them, muffled by several floors, they heard the front doorbell ringing. He opened the door of her room, went onto the landing and found a window overlooking the street. Whoever had rung the bell was hidden by a shallow porch. A car was parked twenty yards down the road. There were other parked cars, but this one was facing the wrong way for the side of the road it was on and there were two men in the front seats.

He went back into her room, locked the door and opened the window as high as it would go. "They're outside," he said. "Your door won't stop them." She hesitated, and he

—

took her wrist. He thought she was going to resist but she let
him pull her toward the window. He sat astride the sill and
helped her across. For a fraction of a second the warmth of
her breast was against his body; he was holding her steady.
Her eyes looked very frightened and her face was white and
drawn. He gripped her wrists. Her leg swung over the sill,
her full weight was hanging from his hands, his bent arms,
astonishingly heavy, her body soft against his outside knee,
sliding down. He heard her breath catching in her throat
with fear. The footsteps were on the landing. He let her
down to the full stretch of his arms, bent sideways and down
to let her drop still further until he could see her feet within
inches of the flat roof.

"I'm letting go," he whispered, and she tried to grip his
arms with her own hands but her fingers slid; she started to
cry out with terror. The handle of the door turned, a
shoulder leaned hard and sudden against the panels. Wood
splintered and a woman's voice said, "What d'you think
you're doing?" A man's voice said, "Shut up," and the
shoulder hit the door again. Eva was sprawling on the tarred
roof. His own legs were outside the window and he was
balanced for a second on the narrow granite sill, his left
hand groping for the lower frame of the window above his
shoulder, his right hand under his hip, gripping the stone,
checking him from falling outward. He found the edge of
the sash, drew it down as far as it would come, held it and
let go with his right hand. For a second he seemed to
balance on nothing. He pulled the window completely shut
and in the same instant was falling.

He landed on his feet, stumbled, nearly went over the
edge. Above his head the door crashed. He pushed her, took
her wrists again, swung her almost bodily off the roof, held
her arms on either side of the down pipe. "Grip the pipe
with your knees." He held her arms close to it. Let go of her.
It was twelve feet to the ground. Halfway down the angle of

—

151

the pipe broke her slithering fall. She gripped at the metal, cried out, went on falling. She was on her back in the remains of a small starved laurel bush. He came down hand over hand as the window above their heads banged up. He was below the angle, out of sight from anyone inside the room. He touched ground, looked down, saw her mouth opening, her body starting to move. He put his foot across her mouth, tried to do it gently, felt her struggling and pressed harder, heard a laurel twig snap, leaves rustle as she moved. Then she realized and lay like a stone. Above their heads voices called to each other. He thought he recognized the voice of the man who had hit him in the Coach Inn lavatory.

"Can you see anyone?"

"There's a flat roof—"

"The window was shut—"

The sound of a cupboard opening, the woman's voice again, and a man saying, "Madam, we're police officers." The drag of furniture. No one came out of the window. Footsteps crossing the room, a voice from further away in the house, someone protesting. Was the window empty? Or was someone still watching, waiting for a move? But they'd have come after them if they'd thought—He realized he was still treading with his right foot on her mouth, lifted it, helped her up, one-handed, his other hand ready to silence her if she tried to talk. He counted to ten and then five more. "Cross to that wall," he said. A brick wall, five feet high, overgrown with ivy, a dead apple tree close to it, like an old woman's hand clawing at the ivy. The grass was long and gone to seed, full of cobwebs and dandelions. There had once been a path and they stumbled over the upright edging. He looked up and back. A man's body moved across the window frame, his shoulder to them.

"Over the wall," Sean said. He knelt, got his arms around her legs, heaved her upward. The same soft heaviness, the

—

sense of womanhood. She wasn't made for any of this. For bed and bread and breeding, the softness of love. He had the same overwhelming sense of wrongness that he'd had with Wilfrid, the matchstick child whispering about evil as if he were gossiping about school. Half her body over the wall. "Hold on to it," he whispered, swung her over, heard someone shouting from the window behind them. He caught the top of the wall, vaulted, ran. She ran behind him. This garden was better kept. A row of lettuce, a row of onions, sweet peas, a rose bush, a scrubby piece of lawn and a gravel path. Wooden steps led up to a built-on room, a kitchen with a coal shed under it. They could see a man in the kitchen. Sean pushed the door open, twisted his face into a smile of apology, propitiation, conspiracy. The man was bearded, heavy horn-rimmed spectacles on a thick, gourmand's nose, shirt sleeves and a flowered apron, stirring something on the gas stove with a long wooden spoon.

"What the bloody hell do you think—?"

"Husband trouble," Sean said, pulling Eva into the kitchen behind him, beginning to push her through the room. The man had stopped stirring and the pot boiled over. The kitchen filled with steam and hissing and the smell of burned curry.

"Jesus Christ," the man shouted, juggled with the pot, burned his fingers. Sean pushed Eva, mumbled apologies, pulled the inner door open, and they were in a tumbled bedroom, socks on the floor, an unmade bed and a record player coming to the end of *Daphnis and Chloe*. "Damn you," the man was shouting, "you've ruined my dinner, you bloody adulterous bastard—oh, Christ my thumb—" Sean closed the door on him. They were in a hallway, lit by stained glass in the front door, filled with a hall stand made of antlers and mirrors. Through the front door, down stone steps, iron railings and box hedges taking rust and soot from each other, into a quiet street of respectable rooms to let.

—

They ran to the right. He ran, dragged her, she let herself be dragged, tried to run; her heels slipped and cracked on the pavement like small sharp hammers, her breath sobbed, she was heavy on his arm. There was no turning, no lane. Two parked cars, a cat, garbage cans, milk bottles on doorsteps ready for the morning. In another street a car gunned its engine. They ran. There was a corner a long way ahead. A man came around it with long athlete's strides. Like a rugby forward on a training sprint.

He saw them coming, his shoulders seemed to widen, his mouth laughed like a dog's that sees a cat, he shortened and speeded his stride, ready for them to turn tail, run helplessly like cats for a wall as the dog comes. Sean let go of Eva, kept on running, swayed his body right, then left. The man mirrored him. They were three, two, one yard apart, the man's hands lifting, one to grab, one to hit. It was the man who had hit him in the lavatory. Sean threw himself down and forward, rolled into a ball, went under the runner's knees. An instep kicked his side, tripped, the second foot caught him, the man went in a flat dive over Sean's back, seemed to hover for a moment and hit the pavement a yard short of Eva, skidded on his face, hit the edge of a jutting stone step with his shoulder, slewed round at her feet. He tried to get up and his shoulder and left arm folded under him.

Sean got to his feet, his hands burning from the fall, his ribs feeling broken, his breath coming harder and shorter than it should have done. He stepped over to the fallen man, and the man looked up at him, one side of his face raw meat, his mouth snarling, blood on his teeth, his legs drawing up to his chest to kick. Sean caught one of the kicking feet, dragged the man into the middle of the road, dropped him and hit the back of his neck. The body lay there, and the car that had gunned its engine came around the corner with a shriek of overdriven gears. Sean dragged Eva, ran with her;

—

there was a service lane to the left, and he swung toward it.

Behind him he saw the car swerve past the body, one of its wheels hit the curb, mount it, snarl toward them, two wheels on the pavement. He felt the wind of it as they reached the entrance to the lane. There were garbage cans and he rolled them, spilled them behind their heels. There was another street ahead of them, fifty yards, thirty, twenty, as someone ran behind them. He looked back as a man jumped a fallen can, misjudged the height of it and fell headlong. Two men behind him, and then a third. They were in the street. Shops, traffic, a bus queue, a bus pulling away from the stop, cars, a taxi. He hailed it but it was taken, and the second and the third. People looked, and he stopped running, walked very fast with his arm around her waist, supporting her. People still looked.

A taxi came cruising, flag up. A man with a white mustache and an umbrella hailed it. Sean pushed past him, opened the door, forced Eva in. "Kensington High Street." He saw the first of the running men come out of the lane. The man with the black mustache, the soldier's face. The man who had hailed the cab with his umbrella was trying to argue. "Two quid says hurry," Sean said.

"Sorry, guv," the driver said to the white mustache, revved his engine into the traffic. "Which end of the High Street, Major?"

Sean leaned forward. "Through Soho first. Forget about Kensington." He pushed the two pounds through the hatch. "And try not to be followed. There's a jealous husband doesn't like me."

The two pounds disappeared. "Anywhere you say, Major." The men behind were finding a cab, four men. He watched, and they piled into it, suddenly like Keystone cops, suddenly comic. He wanted to laugh, half of him wanted to laugh, and he realized his nerves were broken, that if he started laughing he wouldn't be able to stop. He put his hands over his face. His hands were shaking. She lay in the corner where he had half pushed, half thrown her, her own eyes closed, her breath shallow and then dragging very deep.

"Listen," he said. He caught hold of her and shook her. The driver was watching him in the mirror, and he smiled at her tenderly as if he were telling her that he loved her more than anything on earth. "I'm going to send you to a friend of mine. He's in a nursing home, he's very ill, they're going to tell you you can't see him. You've got to see him, you're his daughter, do you understand? You've got to see him. Give him this book. Tell him what's in it. If he's under drugs wait there, stay there in his room till he comes round."

And if he doesn't come round? his mind was saying. If he's already dead? The taxi driver calling him "major." As if it had passed to him, the responsibility, everything. For what? To do what? Fight against something he didn't understand, that for all he knew was official, was the department itself. Albert? Honeywell? Bryce? Why not? Being official didn't have to mean being clean, being boy scouts and Marquis of Queensberry. The Marquis hadn't been such a boy scout. Or so they said.

Life is a conspiracy, Niccolò had said. Get inside it. Why ride at windmills when you can break into them and steal the bread? The other taxi was behind them. They went around Cambridge Circus, were into Soho. He tapped the glass. "I'm getting out at the next traffic lights," he said. "Take this lady to Richmond, Brentwood Road. There's a nursing home called St. Luke's. See her inside, please. A taxi is following you. That one in your mirror. It'll stop when I get out. If it follows you again, try and lose it. Give this lady your taxi number and someone will send you ten pounds in the next couple of days." He hoped it sounded better than he thought it did. He leaned back and whispered to Eva, told

her the major's name, something about him. As an after-
thought he told her Margaret's name and gave her Margaret's private phone number. Lights turned red ten yards in
front of them, the other taxi was one place back, separated
from them by a delivery van that had cut in from a corner.

He waited until the cross street's lights had turned orange,
squeezed Eva's arm, eased the door open. The taxi was moving as he got out. The van snarled past him in a fury of
acceleration, traffic roared toward him from the opposite
direction. He stepped in front of the taxi that had been following him, waved to the driver. Behind the driver he could
see the four men. The black mustache, the other commando
from the Coach Inn, two men he had never seen. The driver
gaped at him, jammed on his brakes. Sean went to the
driver's side.

"I'm a police officer," he said. "The four men in your taxi
are criminals. Drive them to Scotland Yard." The driver
went on gaping at him. The nearest passenger door opened.
Sean kicked it shut.

"Here, 'ere," the driver said. "What you kicking?"

"Scotland Yard and hurry," Sean said. "That's an order.
I'm commandeering your cab." Two of the men were getting
out the far side.

"What the flaming hell is this?"

Sean looked for his own taxi. It was forty yards up the
street, stopped at the next set of lights. He opened the
driver's door, felt under the dash for the ignition wires,
wrenched them out. The engine stopped. The driver looked
as if he were having a stroke, grabbed at Sean's arm. The
two men were coming around the hood, the side door was
opening again. Sean dodged away into the traffic, half under
a lorry, between two taxis, was on the far pavement. All of
the four men were out of the taxi, so was the driver. The
driver shouting, "Police!" swearing, shaking his fists, his face
purple, still not believing what was happening, had hap-

pened. The four men had separated. They weren't following him, they were blocking the ends of the short, narrow street. One of them beckoned the taxi driver, but he was too angry to notice, plunging after Sean.

Sean's own taxi had disappeared. What was she thinking? The taxi driver was yelling, "Stop, thief!" People were turning around, one or two started to run, most of them just stared, laughed, gaped. It was a street of gapers. Restaurants, huckster shops, delicatessen, strip clubs, dirty bookshops. Swarthy men in doorways waiting for clients. Teenagers in plastic macs and bell-bottom trousers. Three girls and two pimps arguing in French. The smell of garlic, roasting coffee, gas fumes, French tobacco, a Chinese restaurant, a hatch in the wall surrounded by pictures of fat girls dressed in feathers.

"Sunset Strip." An unshaven man in the hatch. "Nudest show in town, fabulous beauties, only a pound. Just a pound, sir." Two of the men were ahead of him, working back toward him, one on one side, one on the other side of the street. Two men behind him. And the taxi driver. He wasn't going to get clear. He turned back to the hatch, pulled a pound out of his hip pocket. The man slid him a membership ticket and he went down a dark, narrow staircase into blackness, smelling of dust and sweat and talcum powder and mice. Behind him he heard the taxi driver shouting, refusing to pay the pound, trying to force his way past the hatch.

There was a dusty curtain and he went through it into a tiny theatre. A small woman in a red sweater said, "Five shillings, please, if you're not a member already." He gave it to her and looked for the back exit. There was a bar with a blonde and two men drinking beer. Rows of seats beside him. And the stage. He had to turn back away from the bar to see it. A girl was finishing her act. Drums rolling on a gramophone, a large behind like a white target presented to

—

158

the audience, two fat legs tapering to spindle ankles, black high heels. The curtains closed. There wasn't any back exit. Back stage, or here? At least there were witnesses here, he might get past them, up to the street.

He sat down in a vacant seat, slid along the row to the far end of it. The room was less than half full. With the curtains closed it wasn't possible to see more than that. A dim light behind the bar. Shadows of men rustling in their seats, stretching their legs, sighing. About twenty men. Only the front row was full, surrounding the small apron stage. A couple of men were standing in the aisles, waiting for a vacant front-row seat.

The taxi driver came down the stairs, still shouting. The two men at the bar stood up, moved forward. As the taxi driver came through the curtains they took him by the elbows, lifted him, carried him backward up the stairs. A couple of seconds later the four men who had been in the taxi came down the stairs, paid their five shillings each. One stayed by the curtain. The other three went to the bar, ranged along it. The blonde tried to sell them some beer. They pushed the glasses away and kept the bottles. The blonde began to look frightened. The two bouncers came back. The man with the black mustache at the curtain spoke to them and they stayed beside him, their eyes hunting through the scattered audience.

Sean felt cold and sick. He tried to think that it didn't matter what happened now. He'd done his best, got her away, she'd be halfway to Richmond before they got him. He felt for coins in his pocket to make a knuckle duster, arranged them between his fingers. A man's voice behind the stage curtains said in a dispirited way, "And now—the fabulous Dorita, all the way from Hawaii." The drums rolled again, the curtains opened. A big colored woman dressed in imitation grass revolved her hips. The men in the front row leaned forward. They were surprisingly young. There was

—

only one baldhead. A boy in his twenties was eating sand-wiches out of a plastic briefcase.

The hips revolved, swiveled, the big grass skirt rustled to the ground, revealed more skin, more hips, a smaller grass skirt. The man with the black mustache found Sean, moved toward him. The others started moving too, and the man lifted his hand to stop them, pulled a white handkerchief out of his breast pocket and showed it to Sean in the palm of his hand. Sean nodded, and the man came down the row toward him, smiling. He had small, stained, unpleasant teeth, widely spaced in an ugly, powerful mouth. He sat down one seat away from Sean and leaned closer. The grass brassiere came off to a crescendo of Hawaiian guitars on an exhausted gramophone and the boy stopped eating his sandwiches long enough to suck in his breath.

"Let's go outside and chat," the man said. He had a flat, twanging accent. Australian? South African?

"I like it in here," Sean said. "It's artistic."

The stripper had a forty-inch bust and nipples like purple cones. She looked bored and arrogant and she pushed her pelvis with its grass fringe in and out, in and out in time to the music as if she'd have preferred to knock someone down with it. The fringe came off and she twirled it on a long black finger. The bald man had his head on the edge of the stage like a glowing footlight, gazing up at the great choco-late mass of flesh above him. His eyes were wet with sadness and desire.

The boy stuffed more sandwich into his mouth. The curtains closed. There was tepid applause. The front row shifted in its seats and sighed. The tiny theatre was dark again. "Why be obstinate?" the man with the black mus-tache was saying. "You don't understand what you're play-ing with. Your own boss has told you to lay off. Why not be sensible, and we'll try and see you don't get into too much trouble for what's happened already."

—

"And now, the fabulous Yvonne, all the way from Gay Paree."

The curtains opened on a girl in a black wig and a shiny black satin dress slashed up one side. The gramophone began grinding out. "It isn't what you do it's the way that you do it." The girl made obscene gestures. The men in the front row laughed.

"Suppose I laid off?" Sean said.

The black mustache leaned closer. "We might do a very friendly deal. A ticket to somewhere nice, a couple of thou. Depending."

"—it's the *way* that you do it—" The shiny dress had opened all down the front, was showing black lace brassiere, black lace panties, black lace stocking tops. She smacked her right hand against her left biceps, punching her left fist at the audience on the word "way." The audience sniggered. The girl looked at someone hidden in the wings, crooked her little finger up and down. "Even if you're *little*—" The dress fell off.

"Depending on what?"

"How much damage you've done already."

The girl was undoing her brassiere. Sean heard the movement behind him, began to turn. The bottle took him sideways across the skull, just above the right ear. Then again. He saw the brassiere coming off, the white breasts. They grew bigger, swelled to a fantastic size, pink nipples like great roses swelling and bursting—he was sliding down between the breasts, a smell of mice and talcum powder and sweat and dust. The breasts closed over him, he couldn't breathe.

"Just a friend of ours," the man with the black mustache was saying. "He's had a couple too many. Better take him home to his wife." He winked at the blond girl behind the bar who had seen the swing of the bottle, put a fiver on the counter. She tucked the fiver into the top of her dress and

—

161

bent down under the counter. Two of the young men lifted Sean by the armpits, began carrying him out. The bald man said "Ssssh," two or three other looked around. The black stockings were coming off, the girl sitting on a padded stool covered in tatty, faded cretonne. The men who had looked around turned back to the stage, followed the stocking tops down the pallid, flabby white legs, sucked in their breath mechanically. The boy finished the last ham sandwich, belched delicately and blushed.

"Heave ho," Captain Robertson said. He brushed a knuckle under the edges of his mole-slick black mustache, nodded authoritatively at the bouncers still standing uncertainly by the black curtain that hid the stairs. They moved aside. The small procession went past them and up into the mouse-hole darkness, with its rectangle of dusty evening light at the top. Sean's feet dragged and clattered on the stairs. The two men carrying him had to move sideways, and one of them almost fell. He had already fallen over a garbage can and he was limping. He freed one hand and gave Sean's unconscious body a vicious hammer blow with the side of his fist.

"That's enough," Captain Robertson said. "Pick his feet up." The third man, the boy from the Coach Inn, followed, coming up the stairs backward, ready for trouble. But there was none. Only the sunburst of cracked music as the black lace panties dropped to the floor, revealed the triangle of blackish hair which the men in the strip club had paid their pound and their membership fee to stare at.

Captain Robertson hailed a taxi. The others stayed in the doorway, supporting Sean. The man in the money hatch looked resolutely the other way. The taxi slid into the curb, the two carriers heaved Sean aboard with affectionate laughter and loud remarks about booze-ups. The taxi driver looked bored. The money man looked relieved. Captain Robertson got in and closed the cab door. The fourth man of the group moved unobtrusively across the road to see what might happen before he followed on.

Two minutes later their first taxi driver, still scarlet with anger, arrived back at the club with a policeman. His taxi still stood paralyzed in the middle of the narrow street, traffic flowing around it and past it as best it could. "Now then, now then," said the policeman, who was very young. "What's all this about?"

But it wasn't about anything. No one in the club or in the street had seen anything or anyone. They hadn't seen the driver, or a man running, or other men chasing, or men fighting, or the driver being thrown out. Downstairs the colored woman was on again and the policeman turned beetroot purple and wondered what his mother would say if he ever told her. He dreamed about the woman for nights afterward, twitching in his sleep, until his mother gave him some syrup of figs in his corn flakes.

But no one had seen anything. He threatened the taxi driver with a summons for obstruction and helped him push the cab into a side street.

18

They lay together in the wide bed, their hands barely touching, his eyes watching her in the mirrors, now this one, now that one. He had found a pair of long, soft black boots in the cupboard, as long and soft as kid leather stockings and he had made her put them on, with a black leather jerkin. He was wearing her Chinese housecoat and he lay like a mandarin against the satin cover and the down and silk pillows, watching her in the mirror. When she looked sideways out of the corners of her eyes she could see him watching her, his eyes fixed, his thin, reptilian mouth moving slightly, the tongue touching the lips, flicking out to moisten them, disappearing.

He made her turn over, smoothed his hand over the curves of her naked buttocks, touched the tops of her leather stockings. He hadn't made love to her at all and she lay cold and frightened. "We'll have a lot of fun together from now on," he said softly. He slid his fingers between her thighs, closed them on the inside of her leg. She bit the satin coverlet to stop herself from screaming.

"Relax," he whispered. He prided himself on being able to relax in any circumstances. "Give me a free half-hour," he often said, "and I'll sleep for twenty-five minutes and wake up as if I'd had a night's rest. The secret's perfect relaxation." He prided himself on many things. On his handling of women and cars, and dogs, and subordinates. "They're all pretty much the same," he said. "They all need to know who's master." On psychology, "It's not what you do to a man so much as what he thinks you're going to do that breaks him down. In Cyprus—"

He closed his fingers a fraction harder on the softness of her thigh and she tried to roll free. He held her still without moving his head or looking away from the mirror. He was thinking of Cyprus, as it happened, and of a prisoner who wouldn't talk. It had taken all night but it had been very satisfactory. The most satisfactory night he had ever spent, even in Cyprus. He wondered if Sean Ryan would take so long. He very much doubted it.

"Power is a curious thing," he said. "There's nothing people desire so much, and nothing that frightens them so much when they have it. Or could have it. And it's that fear alone that keeps democracy alive. Nothing else." He ca-

—

ressed the warm flesh, the cool edge of leather, the cold metal of the zipper fastener that ran the length of the long boots almost to Babette's crotch. "Not votes or constitutional rights. Just the fear of being master. And all the time that's what the people really want. A master. To be told what to do. To be made safe." His eyes stared at the mirror, at the white and black, the subtle shadows of Babette. But they saw beyond that to a future in which he would not be afraid to be master. The real master. General "Cromwell," one of the others, they could wear the mask, play at being Britain's De Gaulle, Franco, Salazar, and, if anyone wished—why not?—Britain's Hitler, Mussolini—all born out of the kind of chaos, the kind of breakdown that was coming to Britain. That could be helped to come if necessary. Unemployment, poverty, bankruptcy, a savagely injured vanity, a ferocious inferiority complex, a yearning for lost, irrecoverable glories. Like a chemical formula out of which dictators come like genies forming from the smoke of the chemicals. One of them could wear the mask. But he would be standing behind their shoulders. His hands caressed, squeezed and gentled.

His mind was waiting for the telephone call that must come any minute now from Robertson, to tell him that he had failed or succeeded. But he didn't let it affect his hand, his eye, his breathing, his heartbeat. Not the waiting. Not Babette. Nothing could affect his heartbeat, his nerves. They sang to his own tune, like violin strings. No one else's. Nothing exterior touched them. It was his idea to plan Crystal Night.

"It's very simple," he had said when he first explained it. "The colored immigrants are our Jews. When we need a scapegoat they're ready-made. Poverty, unemployment, housing shortages, disease—immorality, prostitution, rape. You can blame it all on them. And they're spies, they're a fifth column for the whole horrible emerging mess in Africa and Asia. You couldn't invent anything as useful if you tried.

—

When we want to give things a real push, we start a pogrom. We wouldn't need to kill a lot of them, the street amateurs'd do the rest for us. With the kind of panic that'd follow if we handled it right we could have a government of National Emergency inside a week. And General Cromwell—"

The men he had explained it to had been deeply horrified. A month later they had ordered him to draw up detailed plans under the code name Crystal Night. Purely as a contingency of course, remote and unthinkable, to be put into use only in inconceivable circumstances, such as the British government's attempting to use armed force against South Africa, alone or in consort with the United Nations. The plans were to provide for a spontaneous outbreak of race hatred in Honeywell, Paddington, Notting Hill and parts of Bayswater. Although it was outside Oliver Randall's area of authority and knowledge, similar plans were also to be drawn up for other areas, such as Coventry and parts of Birmingham.

Not that the Trust Fund people ever intended the plans to go into operation. They were not the kind of men who ever intend the unpleasant physical results of their purely intellectual requirements. Just as slum landlords never intend the babies of their tenants to be bitten by rats. And when occasionally it does happen they are so horrified that they refuse to hear about it.

Trust Fund was equally squeamish. Its organizers would not even have cared to hear about slums, although one or two of them owned fairly substantial blocks of property that they might—if really seriously pressed—have admitted were a little run down, pending "redevelopment." But most of them had their money in other things. South African gold, Rhodesian chrome, Zambian and Katangan copper, or in some aspect of the immense complex of industries and companies deriving from African metals.

A few of them were in oil or shipping. Some of them had

—

come into industry from the top levels of the army, and all of them, military or civilian, had excellent connections of one kind or another with the men who counted in the War Office, and with the government, as men of money, of substance, of influence. That was why they were in Trust Fund. Some of them were also members of Parliament, or senior officials in the Civil Service, or still serving officers in the army. And all of them, without exception, had the highest conceivable motives.

They believed almost passionately in Britain and in the British way of life. By which they meant their own highly civilized and perhaps rather expensive way of life. But they also believed, in a slightly vaguer, slightly more idealized way in things quite remote from their own selfish interests, such as the British workman, and the essential decency of the lower classes, when not corrupted by shop stewards and materialism and wrong ideas. They would genuinely not have wished any action of theirs to harm any living soul, and if by some mischance or malice of destiny it did, they would not want to think about it. After all, it's no good thinking about what's already done and can't be mended and anyway was never intended in the first place. Better to leave those things to men who weren't quite one's own kind. Like Randall. What a swine the fellow must be to come up with a scheme like Crystal Night. It didn't really bear thinking about. God forbid one should ever have to put it into effect.

In Honeywell the trigger for the pogrom was to be the sex murder of a white girl by Negroes. Oliver Randall fondled Babette's legs and smiled at the mirror. She would be the white girl. It seemed a shameful waste in one way and he had had other plans for her, but on reflection it was best. She really knew too much. The telephone rang. He let it ring three times before he picked it up, listening to his breathing and his heartbeat, his hand not breaking its rhythmic stroking on Babette's skin.

—

In Geneva, Edward Bryce finished his unpacking and sat on the edge of the bed to stare at nothing. If he had drawn the curtains he could have seen the lake and the fountain, and the French mountains beyond. But he kept them closed, as if they could keep out terror along with the view.

His hands were sweating and he dried them slowly and methodically on the legs of his trousers. Suddenly, and piercingly, he felt lonely. Agonizingly lonely. Not for Nellie. Not even for Babette. He didn't really know whom he was lonely for. Just lonely. He was fifty-three and he had two hundred thousand pounds that he could lay his hands on without danger, and there wasn't anyone in the world he could walk up to with safety and affection and say, "Hallo." He was more alone than if he was in a cell, and the injustice of it made him cry, great scalding tears of loneliness and self-pity.

There was a soft, respectful knocking at the door. He went into the tiny hallway to answer it, and stopped himself. His heart started to race. It was difficult to breathe, to control his voice. "Who is it?" he whispered. "I'm busy just now."

"Mr. Bryce?" a voice said, reassuringly foreign, respectful, gentle. "May I speak with you just for a moment?"

Very reassuring, very gentle. But he didn't want to be re-assured. "Go away," he said, more fiercely because he was no longer so frightened, he was almost reassured. "I said I'm busy just now."

"But I am afraid I must speak to you," the voice said. "I am from the police. Just a formality, you understand, but it must be attended to. Immediately."

Mr. Bryce shut his eyes, put his little fat hands together under his heart. The tears ran down his face and he thought of Nellie. She had never helped him, never, never. He opened the door, and the young man in the dark suit smiled reassuringly, looked at his tears without expression of surprise. "I'll only keep you a moment," he said. His accent didn't sound quite so foreign, but in his agony Mr. Bryce failed to notice the shade of change. He backed and sidled into his bedroom and the young man respectfully followed him, feeling in his breast pocket. A wallet came out, a card was flashed. "Immigration," the young man said. He put the wallet back and took out a cigarette case. One of those complicated ones that girl friends give to young men, with watches and lighters built into them. He opened the cigarette case and offered it to Mr. Bryce.

The cyanide needle took Mr. Bryce in the throat, sank into the loose folds of skin and flesh. He started to lift his hand to his throat; his brain started to tell him that he had been stung by an insect. But his hand lost the power to lift itself before it was halfway there. He began to fall, bonelessly, his face surprised, already turning pink. The young man put his cigarette case away, stood watching Mr. Bryce until he was quite sure that he was dead. When he was sure he began to search the room, unhurriedly and systematically—drawers, luggage, Mr. Bryce's pockets, the pockets of the clothes hanging in the wardrobe.

Ten minutes later he walked out of the room, hung the "Do Not Disturb" notice on the door handle, and went down the stairs. No one had noticed him go up. No one noticed him come down. An hour later he was on the express to Berne, where he would change to another train for Zurich and a plane to London. In the hotel room Mr. Bryce lay where he had fallen, his face and neck bright pink. A sweet heavy smell filled the room.

—

19

The car turned down toward Paterson's wharf between the blind walls of warehouses. Above the warehouse roofs the tops of masts showed against the bright evening sky. A seagull swung over "H" shed, screamed twice and settled on the ridge of the roof. The car rolled up to the sliding doors and they opened, pushed from inside. The car eased through the gap and the doors slid shut again. The driver switched off the engine and let the car free-wheel to the far end of the almost empty shed. The watchman followed the car. When it stopped he helped them lift Sean out.

They laid him down behind an empty packing case, pushed back his eyelids to see if he was still alive. When they were sure that he was and that he was still safely unconscious, the driver backed the car toward the roll-doors, the watchman opened them and the car went away. Captain Robertson, with one of his men and the watchman, settled down to wait for Randall.

They had time to smoke a cigarette each and light a second before he came. Sean lay on the concrete floor of the shed, trying to remember what had happened, where he was. It was dark inside the shed but the light of a torch shining into his eye had brought him back to consciousness. Too slowly for it to show immediately, and when he moved his head a few seconds later, the men standing above him in the shadows were lighting their cigarettes and blinded by the flare of the match.

He was lying on a hard floor, men standing around him. Three men. The end of a wall. Not a wall, a box. A big box. He remembered the taxi. He had been in a taxi with someone. Eva Lund. After that there was nothing. He tried to construct something. They had caught him? An accident?

—

The pain in his head spread outward as the muscles of his neck contracted, thinking of an accident.

A long way above him they were talking. "He'll be here any minute." The watchman moved away to the doors again, to listen for a car. Sean felt the impact of his boots on the concrete, the jar and vibration. He had to clench his teeth not to move, not to make a sound. Two men standing beside him. Was there a third, a fourth out of his sight, on the other side? He listened to the voices.

"A tool chest'll do. I wouldn't trust a sack. And some chain."

"Maybe I'd better tie him up now."

A foot stirred, pushed into his side, half rolled him. He made himself stay limp, heavy. The foot drew away and his body sagged again. "He's all right. The commander'll be here in a second." They hadn't tied him up in the car in case some inquisitive passer-by, a policeman, a driver beside them at a traffic light looked into the back. The taxi had taken them to Sean's flat. Sean's own car had brought them to the warehouse. It was on its way to London airport now, where it would be abandoned. They had already removed all the personal things and clothes from Sean's flat. They were in two suitcases, also belonging to Sean, on the far side of the packing case. It was going to be an unremarkable disappearance.

A cigarette end curved through the air, was trodden out. Another one followed it. The two voices whispered, the shadows leaned against the packing case. A match flared in the dark. Sean lowered his eyelids, peered through a narrow slit of vision. A face like bronze, smooth and hard and powerful. A black mustache. The white of a cigarette. The other man's face was hidden. The black mustache and the flash of white, cupped in a hand. The club. It made a difference, remembering. As if it made him stronger. He tried to close his left hand. For a second he was afraid it

—

wouldn't close. But the fingers moved. He opened them again, pressed them on the stone flooring, the concrete. He could feel dust, and stone-grit, and the rough surface. Very slowly, very carefully, he tensed the muscles of one leg and then the other. Not to make a sound, a visible movement, stir his breathing.

There was the sound of a car engine, far away. And then the rumble of the doors. Like drums. The floor seemed to quiver, deafen him, stun his mind. The doors stopped and the engine was louder. Then the doors again. The shadows by the packing case moved, vanished toward the sound of the car. Sean lay. He ought to move. His mind was completely clear, his muscles were working, there was nothing to stop him moving. And yet he couldn't. Another second, let them get further away. Let the noise, the rumble of the doors stop. But that was stupid. He had to move now. Only he couldn't. Just to lie there. Another second.

He drew one leg up, flattened both hands against the floor. He was afraid of the pain. He knew it was coming, and it came like nausea, like being kicked in the brain. He lay flat again and thought that it was better to lie there and let them kill him than to feel that pain. The rumble of the doors stopped; there were voices, the sound of a car door. He gathered things inside him that he hadn't known were there and made himself move, roll over—he was on his face, on his hands and knees, the voices on the far side of the packing case were coming nearer. Randall's voice.

"I'm rather looking forward to this in a tiny way. I've never been fond of Irishmen." Another man laughing. Sean came to his feet, felt so dizzy that he half fell, steadied himself with both hands on the floor. There were shadows, another packing case, some kind of machine like a gigantic clotheshorse of iron bars and cogwheels. He gripped the corner of the case, a bar of the machine, eased himself

—

between them. A pile of old motor tires. A tractor. A stack of timber.

He moved behind the timber, felt rough wood. His eyes were getting used to the dark, and the wood was pale, the iron wall of the shed a pattern of crossing shadows of angle irons. One of the shadows formed a rectangle. A door. He moved toward it. His hand was on the steel doorknob. The voices beyond the pile of junk changed tone, shouted. A torch beam sprang into the shadows, whipped sideways. Probed at the timber pile, the tires, the tractor, found the wall, moved toward him. He turned the knob, tried to open the door. And knew before he tried that it was locked, that it wouldn't open.

The torch beam found him, ran up his shoulder like a golden spider, huge and soft, furry, fixed on his throat and face. He threw himself sideways, started to run, stepped into the middle of a coil of wire rope and flung his arms out and forward to save himself. The shock of the concrete hit his hands, his chest, winded him. A man jumped on his back with both knees, hit the side of his neck with a clenched fist, grabbed his left arm and wrenched it back and up until he thought his shoulder was dislocated.

Another hand caught his hair, lifted his head and smashed his face down onto the concrete. He felt blood running out of his nose, his mouth grinding into the stone-dust of the floor. "Jack him up," Randall's voice said. Hands lifted him, and the torch ran spider-light over his face, his eyes, blinded him, and Randall murmured approval.

"Such a busy fellow," Randall said. "Let's take him on board and find out just how busy he's been."

The hands twisted him around, a key rattled in the iron lock of the door, there was daylight. A stone quayside, railway lines and cobbles, and beyond them the cliff side of a ship, riding high out of the water, the hull plates black and

—

rusting, a gangway slanting up to the foredeck. He opened his mouth to shout, and the watchman stuffed his cap into it to gag him. It tasted of oil and sweat and nearly choked him, thick and hairy on his tongue, the fist ramming it in until he couldn't breathe. He tried to lash out with his feet, aimlessly, in panic.

"Don't hit his head," Randall said. The torch slammed into his kidneys; he was half lifted by the crotch, run up the gangplank and across the deck, iron echoing under their feet. A tug whistled far away, out on the main river. Another iron door opened, they were inside the main-deck housing, through another door into a big room—it had been a messroom once for the ship's officers, until the breakers had begun to gut the ship of its fittings—tables, chairs, brass, copper, anything that could be auctioned.

A foot tripped him, hands threw him down on the deck. There was a coil of new rope in a corner and Randall took it and made a loop. It was one-inch rope, not too thick to be supple. He held the loop in front of Sean's face, swung it to and fro.

"We could play hanging," he said. "That's a very good game." He turned away from Sean and said, "Take the gag out." Then, "Or would you like to tell me all the tiny things you've been doing this past twenty-four hours?"

Sean said nothing. Randall swung the rope, gently, his thin mouth smiling, his eyes bright as a snake's, small and jewel-sharp and close together over the thin, aristocratic bridge of his nose. That was another thing he prided himself on, the aristocracy of his profile. His grandfather had been a gardener on a ducal estate in Yorkshire, and his earliest memories were a confusion of endless greenhouses and stone balustrades and parkland. In his inmost heart he was convinced that that parkland was his by right, if only by his grandmother's indiscretion with Lord Ratcliffe. He narrowed his eyes, swung the loop of rope until it brushed

—

against Sean's face. Swung it further and let it fall over Sean's head. One of the others lifted Sean's head and shoulders a couple of inches from the floor, and the loop slid under him.

Randall tightened it around his neck. "Well?"

Sean still said nothing.

"You're going to tell us," Randall said. "And really I'd be disappointed if you told us everything too soon. Take your time."

When the rope was not quite tight enough to hurt, Randall stopped tightening, made another loop. They lifted Sean bodily and the loop went over his head and shoulders, pinioned his upper arms. A third loop went over his elbows and a fourth over his wrists, until he was tied with a series of turns and half-hitches, like a corpse being tied into its shroud of sailcloth for a burial at sea.

"Take his shoes and trousers off," Randall said. They took them off, two of them holding Sean's legs. He lay on the deck, the raw iron cold against his skin, half-naked, helpless. It was strange how having the trousers taken off made the helplessness worse. Randall looked down at him, at his half-nakedness, kicked him gently between the legs with the toe of his shoe. His eyes said that he had done this often, that he knew exactly what he was doing and why he was doing it and what effect it would have.

He picked up something else from the corner of the one-time messroom. It was an iron shackle, a U-shape of iron with its two ends made into rings. A heavy bolt ran through both rings, was screwed tight into one of them.

"You see this?" Randall said. "I always like to explain to people just what's going to happen. It helps to make the thing more exciting, or so I find." His mouth tasted the words, he narrowed his eyes to knife points to see into Sean's mind, find his fear, dwell on it, increase it. Like a horseman who walks around a roped and sweating horse, a mustang

—

that has not yet been broken, and talks to it and shows it the whip and bridle and the saddle. He ran his tongue out between his lips and tasted a bead of sweat on his upper lip, drew it in like a seed pearl.

"You see how this bolt screws out? It's a kind of makeshift vise, really, isn't it? I can screw it out, and then I can screw it in? You see all that, don't you? Don't you, you dirty little Irish terrorist?"

Sean still said nothing, and Randall kicked him hard in the side. "Tell me you see, Ryan. I like to think you're paying attention."

He had learned the beginnings of the technique in school. There had been a Jewish boy whom no one liked. And during one long Saturday afternoon Randall had discovered the meaning and pleasure of total power over someone else, body and mind, and how easy it is to get that power, and how frightened others are of getting it or using it. But how glad they are if someone else does it for them. Once he had showed that he wasn't afraid to go to the limits with the Jewish boy, all the others had been willing to help. A kind of team spirit. But every team starts with a captain.

He kicked Sean again. "Tell us you understand."

"I understand," Sean said. And Randall breathed very softly, because that was stage one. Once you can get a man to say anything, it's usually not very long before he'll say everything. Just get him to say any words at all, so long as they're words you've insisted on. "Say the Jews are different." An hour later the boy'd been screaming, "Yes, yes, yes, the Jews killed Christ, the bloody filthy Jews killed Christ." There'd been a bit of investigation afterward, but the headmaster hadn't really been very keen on Jews either, and the boy had just been quietly taken away. His parents had escaped from Germany two years before and weren't inclined to make trouble.

The two men holding Sean's legs apart looked up at

Randall with expectation and approval. Captain Robertson, who had done this kind of thing with Africans, was holding Sean's head down with a finger across his upper lip, and was watching his eyes with a professional's judgment. When it really started there'd be a little silence, then some almost hysterical defiance, and then he'd break. He judged it'd take about half an hour.

"Good. I'm glad you understand," Randall was saying. "Because I'm going to use this rather unsuitable instrument to castrate you. Like this." He bent down very fast, hooked one end of the shackle between Sean's legs and rammed it hard up into his crotch. "If I push the bolt home now," he said, "you can imagine what happens." He pushed the bolt down quite gently. It began to hurt. He pulled the bolt out and took the shackle away. "It'll be rather messy, I'm afraid."

Sean felt sick. He shut his eyes, and Captain Robertson forced the lids open with his thumbs. He remembered vividly the last time he had done that, and smiled like a wolf, showing his gap teeth, the brown tobacco-stained pits in the soft enamel, the discolored gums. His breath was stale and Sean tried to turn his head away. The thumbs pushed into his eyes.

"Think about that for a few minutes. While we take you below." Randall stood back and the two men lifted Sean by the legs, so that his head rested on the floor. "We're going down into the engine room," Randall said. "I'll give you one chance down there. I want to know exactly what you've done for the past twenty-four hours. Whom you've contacted. What you've told them. What they've told you. If you're really thorough, and very, very truthful, we might forgo this little business." He held the shackle up, dropped it onto the deck a foot from Sean's eyes. The shock of the iron hitting iron ran into Sean's skull like a knife, and twisted.

The men lifted him, took one leg each, bent it over their

—

shoulders, carried him like a sack, his head hanging, Randall still holding the rope taut in case the half-hitches slackened. They carried him out of the messroom and down the alleyway, turned into another doorway. The iron sill of the door hit Sean across the side of the head. The world spun, spew came out of his mouth, and he thought he was going to pass out again.

There was a different echo inside the engine room, much bigger, the sounds hollower, coming back from much greater distances, higher, deeper. His head was resting on a catwalk, a steel grille railed off from the huge drop into the shadows, onto the curving, mountain masses of the engines, brass glistening, copper and steel pipes curving, falling, huge piston heads, the shimmer of polished valves twenty, thirty feet down below him.

"Heave him over the rail," Randall said, and he was lifted, balanced for a second, another half-hitch taken around his legs between knee and ankle, pushed out, hanging head down, swaying, twisting, face into the bulkhead and then face out to nothing, to emptiness, a thirty-foot drop under his head, the deckhead of the engine room ten feet up above his feet, the faces of the men lowering him leaning over the rail, upside down, grotesque, laughing. Randall staring down, smiling up, like a reflection in a pool of shadow, licking his mouth, his face a mask, white, terrifying. As the rope lengthened, the pendulum swing grew wider, the spinning slower. The engine room turned, somersaulted, spun on half a dozen axes, vomit came out of his mouth and trailed upward into the dark, downward, away, choked him. He tried to scream and heard the echoes before he heard the screaming; bit the sound off. The rope cut into his arms, crushed his chest, tore the skin off his legs. His head brushed past a jutting bulwark, shaved it. He twisted in the air, swung back toward it, helpless, hit it with his shoulder, bounced five feet out into space, spinning like a top, saw the iron valley be-

—

tween engine and hull rush up to meet him, hit something else, spun face in to the engine, a smooth curve of boiler like an iron whale in a river, slid face down, came to a rack of heavy pipes, lagged in asbestos wrappings, fat and cushioned, was supported for a second while the rope holding him went on paying out, slackened around his ankles, around his waist.

He had a hand free, caught at one of the pipes by instinct. He couldn't see, his head was still swinging, spinning, he was still being sick, but his hand gripped the pipe, and the half-hitches, freed from the weight of his body, slackened further. A long way above, the men lowering him looked down, couldn't see what had happened, shook the rope, peered down to see if he was lying at the bottom, forgot that the twists of rope around his body depended on tension to keep them there. He felt his hands free, pulled at the rope. The twists fell away; one of them caught at his throat just as the men above him realized what was happening and began hauling taut. For a second the rope was under his chin, pulling him up and away from the pipes, threatening to hang him five feet from the bottom deck of the engine room, the iron walk alongside the boilers. He got both hands under it, fought it free, saw it snake away into the dark.

A voice shouted, "He's loose," feet ran on iron, another voice cursed, shouted, "You bloody imbecile." A man, a shadow, small as a bat, a monkey in the cathedral height of the engine room, reached a ladder, began scrambling down. Sean rolled off the pipes, slid down to the deck, one knee in a gutter of oil, one on the iron walk, his side rammed against a stanchion, his body half-naked, his legs bleeding, his head sick and dizzy, not able to think, to see. He wanted to lie on his face on the iron and let them come. He couldn't run any more, he couldn't fight, or think. He couldn't even think why he was running, why he was fighting, what they wanted to know. What did they want to know? If he knew he'd tell

—

them. Just lie on the iron and let them come. As if they were
friends. They wouldn't be so angry if he didn't run. The iron
was cold, he could smell oil. It was a strange smell. He felt
the ridge pattern of the iron against his face. Why were the
ridges there? He wished he knew why they were there.

Somewhere high up he could hear sounds—feet scrambling on iron rungs, scrambling down, lower and lower,
closer. Why were they coming? A voice a long way away, inside his head, a long, long way away, so far away he could
hardly hear it, said, "Run, you stupid bastard, run, get up,
run." He tried to tell the voice that he couldn't run, that he
wanted to lie there until they came. But the voice made him
get up, both hands clinging onto the stanchion, onto the
guard rail above it. He pulled himself along the rail, heard
the feet scramble, slip behind him, saw a bulkhead in front
of him, an iron door, the locking-dogs hanging loose, the
door not really closed. It was a fire door, meant to cut off one
part of the engine room from another if fire broke out at sea.
He pulled the door open, fell through the doorway. The feet
ran on the iron walk behind him, the voice shouted, "Ryan,
you bastard." He was through the door and pulling it shut,
his hands fumbling at the dogs, swinging them over, jam-
ming them down into their sockets.

There was an iron wrench, meant for locking the dogs,
stuck into a clamp beside the door, and he pulled it out of
the clamp, tried to fit the spanner end of it onto the first dog.
As he tried, the running feet reached the door, the dogs
moved as the man on the other side of the door wrenched at
his pair. For a second Sean stared at them, stupefied, not
understanding, his mind like cotton wool. He leaned against
the bulkhead, the wrench in both hands, and the door
opened, Captain Robertson started to come though.

He was halfway through, his head and shoulders ducking
through the low, narrow doorway, when he realized what he
was doing. He had been chasing Ryan like a dog after a

—

rabbit, not thinking of him turning. He had seen him hung upside down like meat on a hook, like a carcass, his legs naked, his shirt tails falling away, as humiliated as a hanged man, half dead, vomit streaming out of him like blood, screaming for mercy. Seen him fall on the deck below like a sack of offal, run staggering on naked, filthy legs. A thing like that couldn't turn. He'd expected it to stop dead, fall down when he shouted, when his sergeant-major's bark of command went after it like a lash, to curl on its legs and bring it down. A thing like that couldn't turn. And he was halfway through the doorway before he realized.

He looked sideways, saw Ryan's body, saw his arms lifting, saw the wrench, twenty-four inches of iron bar topped by the jaws of a spanner four inches across. And for a half-second, a fraction of half a second, he was paralyzed, his mouth open in anger rather than fear—astonishment at this insolent, turning worm, as if Olaf Redwin's corpse had got up from the bloody grass in the wood and threatened him. His teeth, small dirty teeth under the mole-mustache, snarled in fury. His hands reached sideways, one to the edge of the doorway for support, one for Ryan.

The wrench came down across the side of his skull, the rounded jaw of the spanner took him just behind the left ear, cracked the bones of the skull. The look of anger turned into astonishment, almost innocence. Ryan beat on his skull with the wrench and he fell down on his face, half in, half out of the doorway. Ryan looked at what he had done and hit him again and dropped the wrench out of hands that couldn't hold it any longer, that were shaking and helpless.

There were more feet running. He pushed the body back through the doorway with his own naked feet and saw blood on them, scarlet over the black of the oil. He pushed the body further through the doorway, dragged the door shut again, dogged it down. He picked up the wrench and hammered at the dogs until no one could open them with bare hands. He let the wrench fall again and stumbled away. Behind him someone was at the door; he could hear voices, shouting, the crash of something against iron, then more running.

The engine room was darker this side of the bulkhead. On the far side light filtered in from a dozen sources: open doorways, air vents, inspection manholes. But here, once the iron door was closed, it was almost dark. A little light sifted into the dark like pale dust, he could see a yard, two yards ahead of him and beyond that the glisten of steel, a brass wing nut like a nugget of gold in a cave, the massive shadows of the engines, the bulkheads, the silver dragon shape of the port propeller shaft, the steel rungs of an emergency ladder up the side of the hull into the total darkness above him.

He went up hand over hand. The rungs cut into his bare feet, he had to take most of his weight on his hands and arms. And all the time he was listening. He could hear his own breath like an engine, like something apart from him, behind his back, above his head. He couldn't see, and his mind's eye felt, saw hands coming at him; he could hear voices, feet running, whispering, breathing. When he stopped, held his own breath, there was nothing except a distant engine slam, muffled by dark and iron and distance. Until he realized it was his heart beating. He remembered another ladder. When? He couldn't remember when. The TV studio. Like this. Like an imitation of this. Playing at death. This was real. They were going to kill him. His heart thudded: "Kill me, kill me, kill me."

He hung on the ladder and shut his eyes, his mouth open, listening. He put his ear against the ladder, and then leaned sideways to reach the plates of the hull, put his ear against the side of the ship. Nothing. He opened his eyes again and looked down. Far, far down he could see the propeller shaft. Light from somewhere glistened on its polished, oiled curve, hypnotized him. He wanted to lean out and down toward it; he wanted to let go and fall. If he fell it wouldn't matter—he'd float down, float down in the darkness to the bright shaft of the propeller.

He was almost unconscious, almost asleep as he hung from his arms on the ladder. He shook his head, felt suddenly so tired that his hands couldn't hold any more. He felt them slipping, sweat-greasy, the pain in the tendons of his wrists like a knife cut. He forced himself up another rung, one more, two more. Above his head an iron door crashed open, seemed to fill the cliff space with light, as if the moon had come up over a seascape, turned everything black and silver. Feet ran, a man shouted, ten, less than ten rungs above his head. The ladder shook, and then the feet were past the top of the ladder.

"He's down there somewhere. No—he's not up here unless there's another door—"

The feet running. Sean went up again, felt the catwalk with his hand, his body was over it, knee, foot, he was kneeling on the catwalk. The running feet came back, the man still shouting to someone invisible. Sean knelt there, paralyzed. He'd thought the man would go on around, he hadn't thought anything, had only scrambled up toward the cliff top, to what had seemed like safety. Or had he wanted to be found, caught, killed, to end it? The man was five, three, two paces away from him, the catwalk shaking, jarring his hands and knees. He waited for the man to shout, to grab him. He couldn't fight, he couldn't run, he couldn't do anything but kneel and wait. His body sweated and the sweat was cold. He felt his mouth opening to scream, felt the cold brutality of the iron shackle between his legs, wanted to scream and scream and go on screaming.

And it was as if suddenly his mind was apart from his body. He could see his shadow humped on the catwalk, the man running toward him, and the catwalk was far down, far,

—

far down below him and he was seeing it like a picture, like something through a telescope, and his mind shuddered at what it was seeing and he thought if I die like this I will be like this forever, I will always be screaming, I will be a coward forever. He knew it as one knows a place one has never seen but recognizes out of the depths of one's mind.

"Get up!" he screamed, and the scream was a whisper, nothing; it couldn't reach down that far to the catwalk, to the kneeling figure. "Get up!" Like an echo in a cave, a whisper. But the figure moved, started to straighten. And the running man saw a shadow move in front of him, realized it was a man, and was driven sideways by instinct, to sway sideways against the attack from the straightening man. The guard rail hit his hipbone, threw him back to the left. His shoulder hit an iron buttress, a strengthener, an angle iron running up the side of the hull, and at the same instant Sean's lifting head took him in the stomach. He went sideways again, his arms flailing, through the gap in the guard rail above the ladder, was flung five feet out into space.

He didn't scream until he was halfway down. His body hit the propeller shaft, thudded on it like a sack of mud with sticks inside. His ribs smashed in, drove their broken splinters into his lungs, the lungs filled with blood, drowned him as he lay there. He had been in the Commandos and he had never fired a shot in anger. In a fortnight he would have been on his way to Rimini with his girl friend for a holiday. Sean gripped the guard rail, stopped himself looking down.

He turned very gently, very carefully on the catwalk, felt his way along it to the open door, the light. He stayed short of the doorway, listening, ten seconds, twenty, thirty. The lighted doorway was like a threat. A trap. Somewhere outside it, in the light, Randall was waiting. He knew that the man who had just died was not Randall. He hadn't seen his face, had no way of knowing who it had been, but it never

occurred to him that it was Randall. He waited on the catwalk, listening, and all he could hear was the echo of the
man's scream as he had fallen, and his own breathing. He
couldn't hear his heart beat. Only feel the thud of it in his
ribs, as if it was swelling, was finding it hard to beat inside
its framework, was trying to force itself through and leave
him.

He put his hand on the edge of the door, dragged himself
through. There was no one there, and he leaned against the
side of the alleyway as if getting through the doorway had
exhausted him. He began moving left and still there was no
one. Light came from side alleys, opening onto the deck, the
sky, the river. He came to a companionway and went up it,
was in another alley with an open door ahead of him to the
left. When he looked through the doorway it was the empty
messroom where they had carried him first, stripped him.
His trousers lay in a heap in the middle of the room, his
shoes scattered away from them, his socks. He closed the
door very carefully behind him, looked for a bolt. There was
none, but he left the door, forced himself away from the
handle, and dragged his trousers over his filthy, blood-
crusted legs, fastened them around his waist, zipped the fly.

He began to feel like a man again, like a human being instead of a victim. He made himself sit on the deck and put
his socks and shoes on. Randall. And the watchman. Two
live men. Two dead. He laced the shoes, stood up. He felt
sick and dizzy and the scream was still in his ears. When he
shut his eyes he could see the other man's skull and the
blood coming, the blood on his foot as he pushed the head
through the iron doorway down below in the engine room.
But he felt stronger. In the corner where Randall had picked
up the shackle there was another, smaller shackle and a
spike for opening and closing them: a steel bar fifteen inches
long like a sawn-off, sharpened billiard cue. He left the
shackle there and took the spike.

—

Outside the messroom door there was still no sound. He went back and got the shackle, carried both things with him down the alleyway. He realized he was no longer running. He was no longer being hunted. He was looking for Randall and he was going to kill him. He saw Randall's face as he had rammed the ring end of the big shackle into his crotch, his mouth thin and curved and pleased, his eyes narrow and gem-bright, looking for the signs of fear and pain and cowardice.

He came to the end of the alleyway. A half-open doorway gave on the afterdeck, a narrow cross section of it above the cargo deck with the two afterholds, and below the boat deck. The warehouse to his right. The width of the dock to his left, other warehouses across the dark strip of oily, silvery water. The open river was away behind his left shoulder, out of sight, hidden by the deck housing at his back. He stood listening, and below him a door creaked on unoiled hinges, footsteps came out onto the lower deck, began moving fast and yet quietly across the deck toward the quayside. Sean slipped his shoes off again and followed, one deck above the other man, hidden from him. He came to the far side of the deck, heard the footsteps under him. A voice calling out softly—Randall's voice. "Any sign of him?"

"No, not a sign of him." The watchman. On the gangway. Closing the one easy way ashore. Watching the other ways. Listening for a splash that would tell them he'd gone into the water on the far side. The footsteps came back, were on the afterdeck again, were coming up the ladder to the main deck. Sean drew back, went up the far ladder to the boat deck. When he was up top he took one of his shoes, flung it as lightly as he could to the far side of the deck. It skidded a couple of yards, slid into the scuppers under a life boat.

In the center of the boat deck was the bridge housing. Once it had held the wireless operator's cabin and the chartroom. The wheelhouse was forward, the wings of the bridge

—

curving out from it over the main deck. Sean went into the chartroom. Through a porthole he could watch the deck. He had to wait several minutes. Then the watchman's head appeared, very slowly and carefully. Which meant that Randall was coming up onto the bridge from the other end of the boat deck.

Sean went through from the chartroom into the wheelhouse, saw the black curtain still hanging where the radar screen had been, moved behind it. Childish, like hide-and-seek. He waited there, holding the spike and shackle, one in each hand. They came very softly, one from either side of the bridge, the watchman so close to Sean that he could have smelled him. They stopped in the middle of the wheelhouse, turned to the wide bridge window looking over the foredeck.

"You shouldn't have called me up," the watchman said. "He's got away down—"

"Shut up," Randall said. There was a strange tone in his voice. The two men looked down from the bridge over the foredeck. Sean came out behind them, silently. When he was a yard from them he dropped the shackle, deliberately. He didn't know why he did it, why he had to do it. They turned, too close together, one turning into the other, and he hit the watchman across the side of the head, a clumsy, glancing blow that went on beyond the watchman, smashed into the glass of the window. The watchman staggered, tried to lift his hands. Sean hit him the second time across the side of the neck, into the hollow of neck and shoulder. The watchman went down onto his knees, his hands lifted, his head turned sideways on his neck like a chicken that has had its neck wrung. Sean swung the spike right across, looked at Randall.

And Randall's face was gray with terror, sweating, nothing left in it but terror—the matinee charm, the cruelty, the hunger gone from it like wax melting. He wasn't fighting,

—

wasn't running. Just standing, flattened against the half of the window that wasn't shattered, one shoulder against the wooden center-bar, his head pressed back as far as it would go against the glass, his hands flattened on the mahogany paneling below the window. Sean dropped the angle of the return swing, hit him across the left elbow, swung again, lower still, caught him across the outside of his right knee.

The knee folded, Randall went down onto it. "I haven't got a gun," he whispered. His mouth shook.

Sean closed his fist around the spike, drove his knuckles into Randall's face. Blood came, and a tooth cut his hand, broke, fell out of Randall's mouth onto the wooden grating they were on. Blood flowed out of his thin, high-bridged nose, and he shook his head from side to side, whimpered something through the blood. Sean picked up the shackle, slid the point of the spike into the ring bolt, opened it. "You know what I'm going to do?" He said.

Randall looked at the shackle as it opened, as the bolt came out, suddenly flung himself sideways, tried to run, his right knee giving way, folding under him, until he was on his hands and knees, scrambling, scurrying, clawing at the deck, the door of the wheelhouse, sounds coming out of his mouth, blood dribbling onto the wooden deck, smearing behind him as his feet scrambled. Sean followed him, caught him as he reached the rail, half lifted, half held him by the slack folds of his coat, his body thin inside the gray, expensive cloth, twisting like a snake, his head shaking, swinging blindly from side to side, his eyes no longer bright, filmed with terror, gray, opaque, like scratched glass.

"No!" he whimpered. "No, no, no, no—" and for a second, he never knew how long, if it was for any length of time at all, Sean stared into the blind, scratched glass of Randall's eyes, saw his soul like a shadow behind a frosted window, shuddering, wringing its hands, screaming in the dark, and he saw himself, heard himself screaming, felt as if his hands

—

were wrist-deep in a carcass, in rotting meat, felt the worms
crawling, soft and wet, and felt their leech mouths bite,
suck, bury their blind heads in his own flesh, until his flesh
and Randall's were one pool of corruption.

He thought of what he had been going to do and tried to
make his hands let go of Randall, tried to tear himself away.
And it was as if Randall were holding him, sucking him
down. He shut his eyes, wrenched himself away, straightened his arms in the huge effort to push the stench of death
away from him. The weight hung on him, clung to his skin,
his hands, dragged the blood out of his body, fastened itself
to him in a dreadful hunger. Then there was nothing. Nothing.

He stood with his arms stretched out, his hands holding
the air. And Randall hung tilting across the rail of the
bridge, his own hands lifted, clawing at nothing, his legs
twisting, kicking desperately. It seemed to happen very
slowly, and Sean watched, not able to move, to shout, his
hands stretched. Randall tipped slowly out, his legs still
kicking, one of them kicking, the other trailing, hanging
from the knee, quivering as the muscles stretched and contracted, tried to kick. The whole thrashing body slid out and
down, past the rail, down out of sight. Twenty feet below
the wing of the bridge it hit the water, a sound as if a heavy
bin of rubbish, refuse from a ship's galley, had been tipped
into the dock.

Sean moved like a sleepwalker, leaned over the rail,
stared down. Three-quarter rings spread out from where
Randall had hit the water. The remaining quarter of each
ring was lost against the side of the ship. Most complex and
delicate counter ripples fled away from the hull, crossed the
primary rings, made lace, made geometrical drawings on the
silvery scum of the dock. Orange peel and pieces of shoddy
wood, dark brown and fibrous; a page of newspaper, a
grapefruit, a rotting onion, cigarette packets, red and blue

and white like fragments of the Union Jack; a plastic bottle that had held bleach or starch or detergent; a film of oil with colors like molten steel, like a sword blade being tempered —all the rubbish of the dock swayed and lifted to the ripples, grew still again. A great bubble of air, gaseous, huge, obscene; a great belch of air came up from Randall's lungs, from his clothes, swelled its silver balloon on the surface, broke and vanished.

Sean hung over the rail and shut his eyes. He was trying to say something, to pray, he didn't know why or what prayer, for himself, for Randall, but nothing came, just words, *Christ, Christ, Christ,* and the surface of the water stilled, became a mirror, the refuse floated in it, still and beautiful, and deep in the mirror, far below the surface, Randall's body began to settle in the mud, the black, oozing mud of the dock, ten feet deep, a cloud of mud in suspension around him, stirred up by his falling, sinking body. The particles of mud resettled, began the work of covering the body, filtered into the staring eyes, the nose, the wide, screaming mouth, the clothes, covered it. And the great parent layer of mud opened, drew Randall down. He was still alive. In a way he was still alive. Something functioned inside his darkened mind, told him that he was drowning, that he was dying. His arms, his unbroken leg tried to move, but every movement only buried him deeper in the mud, drove the particles up and out like ink from an octopus. When they resettled again the body was gone, buried deep under them, and the sea creatures that live in mud, small and mindless, moved inward toward the body, began to scavenge it.

Sean pushed himself away from the rail, walked unsteadily to the door of the wheelhouse. The watchman knelt on the deck, his hands holding his head, cursing and crying. Sean walked past him, and the man cringed, lay on the deck. Sean went on down the ladder from the opposite wing of the bridge, down onto the boat deck and from there to the main deck and down the gangway to the quayside. If anyone had spoken to him he wouldn't have heard them, wouldn't have seen them. He found his way into the dark shed, the warehouse that a long time ago Randall had hired for a convenient place to hide weapons and do other secret things; made his way across it and rolled the main doors open. There was still daylight.

He saw Randall's car, and when he had switched on its headlights, saw his own luggage, his own two suitcases, where Randall had put them down. He got out of the car again and loaded them into the back. The keys were still in the ignition, and he drove the car out of the warehouse, stopped, rolled the doors shut, and drove away, along the cobbled roadway, between the blind walls.

20

MAJOR WILLIS awoke in the dark, lay for a while trying to think where he was, what had happened before he went to sleep. That chap Nicholas. Ridickolus Nickolus. Booze-up. A bloody fine booze-up. Except poor chap had collapsed on him. No good. Young chaps these days no bloody good. No stuffing in them.

And then the tart. The little tart. Throwing her arms around him. Starkers. Absolutely starkers. The little sport. Playing tag around her flat in her altogether. By God, what a little sport. Where had she gone? He sat up, and the top of his head seemed to lift a foot above the rest of him and slam back like a door. It was a painful experience and he lay down again to recover from it. Starkers. Except for that rather dashing little thing around her middle. Twang. Mentally he pulled it again and it twanged back very satisfactorily against rosy flesh. Rosy. Roses and cream. Typical English complexion. Perfect. Good family there, bloody fine stock. His old father had always said, "You can tell a horse when it's running and a girl when she's starkers. Only way." Where the hell had she gone?

He felt around him. Not his bed. Softer, nicer smell. Velvet cushion under head, bloody good thing too. Light? He felt around and discovered a table. No lamp. An ash tray fell, matches scattered out of an ornamental matchbox. He found them and struck one. The flat! The little smasher's flat! He was still there. With luck there'd be a stiffener somewhere around. He found the kitchen, and a bottle of whiskey, poured himself a generous recoverer. The top of his head teetered around and around and settled more or less into place.

His clothes wet. Bloody well wet. Must have been raining. He took them off and left them in the middle of the floor Bed was what was indicated, jolly old bed. He went unsteadily into the bedroom, guided by instinct rather than memory. The light was on in the bedroom and Babette was stretched on the bed, still dressed in her leather jerkin and thigh boots, face down, black and white on the satin coverlet. She had cried herself to sleep an hour earlier, a sleep of exhaustion that came from terror: of the present, the future, of Randall and everything that had happened; of the disappearance of Bryce along with her income and her capital; of what she was going to do, of what Randall was going to make her do.

Major Willis saw her spread out on the bed like a fairy tale, like the Arabian Nights. All his life he had known that this kind of thing could happen, ought to happen, and he

—

opened his arms to receive the gift with a little cry of warm delight and welcome. "Woops," he cried and fell on top of her. She awoke and struggled, but she was so frightened and so alone that she didn't struggle very hard. In the morning they packed what was left of value in both their flats, took out the major's savings and caught the first available plane to Paris. That night they were in Monte Carlo.

21

IT WAS a bleak funeral. The cemetery was on a hilltop, looking out across the gray wilderness of North London and the Home Counties. Gravel paths, straight, monotonous rows of graves, a few cypresses lifting thin El Greco hands to the gray sky. They followed the coffin and the clergyman in a ragged file: the housekeeper, who seemed to be the nearest thing to a chief mourner, veiled, breathing heavily from the lengthy walk up the hillside, supported on her right by a rather smug-looking nephew with a mustache and pince-nez, and a bowler hat. He looked as if he knew all about the will already and was determined to see the major securely buried.

"To my faithful housekeeper, Jane Alisoun MacFarlane, if she survives me, I give and bequeath my house at number 7 Chevel Road, Richmond, with all the furniture, fixtures, fittings and appurtenances that it may contain at the time of my death. And I further give and bequeath—"

The nephew seemed to be counting over the clauses as he supported his aunt. Or perhaps he was saying his prayers.

—

Margaret came next, walking alone, and behind her someone else from the office, the bored, elegant young man imported by Randall soon after he himself had arrived. For decoration apparently, because he never seemed to do any work. He divided his attention between the graves and Margaret.

Sean came next. He had barely spoken to Margaret since the major died. Which had been three days ago. Almost exactly twenty-four hours after Randall had died by drowning under the derelict tramp steamer in Hammonds' wharf. The major had been arguing on the telephone with a very senior official who didn't want to hear about Trust Fund or Shadow Force or Olaf Redwin's coded report or Randall or Sean Ryan or anything in the world that might disturb his even progress toward a knighthood and retirement to a small Georgian house beside a trout stream in southern Ireland.

"And if I go to the papers?" the major said. "I've nothing to lose, don't forget. I'm dying."

The senior official had promised to be at the nursing home within the hour. When he arrived the major was already dead. He had put the phone down, turned toward Sean and Eva Lund with a look of triumphant fury, begun to say, "There's still fight in me yet, by—" stopped with his mouth open, a look of shocked surprise, of childish astonishment in his eyes, started to spread his hands, hold them out to Sean, and folded down gently onto the worn carpet of his private room. Sean lifted him onto the bed, and he was a thin bundle of sticks, dust and ivory, so painfully, so obviously dead, so shrunken and lost in his woolen dressing gown that Sean felt almost a horror of touching him, of carrying him the half-pace to the bed, laying him down on it.

The nurse came in, the doctor. Both of them looked at Sean as if he had done it, became exaggeratedly professional, talking between themselves as if Sean and Eva were no longer there, were ghosts. The senior official arrived, and took no more than a minimum of trouble to conceal his pleasure at the news.

"A sad loss," he murmured, collected the papers, the report, some documents from the major's bedside cupboard, sweeping aside the doctor's hesitations with a raised eyebrow and the mention of the position he occupied. Within five minutes of arriving he was gone again. He neither spoke to Sean nor looked at him. If it ever became necessary, he would truthfully say that he had no idea of Sean Ryan's existence.

During the next three days certain things happened, but Sean was aware of none of them. Even before Randall's death, immediately following his last phone call to Trust Fund, the men who formed that shadowy committee had begun to separate themselves from Randall's operation. If in spite of all their instincts it repaired itself, they could take up the threads again. If it did not, they would be safe long before the crash occurred.

In any event, there was no audible crash. The network in Honeywell that Edward Bryce had built up and that Randall had enlarged for quite different purposes fell to pieces. Other people swiftly picked them up and made their own use of them. The tenants in places like Honeywell Road hardly noticed the difference. There are always victims, and anyone who expects that the death of a man like Mr. Albert, or Mr. Bryce, or even Oliver Randall, will make an end of victimization is expecting too much of human nature.

But at least the idea of Crystal Night, of a Colored Pogrom, vanished for the time being from Trust Fund's plans. Trust Fund had never been entirely happy about it, and the reorganization made necessary by Randall's failures made the project impossible, at least for some time to come. Other ways would have to be found to persuade the government of the day not to do anything too embarrassingly foolish about South Africa. It would probably be fairly easy.

Even so, the reorganization needed was quite extensive. The man who had been the real substance behind the shadow-figure of "General Cromwell" found himself with a barony and a roving commission to investigate the state of disused naval dockyards in the Far East. Various other men who had thought that their connection with Trust Fund was a well-kept secret found themselves surprisingly and suddenly moved from one corner of the official chessboard to another. Shadow Force was virtually turned inside out, and large sections of it were efficiently sheared away with all the cold ferocity that Security can use on these occasions. By the end of the shearing, the Force was no longer much good for its original purpose—perhaps it never had been—but it was certainly not dangerous to Authority.

As for Trust Fund itself, Authority was unwilling to hear too much, and a naïve Security official who insisted on telling someone at higher level all about it was told to report urgently to the Falkland Islands, where he would be vitally needed for several years.

By the day of the funeral the main actions had all been taken, or safely set in train, and those people who needed to be able to say such things would safely be able to say that nothing had happened at all. It began to be time to attend to the details. Such as Sean Ryan.

The funeral reached the graveside, the coffin was lowered into the hole in the ground, the men carrying the coffin slipping and stumbling in the dark brown earth that they had earlier dug out of the grave. The clergyman said what he had to say, and Sean heard one word in five—dust—clay—return—in heaven—the glorious resurrection. The housekeeper wept; her nephew supported her. The rain held off.

Eva Lund was already gone. Back to Norway, driven

—

partly by fear and partly by a loneliness that she thought would grow less in Norway, where Olaf had wanted to go with her. Sean stood listening to the mutter, the sudden rises of the clergyman's voice and wondered what would happen to her. And thought of Olaf Redwin, the bitter man he had never seen and who had begun all this. He wondered what there had been in him to make Eva love him, and looked at Margaret's straight, somehow contemptuous back, and looked away again.

A man he hadn't noticed before moved closer to him. "A cold day for June," the man said. Sean looked at him. A very nondescript man in a mackintosh. Even the mackintosh had no noticeable color. It had faded from a kind of khaki to an off-white. Or perhaps it had originally been white and got discolored. The man's skin had the same blanched, discolored look. He might have been fifty. Or ten years less. "An unpleasant day for a funeral."

The clergyman came to an end. Sean stooped down and threw a handful of earth onto the coffin. The housekeeper's nephew looked at him in disapproving surprise. The grave-diggers began filling in the grave. Margaret shivered and turned away.

"If we might have a word together," the nondescript man said. Sean had begun to turn, begun to follow Margaret, automatically, not really thinking. The man's voice, a gesture of his hand toward Sean's arm, stopped him. The man had surprising authority in spite of his appearance.

"I don't see why," Sean said. He was feeling guilty at having turned away so abruptly from the major's grave and it made his voice rougher than he had intended. "I'm sorry, it's not much of a day for conversation."

"I quite understand," the man said. "Quite understand. But I won't keep you long. Have you any—immediate plans?"

Sean stared at him. The housekeeper and her nephew

—

moved past them. The housekeeper sniffed into a black lace handkerchief. The elegant young man from the office picked his way back to the gravel path, unobtrusively holding his trouser bottoms an inch higher to avoid the mud.

"I don't—" Sean began.

The man squeezed his arm. "Quite right not to have any plans. You don't need to change them then. We"—he dwelt fractionally on the "we," giving it great authority and significance—"we would be quite pleased if you left England for a while."

"Perhaps you would," Sean said. "But—"

"Then that's all right. Naturally you'll be discreet. And so will we. Nothing unpleasant. We don't know where Commander Randall is. Or Captain Robertson. Quite frankly we won't want to. Don't oblige us to find out too soon. I suggest you leave tonight." He held Sean's arm, drew him away from the grave, the gravediggers, seemed without effort to lead him back to the gravel path, to follow the others down the empty hillside.

"What a magnificent view," the man said as if he really meant it. He made a small gesture that embraced the smoke-haze of London, the silver, infinitely distant snake of the river. "I believe you've been driving Commander Randall's car?" He pointed to it beside the other cars at the bottom of the hill. A blue Mercedes sports 230 SL, low and powerful and obedient.

"Yes," Sean said through tight lips.

"I think you might continue doing so. As long as it's far enough away from here. If you drive down to Lydd tonight and put up at this address"— he handed Sean an envelope— "someone will see you on board the air ferry tomorrow and hand you the car's papers. And five hundred pounds in Swiss francs. Please don't argue, we're delighted for you to have them. Together with any rents you may have collected from

—

198

Albert Fetter. Goodbye." He increased his pace, checked for a second and was back beside Sean.

"One other thing. When you go to your flat to pack you'll notice a plain-clothes policeman outside on the pavement. Don't worry. He'll stay on the pavement. So long as you're out again in thirty minutes."

This time he moved away without turning back. He got into a very small car that already held another man, a very large man for such a small car. They drove away. The large man looked carefully out of the window at Sean as if he wanted to be sure of remembering his face. Sean felt cold and hopeless and alone. And afraid. He imagined Eva Lund had felt exactly as he felt. He thought for a moment of trying to find her, somewhere in Norway. She had mentioned a place that she was going, a district or a village, he wasn't sure. But he let the idea go as soon as it came to him.

He thought for another moment of trying to talk to Margaret. She was getting into a car with the smooth, useless young man. He was helping her in, making a cultivated fuss of closing the door, the kind of fuss Sean had never learned to make. She looked in a cool way as if she was pleased with it. It made Seal feel lonelier still and he let that idea go too.

He turned back up the hillside, stopped himself from looking over his shoulder at the very small car just turning out of the cemetery gates, and walked heavily and firmly to where the two silhouettes were filling in the grave. He stood and watched them. They said nothing, and after a few minutes they wiped their spades and went away. The rain still held off although it was in the air, an invisible dampness that made his clothes feel uncomfortable, as if he had been sweating and the sweat had turned cold.

He tried to say a prayer for the major, and all the prayers

—

199

that he knew seemed as stupid and pointless as the ones the clergyman had already said. He took a coin out of his pocket. A penny, dated 1925. George V. How had the world seemed to the major in 1925? Had he already been a soldier then? With his belief in the wall that men like him were born to defend? With chaos outside it and St. James's Park inside? With the nursemaids and the well-bred children and the tame ducks and the well-kept grass. It was a very limited vision to keep a man going to the end. But perhaps only men with very limited visions can keep going to the end.

Sean threw the penny onto the turned earth and pushed it in with his foot. He wished he had a vision.

He drove back into London very fast. The rain had started and the streets shone with silver, and with fools' gold where the shoplights hit them; all the gorgeous swinging city began to unfold itself in the late afternoon, stretch itself toward the evening—the bright white neon evening where the true business of life is making money out of pleasure; where TV is reality, and rocks and trees are made out of rubber-foam plastic and walls fall over when they're pushed; where disaster is followed by the ads and handsome men are never killed; where small black children with legs like matchsticks are only photographs in an Oxfam appeal; where men like Mr. Albert don't exist and no one lives in Honeywell and everyone has scrumptious yummy yum fish-fingers for dinner and tea and Chocky-crisp biscuits whenever they feel peckish; where Black Jesus will only come in the *Reader's Digest* and Jihad isn't even a word; where men like Major Courtenay are a funny joke and men like Edward Bryce and Niccolò are kings. Until Trust Fund comes. Or Jihad.

The streets went past the car like dirty tinsel, and he thought of nothing except the major buried under the sodden mound of clay, and the dusty, brittle lightness of his body when he died. What had he been thinking when he

—

died? That he was winning? That it was still possible to win? Or was it the truth that killed him? That he wasn't going to win, that it wasn't possible, and wasn't worth trying, that the battle he was fighting had ended fifty years before, on the Somme and Ypres, and that everyone around him was fighting a different battle about different things.

The thought of it came up in Sean's throat and choked him, and he found himself praying that the major hadn't known, that he hadn't died of bitterness the way Olaf Redwin had died. That he died still believing in the wall. He found it was difficult to see clearly and had to slow down. He saw a post office and stopped the car and sent a cable to Niccolò. "Joining the Common Market. Expect me Saturday. Sean." He got back into the car, trying to believe that he felt better.

Outside his flat a largish, unobtrusive man stood unhappily in the rain. He looked at his watch as Sean went into the house, and then crossed the road to wait under the shelter of a tree. He looked much more like a man at a funeral than anyone who had been there.

Sean packed hurriedly in a room that already seemed to belong to someone else. Socks, ties, a book he hadn't read, yesterday's newspaper, an inlaid ivory cigarette box that a woman had given him in Baghdad, a bronze statuette of a naked dancer three inches high that he had bought in Cairo, a Greek coin that he kept for luck, some shirts, his other suit. It didn't take half an hour. He strapped the case and looked out of the window. The man was standing in almost exactly the same place as Trust Fund's watcher four mornings earlier. He was lighting a cigarette in the shelter of his coat collar. When it was lit he looked at his watch again and up at Sean's window. Sean turned back into the room, feeling very cold. He tried to believe that they meant to keep their word. He'd know very soon.

He looked around the room to see if he had forgotten any-

—

thing. If they were going to arrest him, would they do it now, outside? Or wait till he reached the coast? He went down the stairs, past the landing with the telephone, down toward the front door. His mouth was stiff and his hand was so unsteady that he missed the catch of the door lock, had to fumble at it. The telephone rang. He had been twenty-three minutes inside the house.

He went back up the stairs to the telephone, not because he thought it was for him, but simply to force himself to do it, to get a grip on his nerves. "Winslow House," he said. Twenty-three and a half minutes. He wondered if there was anyone with the man outside, in a police car. He heard coins dropping in the caller's box. A voice said, "Is that you, Sean?"

He didn't believe it at first. "Margaret!" And then, very coldly, "What did you want?"

"Are you leaving?" she said, her voice quick and breathless and low, as if she was afraid of being overheard.

"You know bloody well I'm leaving. If they let me."

"They'll let you," she said.

"Did you see to that? As a farewell present?"

"There isn't time to quarrel." Her voice still urgent. "Where are you going?"

"What does that matter?"

"Where are you going?" She spaced the words out with controlled violence.

"Milan. I don't know what—"

"I'll write to you Poste Restante. Or don't you want to go on working?"

"Go to hell," he said. But the phone was already dead. Twenty-four minutes and thirty-five seconds. He went down the stairs again, out into the street and the drizzle of gray rain. The man across the street looked unhappier than ever. He watched Sean get into the blue Mercedes, snarl away toward the main road. When he could no longer see the car

—

he turned left and trudged to the nearest public telephone.

Sean worked his way through the homebound traffic, cutting across London toward the South Ring and the coast. He was cursing steadily and savagely under his breath. The High streets went by, district after district, with their coffee bars and bingo halls and boys leaning against shop windows, waiting hopelessly for something, anything to happen. The rain fell out of the sky. A newspaper placard said: "Toto Found." Another said: "Star's Snake in TV WC." In the next High Street a placard said: "England Crashes. Test Disaster."

He thought of the major lying in his sodden grave and Randall buried in the mud thirty feet down by Hammond's wharf. And Randall had fought against Toto and the bingo halls, and the major had fought for them. It was more than bloody strange. And Olaf Redwin. What had he wanted to fight for? And against?

A boy and a girl skittered across the road almost under the wheels of the Mercedes. Jeans and long hair and white faces. It was hard to tell them apart. He remembered the couple in the Wimpy Bar, the girl's eyes. Damn her, he thought. Damn Margaret. Damn this filthy country. The road widened, became suburban, almost country. He let the car out and it leaped south as if it scented freedom. Niccolò should have the cable by tonight. He imagined his face, the brown, hard eyes, the warm, slow smile that said without any need of words, "I know everything and believe nothing." Damn them all.

The road lifted over the North Downs. The rain stopped. It hadn't been raining the other side of the Downs. The road was dry. He saw an inn sign ahead, was almost on top of it before he recognized the building, the parking lot, the low brick wall topped by decorative loops of chain. The Coach Inn. He slowed down, for a second had an insane impulse to turn into the parking lot, go inside and ask the landlord if he'd heard from his friends recently. He drove on, his hands clenched on the wheel. In half an hour he'd be by-passing Learham. Olaf Redwin. Failed poet. Failed patriot. Failed conspirator. And yet at least he'd tried.

Damn him too. Let her write. Let her write any bloody soft-soap rubbish that she liked to Poste Restante, Milan. It could lie there a long time before he'd answer it. The sky to the south was bright, green-blue, like a reflection of the English Channel. Tomorrow, if his luck held, he'd be across the Channel, driving south, toward the warmth. Sun and wine and money and women and to bloody hell with everything else. Particularly Margaret. He began to wonder, realized he had been wondering ever since she telephoned, what she wanted to write to him, what there was to tell him. Damn her, damn her cool, insolent, arrogant voice, her assumption that whatever she wanted he'd do. He wondered if the letter would be waiting for him when he reached Milan.

He put his foot on the accelerator again. The needle shot up to the legal limit of seventy, and a long way beyond it. He was on the Learham by-pass, although he was not really aware of it. On his right there was a dark shape of woods, old, handsome trees covering a slight ridge, no more than a rise in the ground above the fields to the south. Goff's Wood. He went by without a glance. At least he could read her letter. He didn't have to answer it. But he knew that he would.

About the Author

BRIAN CLEEVE, married with two daughters, was born in 1921 and during the war worked with counterintelligence. He lived for a time in South Africa, where he took his B.A. degree, and then went to live in Dublin, where he has taken his Ph.D. degree. His chief hobbies are fencing, reading history, and collecting miniature bronzes. His short stories are enjoyed all over the English-speaking world, many of them having appeared in *Saturday Evening Post,* and he is a well-known television writer in England and Ireland.